Remembrance Sunday

Praise for *All That is Solid Melts into Air*

'A startling achievement . . . McKeon's characters may already have receded into history, but by imprinting their triumphs and tragedies on to the imagination with such visceral empathy, he has given them a deserving afterlife in this powerful novel' *The New York Times Book Review*

'A supremely accomplished social novel . . . What makes McKeon's vision so compelling is that the system this novel describes is not merely Russian, nor communist, but universal' John Burnside, *Guardian*

'This daring and ambitious novel blends historical epic and love story with a moving description of the Chernobyl disaster and the fall of the Soviet Union. A book rich with resonance far beyond its historical moment' Colm Tóibín

'Brilliantly imagined, exhilarating in its sweep; McKeon creates a thrilling appearance of ease, while he delves deep and forges new territory for the contemporary novel. Daring, generous and beautifully written, *All That is Solid Melts into Air* marks the beginning of a truly significant career. I cannot say it loud enough: McKeon is here to stay' Colum McCann

Remembrance Sunday

DARRAGH McKEON

PENGUIN BOOKS

PENGUIN BOOKS

UK | USA | Canada | Ireland | Australia
India | New Zealand | South Africa

Penguin Books is part of the Penguin Random House group of companies
whose addresses can be found at global.penguinrandomhouse.com.

First published by Sandycove 2023
Published in Penguin Books 2024
001

Typeset by Jouve (UK), Milton Keynes
Printed and bound in Great Britain by Clays Ltd, Elcograf S.p.A.

The authorized representative in the EEA is Penguin Random House Ireland,
Morrison Chambers, 32 Nassau Street, Dublin D02 YH68

A CIP catalogue record for this book is available from the British Library

ISBN: 978–0–241–99679–9

www.greenpenguin.co.uk

Penguin Random House is committed to a
sustainable future for our business, our readers
and our planet. This book is made from Forest
Stewardship Council® certified paper.

MIX
Paper | Supporting
responsible forestry
FSC® C018179

How much of him is in me, and how much of me is in him?

Brian Keenan, *An Evil Cradling*

I have a book opened on the desk in front of me: *Van Gogh in Auvers*. It documents the two months that Van Gogh spent in the village of Auvers-sur-Oise in 1890, after his release from an asylum in Saint-Rémy in Provence. By the time of his arrival, he was still fragile but rested, optimistic, ready for work, entranced by the cool, muted light of the north. During his visit, he lodged with the Ravoux family in their auberge. They gave him a small room and a warm welcome. In gratitude for their hospitality, he painted a portrait of Adeline Ravoux, the eldest daughter, who was ten years old at the time.

It's a strange, disconcerting painting. It doesn't become any less strange with repeated viewings. Adeline is dressed in blue, and Van Gogh chose to paint the background in the same colour, which gives it an hallucinogenic aura, the girl's face and hair and hands seem to float outwards, towards the viewer. This effect – although *effect* seems too slight a word – was entirely intentional. On arrival in Auvers, Van Gogh wrote to his sister, saying: *I would like to do portraits which would look like apparitions to people a century later*. But the style of the painting isn't what unnerves me. It's Adeline's face that's disturbing. It's not the face of a child.

On the opposite page, there's a black-and-white

photograph of Adeline as an elderly woman. She sits in a chair and gazes at a reproduction of her portrait. The likeness between the old face in the photograph and the prematurely old face in the painting is so accurate it's deeply unsettling. Underneath the photograph, she's quoted as saying: *The painting frightened me in its violence. I didn't see its resemblance to me. It was only much later that I realized, when looking at a reproduction, that he had been able to perceive the woman I would become in the girl that I was at the time.*

Recently I've been overcome by seizures. They happen daily now. Some force, internal or external, overcomes my body and causes me to thrash and flail on the floor. Usually I come to on my back: groggy, disoriented, flushed out, sometimes with blood in my mouth, sometimes with my trousers soaked with urine. My seizures first came upon me when I was fifteen years old, living in Northern Ireland, at the height of the Troubles. They passed quickly then, with only a few occurrences, lying dormant until they returned to me several months ago, at the age of forty-nine.

To try to explain all this, I've been reading, looking for justifications, but nothing in the textbooks on my desk can bring me any kind of clarity. Modern science is no closer to identifying the source of consciousness than the Ancient Greeks were. We all feel that we're located within our bodies, and yet we don't feel that we're made of the kind of stuff we see when we look inside a human being – organs, tissue, sinew. If we didn't know that human beings experience the world, we couldn't deduce it from neuroscience. There's nothing about the behaviour of neurons to suggest they're any more special than, say, red blood cells. They're cells, doing what cells do – generating flows of ions, sodium, potassium, chloride, calcium – and releasing neurotransmitters as a consequence.

When speaking of consciousness, we still don't know where to even begin looking. It could be that it isn't even located in the brain, that it's something outside of ourselves, and that the organ in our head is merely a processing machine. This isn't a new idea. Aristotle thought that the soul is – briefly – identical with the objects of our experience. According to his thinking, when you see an apple, your consciousness and the apple are made of the same stuff, which he called the *form* of the apple.

All the science I read seems so cold, so removed from the sensation of a seizure, from the *having* of it. They talk about it, but can't communicate what it's like to be in it, to inhabit a fallible body that is susceptible to these electrical storms. So instead, for solace, I turn to Dostoyevsky, the great chronicler of the condition.

In *The Idiot*, Dostoyevsky describes the moment before his seizures – via his character, Prince Myshkin – as *the highest degree of harmony, beauty, measure, reconciliation, and an ecstatic, prayerful merging with the highest synthesis of life*. I recognize the nature of the condition in these words. There's a moment of supreme clarity that often arrives before my body twists into convulsions, where past and present intermingle, where time and memory become physical and spatial entities, released from the vaults of the brain to flow out through my body, flooding whatever room I happen to be in. Perhaps a seizure is the price you pay for experiencing a world without categories, for stripping away the fabrications we each create for ourselves just to get through the day.

I'm saying all of this as an explanation, a kind of confession maybe: I have my own personal apparition. A man who lives with me. A companion. An enemy.

I can't see him, I can't reach out and touch him, but I know he's there. This isn't a ghost that appears, it's a visitor from my past, a memory made incarnate. He — or, more accurately, his shadow — arrives from behind me, whispers into my limbs and speaks a sentence inside my skull, inflected in a Fermanagh accent, those soft vowels. He's a figment of my imagination. And yet not. He's a part of me. And yet not. He is present and yet not. He floats somewhere in that nether region between objective reality and perceptual insight.

Form. The word feels accurate. Every afternoon, a form comes to me or I become form, and am laid bare, time and time again.

2

My desk, this desk, this room, is in Chinatown, New York. Tonight is a Friday, the first Friday in June. I live on the fifth floor of a building that sits adjacent to the Manhattan Bridge. The room is triangular. I'm sitting at my desk in the cupola at its apex. There's a window in front of me and on each side of me. The central window overlooks a plaza. To my right is the bridge; to the left I can see along Division Street all the way through to the trees of Seward Park.

My seizures re-emerged just before I moved here, but I don't attribute this to the space. I think of it as a refuge, a shelter. I don't pay rent – a miracle in New York. A neighbour of mine, a friend of a friend, offered it to me. In the city permits it's listed as a commercial space, so she's waiting for the paperwork to come through to turn it into a residential apartment. For now, it's mine, a sanctuary, a quiet room in which I can be still and remember.

I can't sleep. I don't want to sleep. Instead I sit here and look out into the night. The city moves differently in these hours: it loses its intensity, becomes more individualized, more contained. People stepping across the plaza ward off attention by keeping their gaze downwards, rarely lingering. Around midnight a flurry of recycling collectors arrives, each pushing a shopping trolley and filling it with

5

plastic bottles or sheets of cardboard. When I first moved here, I thought that they worked together, but then I noticed that they never interact. After taking possession of a single side of the street or plaza, they then work their way along the piles that have been left out for the garbage trucks. There's one man who, every night, takes his break in front of the video-rental store. He leans against his trolley and watches Asian war movies for twenty minutes, even in the rain.

I can see people walking from the bus depots on East Broadway, arriving from Philadelphia and D.C., pulling trolley cases or hefting rucksacks on their backs, impatient to bed down for the night. I can see a limousine make its way towards the small casino on Pike Street, weaving deftly through the narrow alleyways, its gleaming white patina so at odds with everything around it.

Above the plaza, down towards the East River, are the Vladeck Houses, a vast development of mid-rise buildings from the 1940s. I spend a lot of hours just following the movements of the lives that are stacked up inside them. Many of the windows pulse blue in the TV-screen light. I watch figures rising to go to the bathroom, or bedroom, moving through the window frames. New York, I've come to realize, is mostly a city of internal light. Its charm comes from the fact that there's an endless array of individual lives on display. I lived in Paris for a while and, looking back, I realize that the night there was arranged around its monuments, lit by hidden sources. It gave the city a more public feel; it imposed characteristics on the buildings themselves.

Here, I've developed an affinity for water towers. I like their air of uncomplicated sturdiness. I can see more than a dozen of them from where I sit – tucked on to unobtrusive platforms, or standing exposed, solitary, on rooftops, their silhouettes identical in the reflected glare.

To my right, just a few yards from my window, subway trains clack unhurriedly through the underbelly of the bridge. As the night deepens, when the bars are long closed and the partygoers are in their beds, the trains are usually so empty that I can count the number of passengers. I guess they're mostly shift workers on their way home. They sit alone or with one other companion, unspeaking. I often see them look up at me, startled.

I find the constancy of the trains to be reassuring. I can feel them rumbling up from the ground at Canal Street, then they trundle along past my right shoulder, a length of bright silver bulldozing into the night. Again and again, I find myself following them as they slide out over the river, traffic streaming above them, an unceasing flow.

Tonight, I've been watching a video on my laptop. It documents a hospital procedure that I went through this morning. My neuropsychologist, Dr Ptacek, sent it over to me. I'm lying on a gurney in an angiography suite. The camera is directly above me. I'm staring straight into it. A green surgical sheet covers me up to my neck. I've been shaven bald, and a nest of electrodes is glued to my scalp, the head of a Medusa.

It's strange to see yourself in such a vulnerable state.

I recognize myself of course, but mostly I just see a patient, a prone body in an indistinguishable hospital gown. It's interesting to watch my reactions: they don't necessarily fit with my recollection of events.

People lean into the shot and speak to me. They're indistinguishable: the camera shows only the tops of their heads, which are covered in scrub caps. They look as though they're about to step into a communal shower. Around my groin, a square patch is cut out of the sheet. I'm being readied to undergo a Wada test to check for damage to my right hemisphere.

My seizures have become frequent enough and serious enough to warrant an operation. Dr Ptacek has charted my brain scans and logged my clinical record. He and his team have identified some scar tissue in my left hemisphere. In the absence of any other answers, they suspect that this might be the source of my ills. The operation carries a grandiose title: amygdalohippocampectomy – so called because it involves the removal of my amygdala (the Greek for 'almond') and part of the adjacent hippocampus ('seahorse'). The hippocampus is a vital component of the brain's memory circuitry, essential for laying down new traces. If we're the sum of our memories, the hippocampus is the means by which we assemble ourselves. Everything I can recall flows through it. The amygdala houses my means of accessing emotion. It links the higher cortical areas of the brain – language, perception, rational thought – to the deeper structures that manage the regulation of emotion and motivation.

I can see my face on the screen so clearly, see right into my eyes. They emanate terror, which – although understandable – is odd, because I don't remember being scared. I felt calm this morning, lying on that gurney. I allowed myself to take solace in the constancy of my breath. I trusted those around me. Then again, our internal state often doesn't correlate with our public selves. We prepare a face to meet the faces that we meet.

The purpose of the Wada test was to clear a path for the operation, to check that the right side of my brain was functioning properly, that there were no silent lesions lurking in its folds. If I became inhibited on both sides, I would be cut adrift, unable to form new memories, be devoid of emotional colour. Despite the precariousness of my position, I find a kind of delicate beauty in the fact that the gatekeepers to our lives come in such simple forms.

Last Monday, Dr Ptacek talked me through the procedure in his consulting suite. The Wada test involves pumping a course of Amytal into my left hemisphere to anaesthetize it (although the word is apparently incorrect in this instance: the brain has no sensory receptors; it's forever in a state of anaesthesia, another mystery I fail to understand). We rehearsed what would happen. He had me lie on a gurney and raise both my arms in the air. As I counted to twenty, he had me imagine – after ten – that my left arm had become limp and that I allowed it drop to my side. Then he went through the motions of the test, asking me to perform simple actions, do some basic maths and name images on a flipchart.

We've come to know each other a little. Over multiple sessions of what he calls his obstacle course – an EEG, an MRI, video telemetry, neuropsychological profiling, various courses of medication – he's told me some details of his life. He comes from the Czech Republic. He confessed to me that he still thinks of it as Czecho-slovakia, which it was still called when he left. He grew up under Soviet rule in a village in the Carpathians. His father was a mechanic. He arrived in New York on a scholarship after his undergrad degree. His voice still carries the inflections of his homeland. It sounds so rich, so measured and authoritative. I find it calming.

He's told me to call him Karl, but I can't. It's a question of trust, I suppose. I need to believe in his capabilities, his ability to tackle any problem that faces him. I need the professional signifier.

On the screen, the anaesthetist approaches and injects a local anaesthetic into my groin. I keep my gaze upwards, straight into the lens. It's strange but I don't remember the camera above me. I think I was concentrating on all of the activity within the room. It was cramped, filled with X-ray equipment and control panels. The cameraman sat in the corner viewing his video feed, headphones on, checking the sound levels. Above my head was an arrangement of monitors, all showing cross-sections of my brain. In the video, you can hear people milling about in the back-ground: EEG technicians in white scrubs, radiologists in

blue, like two teams competing for something. The technicians were keeping track of my brain's activity levels, which
snaked across the monitors in different colours. The blue
lines were dominant and undulated only slightly, which I
knew was a good sign, meaning that my brain was idling in
a languid alpha rhythm.

I can see myself closing my eyes. I turn my head from
side to side. I think I was trying to get comfortable on
the pillow. I remember the electrodes were itchy on my
scalp – I wanted to reach up and yank a few of them out.

Dr Ptacek enters the shot. He leans over to greet me.
I turn towards him, opening my eyes again. He's carrying a clipboard, a stopwatch and a black ring binder. He
hands the clipboard to a colleague.

'How are you doing, Simon?' He touches my shoulder.

'Fine. Nervous.'

'You'll be out of here in no time. Keep taking those
nice calm breaths.' He looks up towards the EEG monitors. 'Everything will happen just as we rehearsed it. I
promise.' I remember once again finding his voice so
relieving, that assured accent.

A nurse approaches from the left of the frame and
holds my hand. They're ready to begin.

The radiologist makes an incision in my groin. I can
tell when this is happening on the video because at that
same moment the nurse brushes a strand of hair away
from my forehead and I flinch with distress, fear washing
over me. The radiologist slips a catheter into my femoral
artery and slides it, expertly, through my body.

'Just the junction with the internal carotid,' she says.

I couldn't tell if she was saying this to herself or to me or to one of the technicians.

I could feel the sensation of the catheter sliding up through my chest, from heart to brain: a stranger winding its way through me. On screen, I make a chewing motion, as the catheter scratches the inside of my neck.

The radiologist sits back, relieved. She has arrived at her destination. She clips the other end of the tube into a machine and then leans in towards me.

'Okay, Simon,' she says, 'I'm going to pump through some dye, to make sure that we've reached the right area of your brain. It'll feel a bit weird, like something has burst. Just relax, you're doing great.'

I can see myself clenching my jaw determinedly, ready for action. My face flushes. The liquid, I remember, felt disconcertingly warm. It flashed underneath my skull, an orgasm, a brainwave, an abandon.

Dr Ptacek approaches again and stations himself on the other side of my midriff, across from the nurse. The nurse places her hands on either side of my face. It was so good to feel her cool touch. The nurse, now that I see her on-screen, seems to have no specific medical function; she's merely there to reassure me. As I watch these three people gather around me, I think how each of them is attending to a particular strand of myself. The body. The mind. The human being.

Dr Ptacek speaks. 'Simon, I'm going to ask you to raise your hands just as we practised. Once we begin to pump the Amytal through, you can start to count to twenty.'

I raise both arms, something hopeful in the gesture, an evangelical in worship.

The radiologist nods to Dr Ptacek. The assistant clicks her stopwatch. Dr Ptacek nods at me and I begin to count. My voice is reedy, nervous, hesitant.

By the time I reach eight, I'm beginning to show signs of grogginess, my left arm wavers, then collapses. Dr Ptacek catches it gently mid fall and places it by my side.

My eyes flicker and then dart up and down, left and right. I can see I am frantic, a feral awareness of danger has taken over.

It's so strange to look at myself like this. Thirty seconds beforehand I'm definably Simon Hanlon, an Irishman, forty-nine years old, single, childless. The face on the screen is the same as the one I see in a bathroom mirror. But once the drug begins to take effect I become someone else. An aggression arises in my eyes; my features line with worry and confusion. I look like I'm straining against something, like I'm pushing against a wall. Half of my brain is now inactive. Does this make me half the person I was just moments beforehand? Or is this feral, frantic creature my true self, one I hide under a veil of decorum?

Dr Ptacek speaks again. 'Okay, Simon, I'd like you to touch your nose.'

I respond mechanically.

When he asks me to recite the days of the week, I reply, 'Fed, fed, fed . . . fed . . . fed . . .' I look like I'm trying to clean some gristle from behind my wisdom teeth. My sensibility has changed again. I no longer look agitated but rather lost, desolate.

'Now can you count backwards from ten?'

At first I appear engaged with the new request. Effort is scrawled all over my face. I say, 'Tew, nipe, accch, seb . . . seb . . . seb . . . seb.' Then, suddenly, my concentration fades. I've given up. Maybe I heard my own distorted voice, maybe I just lost the will to continue. Next, I wink at the nurse and chuckle malevolently. And then I'm overcome with another emotion: I look as though I'm about to cry. I'm as raw as an infant.

(I remember none of this. Afterwards, in his office, Dr Ptacek told me that my disturbed speech was normal. Our language receptors are mostly located in the left hemisphere. It would have been surprising if I were coherent.)

Dr Ptacek takes the black binder and shows me some pictures, asking me to identify them.

I point and repeat the same word about each one.

'De.'

'De.'

'De.'

My face lightens.

I chuckle, again, viciously, wickedly. Then I am stricken, and my pupils dilate.

'Okay, Simon. Close your eyes and relax.'

I close my eyes. My face is blank. He exits to another room while the drug wears off. I can see the tension in my face draining away. A peaceful, benevolent look descends.

He returns after a few minutes to test my memory. He's holding a clipboard now.

'So, then, what images do you remember?'

I pause.

'A fork.'

'Good.'

'A basketball.'

'Good.'

'A bicycle.'

'Yes.'

'A donkey.'

'Yes. Good. Anything else.'

A long pause.

'A flashlight.'

He hesitates, nods, writes something down on the clipboard. 'Okay. Thanks, Simon. How was it, overall, how do you think you did?'

I can see myself smile brightly. 'It was all right, wasn't it? Yeah, I kind of enjoyed it. I mean, it's not like you're asking anything difficult.'

Afterwards, he reassured me that he knew I wasn't lying, that I genuinely believed the whole process to have been a breeze. He explained that it was an example of the left hemisphere confabulating. Apparently, it does this constantly, for everyone, editing our experiences to make them understandable, plausible, palatable.

But there is something we both missed. It happens at 18.32. Just before he returns with the clipboard to test my memory.

I'm saying something. I look at the nurse and say

something. She responds by rubbing my neck. My speech is still garbled, my left hemisphere still partially numb: *Warsurnimsn.*

I didn't notice it at first. And, even then, I had to play it back several times with the volume up before I could make out what I was saying.

My eyes have widened while I'm spitting out the words. I can see myself filled with terror, disorientation. The words, I realize, make up a sentence, one I'm very familiar with, one that regularly rings inside my head. But to see myself speak it aloud is a different sensation – strange, painful, somehow revealing. I play the moment again. I watch my lips move, I hear that garbled speech, that voice that doesn't sound anything like me: *Warsurnimsn.*

I play it again, a sentence that echoes through the chambers of my life: *What's your name, son?*

3

A particular quirk of my seizures is that they happen only in the late afternoon. Such consistency is unusual but not unheard of. Each person's condition has its own character, its own shadings of personality. Mine leaves me free to spend my mornings in peace; I have learned to forestall my dread until lunchtime approaches.

I rise early and take to the streets. I buy a coffee and a bagel with cream cheese from a deli on Forsyth Street and I sit on a bench at the Hester Street playground and feel the pulse of the city and am reminded of everything that I have, until this point, taken for granted. The pallor of familiarity is scrubbed away. Something as ordinary as the hues of brickwork on a school building has the capacity to ignite my nervous system in the same way that it did when I used to sit in a concert hall and listen to an orchestra. The phrase *a symphony of colour* is no longer a cliché for me.

I'm told that this is a side effect of my condition, an aberration in my mental functioning. I still can't reconcile myself to this assessment. No one emerging from a concert hall is told that what they have experienced is merely a combination of instrument and notation. I wonder if colour is always this resonant and that I've just been too insulated ever to realize it.

I sit on a park bench and drink my coffee and eat my bagel and look at a group of elderly people work though the incremental motions of their Tai Chi routine. It's become the focal point of my day. Their movements are so simple and yet enacted with such reverence. Many of them have hands that are obviously arthritic: their fingers stick out at odd angles. And they have difficulty keeping their limbs steady; there's a perceptible shake in their arms as they trace their circles in the air. Still, their concentration doesn't wear on their faces. They are — there's no other word for it — filled with grace. Even when stationary, they give the impression of movement.

And there's joy there too, there's nothing pious about these people. After the Tai Chi, they use the public Citi Bikes as exercise machines. While the bikes are clamped in the docking station, they climb aboard and work the pedals, waving to people on the street, chattering amongst themselves, ringing the bells on their handlebars.

I think about death of course, sitting on that park bench, sipping my coffee. I think about it even more since the Wada test. Its presence looms near now. Of course I'm afraid, but these past months have shown me the possibility of something beyond. I'm not talking about heaven, some palace with white clouds with choirs of angels waiting for my arrival. I'm talking about how we view the world, our need for — our obsession with — order and categorization, how smug and petty we are in our assumed knowledge, our intellectual justifications, our claims of expertise.

It's clear to me now that our insistence upon an objective sense of time – constant, linear, utterly indifferent to how we spend our days – is at the very least naive. Time isn't mechanical, this much is obvious. I'm beginning to appreciate the subjective nature of it, how it arrives and departs in waves, a constant exchange of accumulation and dissipation. And so it stands to reason that the more deeply we are affected by a moment, the greater the accumulation of experience. A season, a day, a morning, can carry such density that it can outweigh a decade, two decades; it can imbalance an entire life.

Dissolving the imposed limits of the ticking clock brings a feeling of intense liberation that carries forward into every other aspect of my senses, and so the lines between myself and everything around me, animate or inanimate, frequently dissolve, or become engulfed by a feeling of unity. I can't express this sensation through words. To do so contradicts the experience; it imposes definition upon something that is, in its most natural state, indefinable. Lao Tsu writes: *The name that can be named is not the eternal name.* This makes complete sense to me. If you can put a name to God, it can't be God that you're referring to. Maybe Einstein got closest to it. He used to call the creator the *Old One*. I like it; it has a clear ring to it. If there is something, some entity, beyond all that surrounds us, it is certainly old, and it is probably one.

The Ancient Greeks called epilepsy the *Sacred Disease*. They believed that sufferers were cursed by one of the gods. The accompanying symptoms would point towards which god was offended. For example, if a patient's cry resembled a horse's scream, it was suggested that Poseidon – the father of horses – was inflicting his wrath. The notion of divinity's link to epilepsy didn't end with the Greeks. Méric Casaubon, a French scholar from the seventeenth century, wrote about a baker who had been brutally beaten by his master and began having seizures. These took the form of ecstasies in which he claimed not to have been on his bed – as onlookers would have him believe – but to have been carried away by angels and entered paradise, where he was welcomed by his dead relatives.

Joan of Arc, another figure from history who was probably epileptic, described her visions at her trial for heresy. A voice came to her daily, always to her right, accompanied by a light.

Dostoyevsky thought of his condition as a possible vehicle for transcendence. *As soon as the normal earthly state of the organism is disturbed, the possibility of another world begins to appear. And as the illness increases, so do the contacts with the other world.*

Perhaps all of these are just examples of our trying to will something into being, sifting through a burnt-out building for signs of an arsonist.

After the park, I go to a market on Elizabeth Street to buy food for my day. It looks like a small butcher's shop from the outside but stretches back a whole block. Inside, the exiting customers pass their receipts to a man in a white coat and red baseball cap who checks them against their purchases. Behind the meat counters, roast ducks hang from metal hooks, their heads twisted towards the door, as though they're trying to make eye contact with the man taking the receipts.

It's quiet there in the mornings. There's no urgency to anyone's demands, no music blasting from hidden speakers. It's another land to me, and I'm enthralled by the place. I walk through, making my purchases, stopping and staring into the display cabinets, and gazing at marinated jellyfish – half the size of my fist, textured and barnacled like loofahs – and at the enmeshments of grey shrimp on beds of crushed ice. There are always white crates on the floor around the fish counters, and I stand over them and peer in to see large hefty frogs staring back up at me, morosely. They pile on top of one another, shifting their hind legs for comfort, and I keep waiting in vain for one of them to blink. In other crates, thin white eels move as slowly and steadily as a twig on a lake.

In the afternoons, I stay here in my room and wait for the storm. Most of my movements are confined to a line between my bed and my chair and desk in the cupola. All of the furniture has foam taped around the edges, and the floor is covered in rubber matting.

It might sound like a sorry state, but I'm not lonely. There are people who come in and out of my days. I've become a curiosity in the area. People greet me on the street, say my name. A community organization sends a musician to visit people in their apartments on Wednesday mornings. Often, other neighbours sit in on these sessions, and by now I have an open invitation to come along. When I do, I try to be as unobtrusive as possible. I stand at the back and listen and look at the joy in their faces that the music ignites, the tender nostalgia that can wrap itself around the exile.

Mr Chunyan, in the apartment below mine, keeps showing me his workout routine. I pay attention. The man deserves respect: he's eighty-five, and several times a day he skips up and down four flights of stairs to the street. I've been given a panic button that I'm supposed to press when I feel a seizure coming on. It's connected to a speaker in Mr Chunyan's apartment. I rarely use it, though. After the first couple of times, when I woke to see the distress on his face, I decided it wasn't worth it. He's earned his peace; he doesn't need to be burdened by the afflictions of a stranger who is decades his junior.

Instead, when a seizure has passed, I often make my way down the stairs to visit him and drink some tea. He doesn't speak much English, but it doesn't really matter, as we often communicate by gesture. He offers me oranges and tells me to rub my knees at every opportunity, get the blood flowing within them. Hing, my unofficial nurse, told me that Mr Chunyan worked in a restaurant in Jersey City until he was well into his seventies. His wife left him four years ago. He explained to his neighbours that one day she just decided to go back to Hong Kong. No one buys this version of events. For three years he was unhappy, and then he shook it off with the callisthenics routine that he does in the park every morning and shows me every time he answers the door. I like being around him. An eighty-five-year-old with a new lease of life is a rare bird, one that gives me comfort, joy.

Sometimes, when we're sitting across from each other, sipping our tea, two strange comrades, a beautiful quiet descends. Mr Chunyan is one of those people who are comfortable with vast silences. I can't tell if this is a result of living alone for so long or if it's something more innate. These pauses can stretch for ten minutes, maybe more. I've never seen him close his eyes, and yet I don't feel scrutinized. His presence instead feels intimate, containing an odd kind of harmony.

When these silences land, I don't try to imagine Mr Chunyan's past – his experiences have been so different from mine that I can't gain any purchase on them. Instead, I am swept away by visceral memories, details of my childhood: smells and sounds and images; things I had no idea I still retained. I can hear the sound of cattle walking into a crush. I can smell primroses and see scarecrows made from used fertilizer bags. I gaze at nettles and dock leaves. I smell the billows of turf smoke that expanded from the fireplace in our parlour when the door was shut quickly. I taste porridge cooked overnight in our range oven, feel the texture of the barmbrack that my mother made at Halloween, with a spent match and a hard pea and a ring inside, all wrapped in slips of greaseproof paper. To find one in a slice meant that you'd receive a great love, or a beating, or a life of poverty. A blessing or a curse.

I remember the way a bullock uses its tail as a fly-swatter. I can see small rotten apples splayed under a tree. Soda bread spread with melting butter. Sparrows bulleting into a crumbling wall. Starlings in murmuration, reshaping the sky. I can hear the rasp of corncrakes announcing the descent of evening.

And I think of soldiers – uniformed or not. I think of armoured vehicles. Of peacelines. Of barriers. I think of burnt-out cars and firebombs.

We regard a memory as a pale re-enactment of a particular moment. I am coming to wonder if, in fact, the opposite is true: that our experiences of events and incidents in the present are scant, without volume, that we merely accumulate them, and it is only later, when they have been released into the landscape of the time, that they can reach fruition.

4

On the 8th of November 1987 the IRA exploded a bomb in Enniskillen, my hometown. Twelve people were killed; another sixty-three were badly injured. It was one of the lowest points in the whole sad history of the Troubles. Myself and my father were present. My seizures began soon after.

The bombing took place at a ceremony to mark Remembrance Sunday, the annual day of commemoration for the British troops who died in the world wars and later conflicts. Neither of us had attended the service before. My mother, as a respected member of the Church of Ireland, always took the duty upon herself. Aside from weddings and funerals, she rarely asked me to go along to any kind of formal service. And my father left this one to her alone. A naturally timid man, he was resistant to all notions of patriotism, all displays of military service – on either side. He simply wanted to work the land, peacefully, in solidarity with his neighbours, irrespective of religious or political beliefs.

My mother wasn't there that day, though. Or the next day. She had died from cancer nine months beforehand. So that morning we were present – as the saying goes – in her absence, a statement that seemed to be true for all aspects of our lives at that point.

I was fifteen years old and alone. I had no brothers or sisters. We lived in a large farmhouse near the shores of Lough Erne, in a place called Lisnarick, not far from the village of Kesh and a short drive to the town of Enniskillen. It had been in my mother's family, the Stewarts, since the Plantations and had been passed to her after her brother, David, died of a heart attack before he'd had time to marry. She returned from Liverpool just before the Troubles reignited in earnest, a newly qualified nurse with a baby and a young husband in tow, a dockworker from down south, a Catholic impostor. And so, in a polarized time, a tribal time, I straddled both sides, which of course meant that I belonged to neither.

It's only now, in adulthood, that I can appreciate the effect that such a return must have had on her spirit. A few years ago, not long before his own death, my father told me that it had been her ambition to join the Nursing Corps, and I can easily imagine her in some of the great cities of the world, wearing that neat grey uniform with her hair pinned up under her cap. After he mentioned it, my recollections of our trips to Dublin and Belfast took on a different aspect. I could understand why my mother would always take time to sit in a tearoom and listen to the ambient chatter that swirled around under the high ceilings, unbothered by my behaviour in such a place, too immersed in the lives of others. Those moments, I now realize, along with her books and the plays she listened to on the radio, would have been her only recourse to an alternative life that was once within her reach.

There was a certain decorum to the way that she held herself in those fine rooms. She would place her cup down on its saucer without making a sound. She would cross her legs and smooth out any creases in her skirt. And the way she nodded to the waitresses, the way she spoke with her head angled slightly to one side. My mother had poise, everyone remarked on it.

The silences that filled our house in the months after her death echoed all the more loudly for the fact that they would have been cast away with the sound of her singing as she mopped the floor in the scullery and by the unending run of conversation when she sat at the kitchen table talking to one of her friends on the phone, tangling and untangling her index finger around its black cord or drawing circular doodles on any scrap of paper she could find nearby. Whether singing or talking, I missed her voice more than anything.

My father didn't grieve openly, instead he collapsed internally. Even the way he sat on the sofa changed: he sank, inattentively, down into its soft interior. When he rose from it, he placed his hands on either side of his legs and hoisted himself up. It was as if he had aged a few decades. Speech required a similar level of effort from him: he couldn't seem to manage to float more than three or four sentences in my direction.

Perhaps if my father and I could have talked about my mother in those lonely months after she died, it would have transformed us both; we may have laid an easier passage for each other. That we couldn't was our small tragedy, and it was an inevitable one. No, *tragedy* is much too grand a word. What occurred between us was slower, more porous, more mundane. A dissolution.

History isn't created from the images that cascade across our news channels, the rhetoric of politicians. It grows from a myriad of personal decisions, quiet conversations. The singular events of each life ultimately cohere into the continuity of communal experience, communal belief, like a stone skipping across still waters, the linear intermingling with the circular. We're all a product of our time, and the time into which my father emerged insisted that he must record every sexual thought that had entered his mind and account for it later, shamefully, to a priest, in a small darkened booth. It decreed that he should do his best to avoid all physical contact with his child and should discourage any questions that could not be met with a solid answer. The borders that entangled my youth were not only geographic, they were also internal. They segmented and categorized every thought and word and gesture with unwavering definition. It felt at the time, moving past each other to occupy separate rooms, that neither of us had any more influence over our silent estrangement than we did over the British squaddies that milled around our country lanes at all hours of the day and night.

At home, the main accompaniment to my thoughts, aside from the TV, became the sharp ticking of the gold carriage clock on our mantelpiece, a boxy affair with a flywheel that ran underneath its face, parallel to the marble mantelpiece. The clock was one of the few items of furniture that was definably his, a departure gift from his former employers, Watling & Sons, whom he worked for in Liverpool until just after I was born. It was run, he pointed out to any visitor that came into our house, on barometric pressure. His fascination for this marvel never seemed to lose any of its freshness, and because of this people, or more specifically men, didn't have to feign interest. Instead they peered into its glass box – as I sometimes did when I was alone – to try to discover its secrets. No doubt they felt that they too should automatically understand how such an instrument went about its business. Maybe some of them did. Certainly, they always leaned in and then stood back to take a rich, deep pleasure in the endless inventiveness of precision engineering, and then they often talked about some other piece of mechanical ingenuity that had once struck them as a combination of original thought and fine craftsmanship.

The clock was the centrepiece of the lunch that followed my mother's funeral. The two branches of my family couldn't bring themselves to be in the same room together, and so they searched out practical tasks to make some superficial sense of their division. The Stewarts congregated in the dining room, where they supervised the handing out of plates and lifted and replaced the lids over the hot dishes on the buffet trolley. The Hanlons were in the kitchen, cleaning and drying any glassware or cutlery or delph that made its way back to them. The two catering staff that our nearest neighbour, Trudy Irvine, had insisted on hiring were delighted with how the whole arrangement played itself out. My father and I, not having the energy or the inclination to act as mediators, placed ourselves in the parlour, and so that was where all of the focus of the gathering was centred. Both of us stood by the fireplace, where my father deflected all expressions of sympathy towards a discussion of the clock, while I stood to the side and gazed at people I had known my whole life and who, inexplicably, had lost the ability to speak to a teenager. Women sat on the assembled furniture and spoke to each other in low tones, stealing an occasional look at me, while their husbands gathered in a semicircle around the fireplace and scrutinized the mystery of a mechanism that never needed to be wound and didn't rely on batteries. I never came to understood how this phenomenon actually worked; I had a vague notion that it had something to do with the density of air, and possibly an influence of tidal movements. I never asked my father about it in any more detail, because either he would have given a long, convoluted explanation, at the end of which I'd be even more confused, or he himself would have been stumped, and then have nothing to point out to strangers, frozen in the fear of their asking the same thing.

During the previous winter it had served as a more gentle accompanist to my afternoons. In those – now precious – days, I came home from school and was allowed to eat my dinner off a tray in front of the fire, across from my mother, who sat on the other armchair darning our clothes. This happened in the weeks between chemotherapy sessions, when she no longer had to lie in her room, feeling nauseous for days on end and vomiting into a brown tub, which I would empty out into the toilet and wash clean with lemon washing-up liquid before placing it back under her bed in anticipation of her next bout. When the toxins eventually abated, she moved into the parlour and sat by the fire that my father lit in the mornings, wearing a wig that was nothing like the way her natural hair had been – it was much blonder and much shorter and poked upwards around the crown in stubborn tufts. When late afternoon came, I joined her, and we listened to the spit of the logs and the ticking of the clock, grateful for the temporary reprieve of her illness, and she told me stories of her childhood in the house. How she once played with a Ouija board on the dining table with her brother and their friends and a fuse blew at exactly the wrong moment and they were plunged into darkness and ran screaming into the kitchen, where Willy Brady, the stableman, sat puffing on his pipe and reading the racing results in the paper. Willy stood up and walked down the hallway and screwed in a new fuse and sat back down again and did all of this while hardly taking his eyes off the page. Or when her father brought home his first car and taught her that afternoon to drive on the laneway and how, when she was put behind the wheel, she stamped the accelerator to the floor and they shot off down the lane and her maiden voyage ended abruptly against the stone gatepost, and how her father wasn't in the least bit annoyed.

Instead, after checking that they were both uninjured, he threw back his head and laughed heartily and told the story at every opportunity and people invariably responded to it by looking at her and winking and telling her she'd do all right and how she never knew what this was supposed to mean. For the next year or two she thought that maybe crashing cars was a well-established profession for women that she could one day apply for in some car factory in England.

I, in turn, offered up the details of my school day. A supply teacher struggling to keep control and fights in the yard and failed a chemistry experiment and a food fight on the bus, where the older boys bought mandarin oranges and onions in Flannery's grocers and fired them at their captive targets – the oranges made a mess, the onions did the most damage – while the driver kept looking forward, deliberately oblivious to all of the action behind him.

They were fragments of my life that I never would have voiced before her illness. By then she had mellowed and listened without judgement, feeling no need to correct me or offer guidance. She nodded along and fixed patches on to the crotch of my school trousers and inside the heels of my socks so that they didn't wear out as easily, and months later, when my feet itched underneath my school desk, I'd be taken immediately back to the image of her by the fireside and feel a small solace within the sadness, that she was still, in her way, taking care of me.

A month after the bombing, the clock took on another

significance. But before I go into all that, I should talk about the explosion itself.

The bomb exploded at the cenotaph at the top of Belmore Street at 10.43 a.m. The cenotaph is a statue of a soldier leaning on the butt of his rifle, its muzzle at his feet, a pack on his back, a cap on his head. It's still there, it wasn't affected by the blast. My old school, St Michael's, is a fifteen-minute walk from it. The gates of Mount Lourdes girls' school are twenty yards away. I remember the statue well, we played football against it. Our school finished a half-hour before the girls' and so, while we waited for the buses that served both schools, we killed time by playing soccer on the street, using a tennis ball. The plinth on which the soldier stood was one goal, the steps of Forthill Park the other. These targets, when combined with the size of the ball, meant that we didn't need goalkeepers, a situation that suited all of us, leaving us free to swarm up and down the street, and slip on to the pavement when a car passed through. The soldier looked down disconsolately upon us; even our frenzy wasn't enough to shake him from his stupor.

Between the cenotaph and Mount Lourdes' gates sat an old building known as the Reading Rooms. It belonged to St Michael's parish and housed our school until the 1950s, when there was a funding push for education and the local council built something more fit for the purpose. In the 1980s the top floor was used as a storage room for the boy scouts. They kept their canoes and some other equipment up there. The ground floor was a large open space with basketball hoops on either end and functioned as a community centre. In the basement there were some snooker tables and a card table where the caretaker, Jim Dunlop, occasionally played poker with his friends.

On Saturday nights, there was a bingo session in the main hall on the ground floor. About fifty women attended religiously. Seamus McCarney pulled the balls out from the machine and called the numbers. His son, Young Seamus, manned the cash box and handed out the bingo cards.

On the evening before the bombing, those women – who we called 'the headscarf brigade' – arrived around quarter to nine and readied themselves for action.

The game finished at half ten, after which Seamus and Young Seamus walked down to the basement to join the poker game that was in play. Jim Dunlop used the disruption as an opportunity to drop his kids home. He promised to return soon enough, a promise which he upheld: he was back within the hour. By that time Seamus had left, but Young Seamus was still there, along with Damien McGurn and Eamon Goodwin.

Around midnight, they heard some sounds in the bingo hall. They went quiet for a moment, but heard nothing more, so they continued playing. Ten minutes later, they heard the sound again. It wasn't any cause for concern. It was an old building and it was wintertime, creaking noises were commonplace.

Eamon stood up and went to check on the bingo hall

but didn't find anything and returned to the game. About an hour and a half later, when they had finished and Jim was locking up for the night, Eamon shouted into the hall that they were on their way home and that if anyone was around they should come out or they'd be locked in.

No one answered.

At about the same time as the bingo session was finishing, I was going to bed. My father and I were watching TV in our parlour. I stood up from the sofa and made for an early night. My father said my name just before I left the room.

Simon.

He didn't need to continue his sentence and ask me to wait a minute, the word itself was enough to cause me to pause. My father never referred to me by my name, unless he was introducing me to someone else. He said that he'd be going to the Remembrance Parade in the morning and asked if I'd like to come along. I told him that would be fine. He said we'd need to head to Mass beforehand, and I nodded as agreeably as possible and made my way to bed.

In the morning, I woke early and stayed in bed, staring at the wallpaper that my mother had picked out years before in Dickie's Hardware Shop. Scarlet roses, their stems knotted in curlicues. I stared at my breath, which rose in wispy drifts in the chill of the room, delicate as the sprays of lily of the valley that she put in the small glass vase on the nightstand of the guestroom when people came to stay.

After a while, I heard my father pad down the stairs and clatter about in the kitchen. The back door opening and closing. The crackle of his footsteps on the gravel that he had laid down in our yard, another of the touch-ups he had undertaken in previous months to keep himself occupied. That autumn was a particularly bad one: it had rained solidly since early September, and the grass had had no chance to renew itself, so he'd had to begin feeding hay to the cattle much earlier than he would have liked. He was already worried that he might not have enough to last him through to the spring if the early months of the next year proved to be similarly unkind.

I listened for the Massey Ferguson to splutter into life. The model was a 35. My uncle David had bought it in the early 1960s. It was a durable little machine. I was fond of it, not only because I learned to drive on it, but also because it was stubborn and its gears were simple to work. My father used it for smaller jobs, the type that once would have been carried out by a donkey. Carrying a hay bale down towards the lake was about the limit of its capacity. I thought that it had some of the character of the animal it replaced. It was even similar in size. When I filled it with diesel it felt like I was feeding it, and I had to resist the urge to pat it on its bonnet and thank it for its work.

I heard my father turn the engine a few times; it growled before the ignition kicked in. The gears grinding under the weak clutch. I imagined him rounding the corner into the upper yard, where we kept one stock of bales. There was a brief thud, when he shunted the tractor backwards into the bale, the forks of the back loader stabbing into it, and then a revving of the engine to put power into the hydraulic lift and a rasp of the clutch as he bolted forward and puttered towards the gate, a pause into neutral as he opened the gate, another rasp, another forward movement, another pause while he closed the gate again and then a louder revving as he worked his way through the gears, gathering speed, rumbling down the slope. I had done it all so many times myself.

I turned to look out through the window and stared at the chestnut tree that sat just beyond our garden wall. The wall was high enough to enclose a metal door, which led into the Orchard Meadow. The tree dominated it benevolently, rising up five times higher than the stonework. Its leaves still clung to the branches — russet coloured and almost translucent in the harshly chromatic winter light.

In the weeks after my mother's death, I would come home from school and lie in its branches. The boughs were thick enough for me to rest with my back against them and let my limbs dangle below me without fear of falling. I would drop my schoolbag in the kitchen and make my way out into the garden, lifting the metal door by its clasp to take the weight off its failed hinges, and clamber up the trunk by gaining purchase on the scraps of timber I had nailed into it when I was ten years old. I drew comfort from the great branches. The blood, the frailty of a body – I saw them as emblems of infinite regression. I would trace my eye along their lines, following the thick boughs as they tapered down into thinner branches, finally dwindling into stalks as slender as a candlewick. Looking at them, I found it easy to understand that everything inside me and everything surrounding me could be traced down into atoms, could be traced down further still. The leaves shuffling timorously above reassured me that my mother's frailty as she approached her end was not a diminishment of the self, that it was merely a progression towards something less definitive.

Beyond the Orchard Meadow, out where my father was headed that morning, all of the fields were named after activities that had once taken place in them. The Hunt Field. The Cricket Field. The Festival Field. The Race Field. I never found the grandeur of our home intimidating. The farm I knew no longer had any labourers. My father took care of everything himself. All that remained of the farm was a beef herd that he had bought as yearlings and sold on to the meat factory once they had reached their full bulk. But it was comforting to think of our house and fields once being populated by carpenters, stablemen, cooks, labourers, gardeners. I imagined the place to be full of life, and I took pleasure in the workmanship that was still apparent all around me, from the neat and sturdy floorboards in my room to the sunburst tiles around the fireplaces, to the stone wall running around the perimeter of the garden that even after a couple of centuries showed no sign of subsidence.

On the front lawn were coopers' barrels that had been cut in half and used as flowerpots, the wood so old that it had a bluish tinge. Near the gate at the top of the Festival Field was a drinking trough, which was made up of an old enamel bath that had been converted long before my father was on the scene. In the side pouch of the Massey Ferguson there was a bread knife with a mother-of-pearl handle and a stamp on the blade from a silversmith in London. My father used it to cut through the twine of the hay bales.

The sky that morning held the potential of more rain. Despite the bright beginning, I could see dense clouds rolling in from the lake. I knew that they loomed over my father. I could picture him delivering the bale to the cattle in the Race Field and looking up and cursing. I could see him dismounting from his seat and crumping through the frosted grass, cutting the blue cords of the bailer twine and the bail being released, giving off that peculiarly sweet and rancid smell that accompanied its freedom. There would be expansive spumes of condensation leaking off the cattle, rising into the morning chill as all of them gathered around in a tight circle, jostling each other for space, a great roll of compressed muscle under a threatening sky.

When I heard the tractor returning, I rose and was in the shower by the time I heard him walk back into the house. Still, I managed to make us late. The minutes between drying myself, brushing my teeth and dressing managed to slip away without my realizing, until there was the familiar bang of a fist on the bedroom door.

'Jesus Christ, would you get a move-on? Is it too much to ask that we're on time?'

'Aye, I'll be right with you.'

The car park was full by the time we got there. He suggested that I get out and go in ahead of him, but I refused: I told him we needed to arrive in together. A late entrance was a public act and with all those eyes upon me, I wanted him there with me. I only rarely contradicted him, and, whenever I did, he made it a point not to react. In the midst of a silent war, he was decidedly conflict averse. In this instance, he busied himself by looking in both directions for a parking spot.

At the entrance to the church he stopped and dug in his pockets and gave some change to the woman collecting for Guide Dogs for the Blind. He dipped his fingers in the font by the door, made the sign of the cross – forehead, stomach, shoulder, shoulder – and entered.

I kept my hands in my pockets. It had been a few years since I had attended Sunday Mass. My parents excused me from any kind of worship. It wasn't a decision that they took lightly. When the time came for me to leave primary school, there were tense discussions as to where I should go next. In Northern Ireland a school functions as far more than just a building where education occurs, it defines your affiliations. The secondary school they chose, St Michael's, was for Catholic boys. It was what we called a 'maintained school'. The Protestant schools were 'controlled schools'. How we came up with such meaningless vocabulary is beyond me.

I'm sure my father had some concerns about his beliefs

being consumed by another tradition, but I suspect the main reason for excusing me from worship was that they didn't want to take sides. The same idea probably explains their decision to send me to a Catholic school, which would balance out the Protestant lineage of the farm. Whether through luck or caution, we never got any bullets posted through our letterbox. There were estates that I couldn't go into and a few scrapes here and there, but very few threats ever came my way, and I didn't get bullied in school, which is kind of remarkable in retrospect. I suppose I became skilled at keeping my head down. The fact of my mother's being a nurse probably worked in our favour, as did my father's decency and humility. He was around enough to be familiar and still he made sure he was as unobtrusive as possible. His technical skill was also a factor. If a tractor cut out in a nearby field, he would perk up as definitively as a dog, and if there were no restarting of the engine he would drop whatever he was doing at the time and stride across the distance between himself and the problem. His mechanical ability was known for miles around, so he was welcome no matter the colour of the land.

At St Michael's, I was allowed to forgo religion classes. I used the time to do my homework. Notes would trickle down to me – 'Hanlon, you're a sheepshagger' – then the author would turn his head and look slyly back at me and I'd flip him the finger and that would be the end of that. I played soccer in the yard and on Belmore Street while we waited for the Lourdes girls. I didn't play any sports for the school, though, or the GAA club. It was thought better by everyone, including myself, that I didn't slip on any kind of jersey. And my school friends were just that. We hardly ever saw each other when we weren't wearing our uniforms. I didn't resent any of them for it. The cards just fell that way for me.

Even though we were late for Mass, I knew my father wouldn't stand near the back, with the other stragglers. We shuffled our way to his usual seat in the left aisle, shoes clacking shamefully on the stone flags. I looked all around me: the same faces occupied the same pews in the same sections. Dinny Grennan, who trained the junior hurlers on Wednesdays. Tom Metcalf, the barber. Breda Donoghue, the teacher, whose daughters were also teachers, one in Galway, one in London. I stood beside my father, knotted my hands and stared at the candles and the statues and at the paintings of the Stations of the Cross, depicted in lustrous gore.

The organist finished his prelude with a flourish and Fr O'Reilly emerged in his lace-trimmed vestments, an imperious look on his face, trailed by a phalanx of altar boys. They took their positions, kneeling on the stone steps, while Fr O'Reilly made his way to the lectern and raised his arms to begin, his vestments billowing out, his hands splayed open. Recalling the grandness of the pose reminds me now of something ancient, a witchdoctor standing in front of a fire, ready to divine a greater power.

Although I rarely attended Mass, the recitations came back to me easily, though I didn't speak them out loud.

They didn't come like an echo in the mind, more like putting your feet back into a stream. A sensation you can't replicate until you do it again. The unchanged can be as surprising as the changed.

The motions, the gestures, the words.

The genuflections. The creed. The eucharist. The consecration. The confessional boxes. The thurible. The incense. The crucifix. The chalice. The sacristy. The nave. The apse. The vaultings. The stained glass. The Gothic arches. The baptismal font.

There were pensioners around me who worked their rosary beads, mumbled under their breath throughout, still obeying the practices of the Latin Mass, the reforms of Vatican II – when the liturgy changed to English – still, decades later, too radical for them to countenance.

As Fr O'Reilly made the community announcements before he gave the final blessing, I can remember my gaze drawing upwards to the stained-glass windows: it was difficult to make out where the glass ended and the ceiling began, the delicacy of the morning light softening all distinction, Bible stories becoming vague as they rose up the stitched panes.

More faces to recognize as we made our way out. Michael Carragher, the chemist. Frank Devine, the draper. Joe Burke, the auctioneer. The women around us hurrying home, needing to get the dinner on. Most of the men intent on heading down the road to Blake's pub.

After Mass, my father and I walked the high street. The rain fell hard and determined. We had only one umbrella between us – I had left mine on the coat-rack in our porch – and so we were forced to press close together, him leading, holding the umbrella high above us, me staying close behind, trying not to stumble into him, both of us uncomfortable with our intimate proximity.

We positioned ourselves opposite Quay Lane and waited for the ceremony to begin.

Down the laneway, I could see the Ballyreagh Silver Band shuffling impatiently in a storage yard, their green-and-red uniforms lending a burst of autumnal colouring to the slate-grey scene.

We were surrounded by families. Fathers with toddlers on their shoulders, mothers holding tightly to the hands of their young children, who were doing their best to run on to the vacated road. I missed my mother then, I regretted not accompanying her to this event in the past. It saddened me, that I had never attended the parade with her.

As the seconds separating 10.42 and 10.43 ticked away, my own sense of time became displaced. I've never since managed to fully secure it.

Each moment returns to me with the clarity of a tableau. Time stretched out in a lingering calm. Everything that came to me in those seconds came to me in the form of a physical escape, a kind of conjuring trick. I was both present and not present. I viewed, tasted, smelled it from another angle, assimilating it, as though the cartilage connecting my body to whatever was inside it had been loosened and I was floating outside of myself.

Down the alleyway, I saw a trombone player check his watch.

A leaking gutter.

A pigeon alighting upon a windowsill.

Rain skipping from the top of the post-box, like oil spitting off a hot frying pan.

An acrid smell in the air.

A burglar alarm ringing out. Thin, insubstantial.

Vibrations in my feet.

Another burglar alarm.

The vibrations running up my legs, into my torso.

Everyone oblivious, doing what gathered crowds do.

I turned right, my gaze resting upon the wall of the Reading Rooms. I saw the wall expand, inflate.

Then a void.

When I opened my eyes, the street was no longer the street I knew. It was shrouded in dust, blanketed in screams. It had one end only – no longer a thoroughfare but a site. Men stood on the road in their bowler hats, poppies fixed to their lapels, standing in stillness, as if waiting for a train. People had their hands to their ears. There were teenagers in clothes similar to my own – anorak jackets and skinny ties – and there were women in red tunics and other women in grey coats, nurses from the St John's Ambulance Brigade. A nun floated in front of me, her habit lifting with the breeze of her motion. Retired RUC policemen in dress uniform, bottle-green, some with the orange sash draped across their chests. Soldiers in combat gear, helmeted, booted, in camouflage fatigues, carrying SLR rifles. War veterans in suits, medals pinned to their chests, carrying poppy wreaths. The Ballyreagh Silver Band arriving en masse, brass instruments still slung across their shoulders. Children sought refuge in their parents' arms. People didn't run away from the blast site – they staggered. Moved towards each other. Stood still. Watched. If they did run, they ran towards the collapsed building, added their hands to the chaos, the scrabble of bricks and bodies, Sunday wear caked in dust. A scrum of people casting bricks on to the road, my father amongst them. The folded building framed the scene. Slates vanished. The latticework of the roof joists was exposed, a shattered ribcage. I watched a drummer excavate a man's leg. With one hand he quickly scattered debris, with the other he still held his set of drumsticks. People streamed out of nearby houses. Someone helped me to sit up. They spoke to me and I shook my head. I watched my father drag a body out by the armpits. Someone helped him with the feet. They placed the body on the ground and stood over it and then knelt down beside it, then my father removed his jacket, left arm first, the way I had seen him do hundreds of times, placing it over the head of the body and returning again to the fray.

A woman followed in his wake, lifted the jacket, stared, replaced it gently.

We didn't go to the hospital, my father and I. There was no need for us to be there, and we didn't want to be taking up room. The army arrived and cordoned off the bombsite and used megaphones to encourage us to go home; they probably reasoned that the longer people stood around, the more chance there was of trouble. They were wrong, though. The prevailing mood wasn't one of anger, it was abject sorrow. The crowd didn't have an appetite for more destruction.

Down near the river a couple of ambulances were being used as first-aid stations. My father brought me there so they could look me over, since I'd been knocked cold. The doctor shone a torch in my eye, asked me some questions, checked my balance and told me I'd be grand.

A few people came up to us to talk about what a terrible thing it was and we agreed and then they moved on to the next cohort. We were left with nothing to do. The only thing for it was to return home. We wanted calm, sanctuary, the blast still vibrating within us. My father said he had a sick calf he needed to check on. It was as decent an excuse as any, and so we walked to our car, dazed, disembodied. Despite all the movements, the ambulance sirens, the army trucks moving, the wails of people in shock, the place had a profound stillness to it.

The air hung heavy. I remember a sensation of feeling that I was living in a painting, that all of this was a painting, or a moving mechanical toy, like those old automata that would come to life if you put a coin into the slot.

When we got back home, we showered and ate lunch and my father left to check on the calf and do some odd jobs. I don't remember what I did, maybe read a book, maybe pottered around that lonely house. We couldn't talk to each other, even after that shocking, murderous event — we just didn't know how.

We watched the news together that evening. The IRA had released a statement admitting responsibility. Their target, they declared, had been the soldiers from the Ulster Defence Regiment, who were due to parade in front of the cenotaph. As it happened, no active members of the military were harmed. At the moment of the explosion, they had just begun marching in formation from a nearby car park. They were late, their commanding officer had been delayed.

Even if they had been in place, the IRA's claim would still have lacked validity, because of the crowd that had gathered, as usual, between the Reading Rooms and the cenotaph. They were so tightly packed together that they pressed up against the blue steel railing that cordoned off the pavement. It was those people who soaked up the impact of the blast.

The IRA maintained that the bomb was operated by a remote-control detonator which had been triggered unexpectedly by the army's radio equipment. But in the following days, when the security forces came upon the remnants of an electronic timer, this assertion was proved to be a lie: a timing device left no room for manoeuvre.

Eventually, the army's forensics unit concluded that the bomb had been placed in a small room on the ground floor of the Reading Rooms, just underneath the staircase. It was probable, based on other IRA operations, that there were two men involved in planting it: one to put it in place and prime the timing device; the other to keep watch. It was also likely that the one doing the watching was a local, someone who wouldn't arouse too much suspicion if Eamon Goodwin had kept looking and come across him. The other, according to the word that spread around town afterwards, had been from the South Fermanagh unit of the IRA. This assertion seemed logical on a few levels. The South Fermanagh unit had considerable bomb-making experience. That particular bomb was put together using a mixture of fertilizer and petrol. Considering the volatility of these materials and the bomb's size and effectiveness, it was obviously made by someone with no small amount of expertise.

Once the two men had planted the bomb and set the timer, there was no way of controlling the blast. Timing devices were typically used only in unpopulated places, or at the very least timed bombings were pre-empted with a warning to the RUC, who would then evacuate the area. We searched for explanations but couldn't find any. The IRA's intelligence about the ceremony's timetable and layout couldn't have been mistaken. It was always done in the same location and to the same schedule. A timing device meant that the IRA had deliberately targeted civilians. It was a slaughter. And it could have been even worse. Another bomb was planted in Tullyhommon – about fifteen miles away. Most of that parade was made up of teenagers. That they went on to live full and active lives was nothing but a stroke of luck: that day a 200-pound bomb, placed beside the parade route, failed to go off.

No one was in any doubt that a line had been crossed and that we had all moved into a new territory. The ramifications of this fact started endless debates in newspapers and on the radio and television. Political analysts were predicting an entirely new phase of conflict. Margaret Thatcher was promising a greater influx of troops. And, throughout these reports, they kept reasserting the time of the explosion: 10.43. I suppose that mentioning the precise moment helped to memorialize the event.

As I write all this down, I realize it might seem strange to an outsider that my father decided to keep the two of us in the house after my mother passed on – considering how exposed we were out there. Kesh, a loyalist stronghold, was only a few miles down the road. The people there wouldn't have appreciated seeing a Catholic take control of Protestant lands. We must have been in danger of being burnt out, or worse. Despite this, though, I doubt the thought of leaving even occurred to my father. The farm was legally his, but he didn't own it: a farm is never owned, only maintained, preserved for the following generations. None of it was his heritage, but it was mine. My father would have considered it a dereliction of his duty to give up on it. I don't know when he went into the office of Mr Hogan, our solicitor, but it can't have been easy to see my mother's name removed from the deeds, to see it written in officious, unsympathetic language that he was the sole proprietor. To continue to run the place, to complete his usual tasks and then take on hers as well – the accounts, the ordering of feed, the various bouts of paperwork required by the Department of Agriculture – all of it must have felt like he was waltzing alone.

Perhaps the people around us could see that my father had enough to deal with. Either way, no one ever knocked on our door at night to tell us that Lisnarick might no longer be the best place for us.

In the weeks following the bombing, I don't think I'm overstating it when I say that the tragedy provided some solace for him. As the whole town fell into mourning, it must have seemed that everyone had caught up to what he himself was feeling. It certainly gave him purpose. He began volunteering as an organizer for the peace rallies that sprang up in its aftermath. He developed a reputation as a sound technician. A few times I went along with him to one of the community halls and drank flat Coke and ate the warm sandwiches and helped him lug his loudspeakers on to their stands, then load them back into our car when it was all over. He gained an offhand notoriety in the area because he would always give the microphone one more check when the dignitaries were lined up in their chairs on-stage, tapping on it and then mumbling three quick words, silencing everyone, so the moderator could begin. He did this so often that my school friends named him *Testing-One-Two*.

It was the formality of his action that quietened the crowd – the readying of the microphone was an official signal that everything was finally in place – but I also think their silence had something to do with the fact that his countenance was one that they could recognize within themselves. His sadness was of a kind that pulsed resolutely: it was obvious that he would never fully be undone by it and yet it would never leave him; it was just something he would have to learn, we would all have to learn, to assimilate.

For myself, I remember my predominant feeling in those weeks was a longing for touch. I needed to hold or be held. It's a simple act that can feel like an impossible feat if you have no access to it. I missed my mother more than ever. I slept without dreaming. I probably walked around without feeling anything. Another boy in my situation would have rebelled, raided his father's drinks cabinet, stolen his car. But that wasn't an option for me. We were living on a precipice.

On the 8th of December, exactly a month after the explosion, I woke up feeling nauseous. I remember the date because we had the day off school: it was the Feast of the Immaculate Conception. I could hardly bear to look at the wallpaper: the roses seemed to shift around each other, bending and twisting. I got out of bed and put on my slippers and shuffled down into the kitchen. My father was having his breakfast. He put his newspaper down and took a good look at me.

'You look a bit peaky.'

'I'm not feeling so well.'

'Well, get some porridge into you. It'll do you some good.'

I ladled some porridge into a bowl and ate a few spoonfuls. I couldn't stomach much. The kitchen had small windows, so the light was on, even in the morning. The light was a fluorescent strip over the table. I hated the fucking thing, and I hated it even more that morning, the bulb was burning my eyeballs. My father watched me sift through the porridge and then he stood up and went to the sink and filled a glass of water and put it beside me.

'Here,' he said, 'go back upstairs. Leave the bowl and take this up with you.'

I tossed and turned in the bed, tried to sleep for a while. I couldn't settle. The bedsheets felt like sandpaper, the roses twisted around each other, and the chime of the clock from the parlour resonated under my skin. I felt like I was inhabiting someone else's body, folded inside a frame that had shrunk around me. The clock chimed on the hour, with a shorter ring on the half-hour, and a ding on the quarters. Eventually, I decided I had had enough. I would go downstairs and move the fucking thing, cover it in a blanket and put it in the back kitchen. My father would understand. I puttered down the stairs, legs unsteady beneath me. I hadn't bothered to put on my slippers this time. The carpet was like sack-cloth under my feet. Then the tiles in the hallway. Then the thick carpet in the parlour. When I approached the clock, I couldn't help noticing the time on its face. 10.43. A coincidence, of course, but it caused me to pause. I looked at the two hands and listened to the ticking and felt even more nauseous. The floor listed like I was on a boat, and then someone entered the room behind me. A sweeping shadow that I could sense past my right shoul-der. And then I heard a man's voice whispering into my ear, urgently whispering a question.

What's your name, son?

I looked in the mirror. There was no one there. I turned around to face the door. My arm whipped into the air, haywire, a machine part coming undone.

Then a void.

I woke to my father's face looking solemnly at me. He was kneeling over me, one hand on my forehead.

'Are you all right?'

I said something, I could feel my lips moving, but I couldn't hear the words coming out of my mouth. Relief washed over my father's face.

'For the love of Christ, you had me worried there.'

He sat me up. All my joints were throbbing. I thought I must have hit the floor hard. I put my hand to the back of my neck. It still felt like someone with enormous strength was squeezing it.

'What happened? Did you have a turn?'

'Aye, must have,' I said.

I looked down and realized I had pissed myself: my pyjama bottoms were soaked from my waist to my knees. My father was still speaking to me. I reckoned he hadn't noticed.

'Could you get me a glass of water, Da?'

'I can, son, I can. Just wait there now.'

He left the room and I stood up. I felt like I'd been in an almighty scrap, but I was steadier on my feet now. My skin felt my own. I walked up the stairs and into the shower and washed myself off and wrapped myself in a towel and bundled up my pyjamas in a ball and put them in a plastic bag which I sealed with a knot – I didn't want my father to smell anything. When I opened my bedroom door, I saw that he had put the water on my side table. I got dressed and went downstairs to the kitchen again.

My father was still in his work clothes. He was leaning on the sink, looking out at the weather. It was a fine day.

'You're feeling better so?'

'I am, aye.'

'Here' – he handed me a thermometer – 'stick that in your gob.'

I slid the glass tube under my tongue and held it in place with my teeth. The metal tip had a horrible taste. My father cut some bread and made me a sandwich and lifted the kettle off the range and dropped a teabag in a mug and poured in the hot water. He went to the fridge in the back kitchen and returned with a jug of milk. Once he had done all this, he opened out his fist and I took out the thermometer and handed it to him.

He turned it until he could see the strip of mercury lined up against the gauge, then shook the thing so that the mercury went back down again.

'Normal,' he said. 'I thought it would be high.'

'Aye, well,' I said.

He leaned forward and put his index finger and thumb around my eye socket, separating my eyelids so he could get a better look at my eyeball. He told me to look up and down, checking the whites of my eyes.

'You're sure you're feeling better?'

'I am.'

'Do you reckon I should call Dr Murray?'

'No, I'll be fine. It was just a turn, Da, that's all.'

Another kid would have milked the situation, but I didn't want to be stuck inside all day, no one around.

'All right. Get your sandwich into you. There's a fence down in the Race Field. I need to take care of it. Do you want to give me a hand? Or you can read a book or something?'

'Aye, I'll come with you. The air will do me good.'

It did. On our way down to the Race Field, standing in the back loader of the tractor, I could feel the lingering sense of someone near me, around me, like when you're being watched from a distance. But after a couple of hours of mending the fence – stringing out the barbed wire and sledgehammering fence posts into the ground – I'd shaken it off. It was just something strange that had occurred. It was just one of those things. That night I ate my dinner hungrily and slept well and I didn't think much more about the incident until a month later, when I was in Mrs Moran's chemistry class. Sitting on my laboratory stool, I felt imbalanced. And I had a metallic taste on my tongue and felt the ripple of a shadow approach me and I heard a man ask that question again, whisper right into my ear – *What's your name, son?*

Then a void.

I woke in the office of Mr Conway, our principle. I was lying on the floor and Mr Conway was kneeling next to me, holding my hand. Being magically transported from my stool in the chemistry lab to his office was strange enough, but what was even stranger was that Mr Conway was holding my hand. He was speaking softly to me. I could taste blood in my mouth. He was wiping blood from my chin and saying reassuring things. It was only after I had sat up and drunk some water and read some of the wallcharts that I allowed myself to believe that I wasn't living through a dream. It had such a dreamlike quality. Everything was familiar, but the context was completely wrong.

When I finished my water, Mr Conway sat beside me and explained what had happened: that I probably had epilepsy. His brother had it too; he said it was nothing to worry about. He said they had put him on a course of medication and he was as right as rain again. The ambulance arrived, and Mr Conway came with me. He talked to keep me distracted. He told me he loved greyhounds. He had a few and described them for me. It didn't help ease my sense of dislocation. He might as well have said that he was a champion gymnast.

In the hospital, filling out the admission form, I looked at the date: January the 8th. Mrs Moran's class lasted from ten until eleven. I couldn't confirm it, but I felt certain that my seizure had come at the exact same time as the last one: 10.43. I didn't tell anyone about it, it would sound too ridiculous. And when the doctor asked me if I had sensed anything strange that morning, I said no. What difference would it have made?

I don't remember if I thought again about the voice while they kept me in for observation for a few days. I must have, but nothing remains. Soon I was being sent back to school, on a course of medication, and life resumed its normal pattern. I'm quite sure no one gave me any shit about the incident. No one called me a spastic. I think the bombing had sobered all of us up.

I remember that Philip Cooney, my bench mate, told me what I had looked like. He said I'd been tugging at my shirt, then smacking my lips and wiping my nose with the back of my hand. He said that he tried to get me to stop but that I ignored him. And then, all of a sudden, I was writhing on my stool. He said it looked like someone was strangling me with an invisible rope. He said, when I fell, I dropped so hard that everyone was terrified I'd cracked my skull, and my mouth spurted blood as my teeth clamped into my tongue.

But that was it. There were no more episodes. The medication worked so well that I often forgot that I had a condition. Later, at university, I often neglected to take my pills, and, since I never showed any after-effects, I just stopped taking them altogether. By the time I reached my mid twenties the episodes had become just another strange element of my past – unknown to those around me, as I never had any cause to speak of them – until they returned again decades later, on a different continent, in a different life.

I keep thinking back to that description of me, flailing around on the floor of my chemistry class, gone to the wraiths. I have to ask myself if the automaton that Philip Cooney saw in that state was a version of me. It doesn't seem like it. Or feel like it. How can my body move unconsciously while I'm awake? Where is it that my mind goes while I'm acting out my purposeless, robotic routine? And what is it that's being strangled out of me?

I write 'I', while at the same time being aware that neurologically speaking there's no such thing. I've done enough reading to know that the mental processes that underlie our sense of self – feelings, thoughts, memories – have no point of convergence; they're scattered throughout the brain, linked only by random electrical impulses. Hold a brain in your hand and you'll search in vain for any semblance of a self within its gloopy matter. If you examine the organ closely, you can only conclude that we don't have a centre, a place that we can point to and say, 'Here I am.' We're all divided and discontinuous. 'I' is a story told by a storytelling instrument. It's something you realize only when the instrument shows its flaws. Except 'I' and 'We' don't tell the story. The story tells us.

Epilepsy is caused by abnormal bursts of electrical activity in the brain. These surges lie dormant until they're triggered, and, once that happens, there's no going back. The first seizure causes a chain effect that can be quelled but not expunged. In Dr Ptacek's waiting room I read a pamphlet that said, 'Every seizure may be said to be the result of those that have preceded it, and the cause of those that follow it.' It brought to mind my father's routine on winter mornings, when he finished his newspaper over breakfast and then moved to the sink and ran water over the pages and carried them into the parlour, where he knelt by the hearth and shovelled the remaining embers on to the damp newspaper, parcelling them up and leaving them to lie there, muted, until it was time to light the fire once more.

It's been explained to me that the premonition I had, still have – that shadowy approach, that whispered question – falls into the category of a sensorimotor aura. Seizures are usually accompanied – maybe 'pre-empted' is the right phrase – by an aura. Auras take different forms. Some people smell burning rubber. Some people experience a metallic taste at the back of their tongue. The musician Neil Young describes it well: 'Before you slip into that other world, you start to feel all weird and echoey.'

The nineteenth-century neurologist William Gowers recorded a patient whose seizures were foreshadowed by a painful, cramping sensation rising up the left side of his chest, which changed to the 'hissing of a railway engine' when it reached his left ear. And then suddenly, and invariably, he saw an old woman before him in a stiff brown dress who offered him something that had the smell of fried beans.

A bus conductor in Edinburgh in the 1950s heard angelic voices. Passengers would see him laughing joyously from his state of ecstatic bliss. He would tell them how pleased he was to be in heaven before collapsing in the aisles. A patient in the Maudsley Hospital in London was recorded as reaching a high level of sexual arousal and then crashing into a seizure whenever he saw a safety pin. A soprano in Hanover would always feel a raven perched upon a branch within her lungs. At first she would struggle to breathe, until eventually the bird beat its wings and took flight through her throat, releasing an aria as her convulsions set in.

What's surprising to me, in retrospect, is that I stopped wondering where the voice came from. In fact, I forgot about this figure entirely. Even though my seizures stopped, and I had no direct cause to think of the man whose voice I'd heard, I now find it surprising that I didn't dream of him, draw him, envision him while day-dreaming over a coffee. I never looked at a face in a book of photographs and wondered if that was what he looked like, this figure in my head.

6

Why have my seizures returned to me now, here, at this time of my life? Their arrival is perhaps not entirely random. They come with the exit of a loved one and the entrance of another – one wave accumulating while another dissipates.

Six months ago, at the end of November, I walked away from my marriage. My ex-wife (I still find myself hesitant to use the prefix) and I had driven back to Brooklyn from a wedding in Chicago. Camille had an intense fear of flying; we avoided airports as much as we could. It was snowing heavily that night. In normal weather the trip would have taken around thirteen hours. I don't know how long this one took, but it felt like an eternity.

When we got to Clinton Hill, I stopped the car in front of our building and asked Camille to make me a cup of tea while I looked for a parking spot. She nodded, unbuckled her belt, leaned over, kissed me on the cheek and ran a soft hand through my hair.

'Thanks for getting us here,' she said.

I didn't respond. I waited until she had stepped inside our building, then parked the car as close as I could, took my bag from the boot, locked it, dropped my keys and phone into a rubbish bin and walked away from everything.

We'd been in New York for two years at that point. We'd met in Paris, where I'd been immersed for months in a large-scale project – designing a library near the Gare de Lyon. Our meeting was by chance, we sat beside each other at a café. A couple of months into our relationship, Camille's son, Étienne, decided to move in with his father and her life was thrown into turmoil.

Not long after, I was offered a job with an architectural firm in New York and we decided to get married, to take a leap into the unknown, our love still fresh, absorbed by possibility. But we still hadn't adapted. Camille was an actress without a foothold in the city, still coming to grips with the language, at sea with all the social nuances of a new country.

We knew we were reaching the end of something; we both could feel it. Camille called me every day at the office. I caught her sobbing in the bath. She grew flowers but then ignored them, she took classes which she didn't finish, started waitressing jobs, then argued with her managers. She was on a perpetual roundabout of fresh starts, new intentions, and nothing seemed to hold. Étienne sometimes didn't return her calls, and sometimes when he did, his father would be hovering in the background, vigilant, protective. We fought long and hard, late into the night. I slept on the couch for weeks. I began to dread coming back to our apartment. I accepted invitations for drinks after work, anything to delay the moment when I walked in the door and had to answer to Camille picking apart my day.

We were driving back from the wedding of a couple that neither of us knew well – one of those invitations you accept when trying to establish a social circle, something you hope will fix you in proximity to others.

We spent the wedding in a state of perpetual tension. I backed away from conversations. I stared at my shoes a lot. I was careful with how much I drank. Our entire relationship seemed choreographed, a series of moves enacted for the benefit of others.

We headed back to Brooklyn on the Sunday morning, a day early. Camille wanted to get out of Chicago as soon as possible, despite the heavy snowfall. She was determined to drive. When I came out of the shower, I noticed that the car keys were no longer beside my wallet. I didn't question her decision. She had that alert quality about her that meant I shouldn't approach. As she fastened the buttons on her dress, her hands moved in staccato bursts.

At breakfast, we told the others we wanted to get a jump on the New York commuter traffic. Maybe if we'd known some of them better they would have talked us out of it, but instead there were just a series of nods and a few raised eyebrows.

The question came as expected, after about twenty minutes. Snowploughs were out on the highway, speeding trucks flanked us.

'What's wrong?' she said.

In other circumstances, I probably wouldn't have answered. I'd have staved off the question until her mood had settled. But we had a long road ahead of us and I couldn't muster the stamina needed for hours of sustained, crushing, deliberate silence.

I answered calmly, no melodrama, no accusation. I played out the previous day, just a list of events, circumstances, and a refusal to repeat them. I didn't know what I wanted. I wanted to be clear. I wanted us to stop pretending and have a straightforward conversation, one without tripwires. I knew what I didn't want: I didn't want more silence.

She took her hands off the wheel.

Her hands were on the wheel and then they weren't on the wheel, they were over her head.

She had taken her hands off the wheel.

It didn't happen slowly – it wasn't a decision, a threat. It was as if the wheel were scorching hot. She screamed and wailed. Her arms flailed into the air, her body shook, her foot stayed on the accelerator. We didn't gain or lose speed. Things became simple. Simple choices. I clutched the wheel with one hand. The other hand I placed on her shoulder. I spoke to her quietly, calmly. The wheel vibrated in my hand. I was aware of how calm I was. I was aware of the necessity of this. There was only us. In that moment. She roared, screamed. Her hands still flailing above her head, her foot still on the accelerator.

I don't know how long it lasted. I know we passed four exits.

Eventually she retook the wheel, guided us towards

an exit ramp and pulled in beside a fast-food restaurant. She turned the engine off. I remember the colours of the place were so bright. Lurid, childish pastels. Pictures of burgers. We sat, watching people entering and exiting the restaurant. Cars inching along the drive-through.

I drove us home. I don't know how or why. In retrospect I should have pulled into a motel, called the emergency services maybe, but what would they have done? There was no one to call: all our friends and family were an ocean away. I wanted to get back to New York and make my decisions there.

When we reached New Jersey, we settled into a strange kind of equilibrium. Darkness descended. I focused on the functional motions of driving, concentrating on what was immediately ahead. I was running on fumes, barely holding it together. I just needed to get there. I kept telling myself this, saying it under my breath: *Just get there*. Camille drifted into a hesitant, shaking sleep. Tired of this sentence running through my head, of the vibrations running through my bloodstream, I turned on the radio for solace and came across a simple piano tune. I recognized it. The *Goldberg Variations*. It was slow and lilting, gently uplifting, and it progressed with a kind of stuttering momentum that was in keeping with the snowfall. Gradually, I was lost to Camille and the resonances of that dreadful morning, abandoned not just to the music but also to the past, to an incident from those opaque months between my mother's death and the bombing.

A long-forgotten friend was suddenly present in the car with me. Her name was Esther. She was a woman – a girl really – who had lived, temporarily, in Lisnarick, with our nearest neighbours, Brian and Trudy Irvine. I hadn't thought about her in years, but the music – or, more accurately, the pianist – brought me back to the evening that she arrived into my life.

I was on the lake with Brian Irvine that evening, fishing for eels. It was a soft April evening – moisture hung in the air. My mother had been dead for almost two months and the finality of the situation was closing in on me. A fortnight beforehand, my aunt Jackie, who had come to stay with us, had returned to Kerry. I was grateful for the chance to sit in a boat, not only because it got me out of the house, but also because Brian wasn't taking pity on me, inventing something for me to do. On the water that night I could pretend that my mother's death had never happened, I could carry on as I once did.

Brian and Trudy were a brother and sister – solid Church of Ireland people like my mother. He was at least thirty years older than me, a former theologian who abandoned his ministry and eventually became an RUC man. But we had an affinity. He didn't take the place of my father, but maybe filled the role of an older brother. He allowed me into his presence indirectly, by getting me to help him with whatever he happened to be immersed in whenever I was around. He taught me how to mend a cooper's barrel by hammering a pencil-shaped wedge into a flaw from the inside, so that the wedge would expand when the barrel was filled with water. He taught me the names of birds and wildflowers – both the English and Latin versions – and had me repeat them back to him: a chaffinch is a *Fringilla coelebs*, a snowdrop is a *Galanthus nivalis*. I can weld a join because of him, and slate a roof. He handed all of this information over freely, more as a statement of things as they were than as a form of instruction. 'These,' he seemed to be saying, 'are the codified rules of the world. Do what you will with them.' He left little room for preference or interpretation, and so, as a consequence, he was frugal with his praise. I listened and observed and repeated, and when, occasionally, a word of encouragement left his lips, it invoked a glow of warm pride within me, even though the word was invariably dropped in a low murmur, a momentary lapse, a coin he had let fall from his grasp.

Twice a week, from the age of twelve until a few months before the bombing, he took me night fishing. We fished for eels. They were always in season. On our first night out, Brian told me that eels spawn only once, at the end of their life, and in those final years they make the long journey to the Sargasso Sea, a collective pilgrimage, in order to spawn and to die. Every evening for the rest of that week, doing my homework in my bedroom, I took our atlas down from the shelf and turned to the Atlantic and traced my finger along the white lines of the currents, across the spine of the Mid-Atlantic Ridge, ending at that azure sea in the middle of the ocean.

Once I had proved myself, Brian showed me how to

build a Dyson rig. He explained that eels couldn't be caught like other fish. Because they could move backwards as easily as forwards, they didn't grab at the bait like a pike; instead they placed their lips around the bait and then backed up without swallowing, so that the pull on the line would be insignificant. If they came upon resistance, they let go and reversed away immediately. To fool them, you needed to create a line that had very little tension in it. The Dyson rig had a float at the end of the line, from which extended a weight that dropped to the lake bed and kept it taut. A few feet away, nearer the boat, ran a trace line, falling loosely. At the end of the trace was a hook that dangled a lobworm, wriggling in protest.

We arranged the lines on the jetty. We carried very little inside the boat: a net, a wooden block to stun the catch, a bucket of worms and a small torch. I rowed and Brian sat in front, watching for an appropriate spot. He signalled right or left with his corresponding hand and told me to stop by raising his closed fist. We rarely repeated our direction. There are so many tiny islands scattered about Lough Erne that even if we had three lifetimes we couldn't have reached every potential site.

When we found a dark cove, we sat and waited, leaned the oars inside the boat. It was usually so quiet that I could hear the gloop of the shifting worms in the bucket by my feet. In those hours, we became part of the lake. Over months and years, it revealed itself to us, accepting us as its own, at one with the reeds, the lilies, the waterfowl with their dainty strides – like a child afraid of getting its ankles wet.

The lake was our sanctuary, its effortless tranquillity held a stillness that ran counter to the tensions of the time. The deep darkness brought comfort and security; it was the lights around its perimeter that harboured a threat. The water was dark as oil, except where the moonlight struck it and it tore apart in a silver foil. On midsummer nights, the evening lingered in the sky. It held a cobalt blue until around midnight. We could watch the dew webbing the grasslands around us. In spring and autumn, condensation whispered above the water, rolling over upon itself, struggling to lift.

The herons on the shorelines were our sentinels. When a heron unfolded into flight, it always seemed a significant thing. It was easy to predict its motion. Its neck settled into a question mark, then stretched out gradually, as an answer spoken softly, and this elongation caused the body to ascend, its wings merely unfurling incidentally, punctuating its soar into the darkness.

When one of us caught an eel, the other placed his rod inside the boat and joined in the pull. Eels are strong, determined. Our rods were thick enough and pliable enough to deal with the eel's dance. We always spooled it in gradually, letting it tire itself out. Inside the boat, our routine never wavered. Brian placed a calm, firm hand on the creature, its eyes searching all around, ready to spring again when it had a moment. When the line was cut, the eel always spat out the hook in disgust. I slipped the net over it, the head entering last. Inside the net it fought and writhed, until Brian struck a blow to its head with the block and slit it with his knife.

Like us, eels grey as they age, and when we pulled up a silver one and managed to finagle it into our net, I would stare at it, thick as a drainpipe, a pound in weight for every decade of its life, and imagine its companions, others exactly like it, making their way through the islands and slipping into the Erne River, winding between Magheraboy and Belleek, trickling through the narrows before entering Lough Assaroe and then out into the ocean from the Ballyshannon Estuary.

That night, we had a catch, one of the dozen times a year that we were lucky, and headed back earlier than usual. As I worked the oars, Brian broke the silence. 'We've a visitor tonight,' he said. 'She'll be staying for a bit. A Dutch girl, a lassie not much older than yourself. She should be there with Trudy by now.'

Trudy was a retired nurse. I imagined the girl to be a nursing student, down from college for some practical experience. My mother would occasionally take in girls for a month or two, and I thought Trudy was doing the same. I didn't like those girls. They saw me as one of their patients, spoke to me in deliberately cheerful tones, as if I were senile. When they were in the kitchen with my mother, they'd stop talking as soon as I entered. I imagined the new arrival to be like one of them, dressed as conservatively as a nun.

When we arrived back to the house, the Dutch girl was sitting at the kitchen table. She stared at me as if I were a museum exhibit. She had a smattering of freckles around her nose and only her head moved – the rest of her sat very still. She was only a few years older than me. I held the sack containing the eel in my arms. A four-pounder, Brian reckoned. Through the sackcloth, I could feel it curled up, a tubular thing.

There was a man in Brian's chair, wearing a pristine black suit; the firelight glanced on his neatly trimmed hair, bringing out brilliantine flashes. The table was laid out for supper.

'You got one!' the man said, clapping his hands exuberantly. 'Out with it there, lad.'

I offered him the sack and he reached inside, took out the eel suddenly, his firm hand clutched expertly behind the head. He plunged it towards the girl and she recoiled, flattened herself against the wall. The others laughed. I didn't join in. The thing was serpent-like in the bright light of the kitchen, otherworldly. I also took a step backwards, although no one noticed.

'A fine specimen,' the man said. 'Trudy, would you think about cooking it up for us?'

Trudy cut the eel into thick slices and fried it until the meat was golden. It looked like a small log on the plate. I watched the girl as she ate. She worked hard to overcome her revulsion, her head involuntarily pulling backwards as she brought the fork to her mouth.

'What's your name?' I asked her, after we had finished.

The man answered for her, 'Lord save us, did we not introduce each other in the kerfuffle? I'm Andrew. This is Esther. She'll be staying for a bit. She's here to relax, spend the summer.'

'It's not summer yet, though,' I said.

'Aye, but it'll be a fine one, won't it?' Brian said.

Brian looked different in the company of these strangers. He stood tall, his shoulders square, his face lined and alert. I had never seen him go about his duties; the only time I saw him in uniform was around his own home. His protectiveness had always come in the form of a kindness towards me. In the kitchen that night, his body took on a rigidity, a definition. I understood then what Brian was capable of, if it came to it.

The girl gazed up at the laundry drying on the rack above our heads. She looked puzzled, as though she had never seen clothes being dried that way before.

'That fish was a tasty one,' Brian said. 'You've a knack for it, Simon.'

'You'll eat forever so,' the man named Andrew said.

While clearing the table for tea, Trudy suggested that Esther should play the piano for us.

Esther nodded and made her way to the piano and sat upright, poised on the stool. She was wearing a thick blue jumper. I remembered her anticipation before playing, the way her silences seemed to clear the air around her. And I remembered how, as the tune gained momentum, she began to hum along with the notes, so captivated by the melody that she seemed to forget that there were other people present. Watching her play, I felt that I had walked through a door and stumbled upon an intimate act. Her music wasn't a performance; she was merely following an impulse. It was the first time I had witnessed that kind of freedom; everyone else I knew was locked inside who they were and, consequently, who they would always be. And in that simple act of humming to herself, she slipped away from the binds of tradition that had entangled all of us.

The memory flowed through me as we approached Brooklyn. I could picture the moment so clearly, and what resonated most deeply was the confidence with which Esther had followed her instinct. And by the time we reached Clinton Hill and Camille was climbing the steps to our apartment, I realized I no longer had to live a life based on obligation, on some abstract notion of duty. I understood that same sense of freedom awaited me, if I had the courage to move towards it.

7

I walked and kept walking. The snow had muffled the city. Taxis slithered, lights glowered. People, the few that were out, leaned into the weather, shouldered it. I walked until the buildings looked different. The brownstones bled away and I was surrounded by drug stores and parking lots. I had no idea what direction I was travelling in. I didn't care about direction, I cared only about distance. Eventually I realized I'd made my way to Queens. I walked all the way to Astoria. I found a cheap hotel. The woman at the reception desk smiled at me when I stepped in – she didn't seem surprised, and I took it that she was used to strangers washing up in the middle of the night.

'Stranded?'

'Yeah,' I said.

She asked me how long was I planning on staying in New York. Did I want to reserve the rest of my visit?

I handed my firm's credit card to the receptionist. I knew that Camille would track any payments on our personal account.

'Let's do a week,' I said.

She swiped my card and gave me a room on the third floor and pointed towards the elevator. I dropped on to the bed, slept in my clothes.

I dreamed of Fermanagh. There were men in caps playing cricket in the field behind our walled garden. A woman played with a diabolo, tossing the wooden spool high in the air and catching it again on a string that she held taut between two sticks. Our chestnut tree was there, with a tyre-swing – an addition that never appeared in reality – that my classmates from St Michael's had found and flocked to in their dozens. I was standing at the base of the tree, looking towards my home. I wanted to walk in through the garden door and stand with my back to the range oven and be enveloped by its warmth. But I couldn't seem to scale the garden wall. The house was a place that I couldn't enter, though it seemed welcoming, functional, lit up like a cruise liner, warm light pouring through the various rectangular windows, smoke billowing out of chimneys that looked like funnels, the engine of my former life still turning along inside it.

The cattle lowed behind me. I turned around to face them and saw Esther there, amongst them. Her brown hair hung in thick strands around her shoulders with that choppy, hard look about it, its ends lightened from the sun into the same shade as the hay in our barn, a lush dirty gold that always gave me the impression that she too had been culled from the earth and tempered by the weather. Her body faced me but she didn't look at me. She was turned away, staring out towards the lake.

I woke up longing to see her face. And I had a strange sense that it would happen soon – the shock of the previous day had opened up something in me.

The next few days blurred into one another. I walked and looked. I stared at the snow drifts that gathered on windowsills, like cooling loaves of bread, and saw how the snow made toadstools out of rubbish bins. I nodded to the men who shovelled channels from their front steps to the street. They shovelled out their paths and threw down salt, then scraped the area around their car tyres clean and tucked sheets of newspaper behind their wiper blades. In Astoria Park, there were snowboarders working the inclines of the wide picnic areas. I listened to their smooth progression and the crimp of my own footsteps and the faint hum of the streetlights and the surf of traffic from the 278.

At some point, I found myself in a second-hand book-shop. I wandered aimlessly, killing time. I picked up a book of etchings, printed a few years ago, swirling trees and owls and departing hares and crumbling stone walls and cows with a manic stare. Each image carried a sense of expansion and contraction – everything seemed to coalesce into the centre of the picture and then dissipate into fine lines that continued off beyond the boundaries of the page. And there, on the back cover, was Esther, staring back out at me.

I'd no idea what had become of her. I recognized her instantly, could see the young woman underneath the image, see the twist in her mouth as she contemplated a question, the alert eyes that soaked in everything and gave little back. Her name had changed – with marriage I presumed – Esther Hak had become Esther Ascencio.

Writing this down, I feel almost obliged to say that I was surprised by the coincidence. But I wasn't. It felt natural somehow, inevitable, a door swinging back open to a life I hadn't fully lived.

I took the book to the counter. The shop assistant was in her late twenties. She had dyed black hair riven through with blue highlights, a bowl cut, a sharp fringe crossing the middle of her forehead. She had some physics textbooks laid out in front of her and a notebook with quick diagrams sketched out in green pen, large arrows denoting torsions and forces. She took the book from me, checked its front and back pages for a price written somewhere – which it didn't have – and then held it away from her, turning it over and back, appraising it, as though it were an antique whose value could be estimated based on a knowledge of the period and the level of craftsmanship involved. I wasn't sure if she were making such a display because she was waiting for me to make the first move, if this were the standard bargaining ploy in Queens. I stood there and watched. Her final estimate was irrelevant to me. I would have paid five hundred dollars for the thing.

Finally she hit on a number. 'Seventeen?'

'That's fine,' I said, disappointment in her face.

She held the book out and returned her attention to her notes while I dug around in my pockets, finally coming out with a few rumpled singles, and then, realizing that it wasn't enough, turned to my wallet, which I'd filled with crisp bills from a gas station. I placed a folded twenty on the counter and she picked it up and straightened it out with a snap and looked at it, and then at me, with disdain. Clearly, I didn't know the value of a dollar.

The book was just about too large to fit into my coat pocket and I didn't want to ask her for a bag. I'm sure she would have shuffled into the backroom and emerged with something, but I wanted to avoid further conversation. When I stepped out on to the street, a light snow was coming down, so I tucked it into the waistband of my jeans. It pressed against the small of my back, only barely perceptible, assuring me of its presence, like the way Camille would touch me in passing at a party when we were first together. 'I won't interrupt. Come and find me later.'

Back in my room, I picked up the book again and stared at Esther's face. It was reassuring to look at her, to hold the book in my hands. It was a limited edition from a small art press, the accompaniment to an exhibition in Chinatown held a couple of years earlier. She too had travelled a distance from that place, had transformed, transfigured, she too would understand the loneliness of exile. All of that distance culminating, condensing into images.

After that initial meeting over supper, I watched Esther from afar. From my position in the chestnut tree, beyond our garden wall, I could sometimes see her hanging out the washing or digging in the Irvines' vegetable patch. Her step was heavy, she seemed solidly in contact with the earth. Her shoulders were broad for a young woman's.

She wore layers of clothes, a wax jacket even when it wasn't raining, her face flushed as she worked the small shovel. She sang during her work. Just as my mother once did. Her voice carried in the still air. It was surprisingly light. I think I expected her to sing in a lower register. The songs were like folk songs, or maybe even hymns. I wasn't deliberately spying on her, there was nothing sinister in my gaze as I sat amongst the great branches.

A few weeks after she arrived, I started playing the piano in our parlour, probably – in retrospect – inspired by her. I began with some Christmas carols that I remembered from the lessons I went to as a little kid. 'Away in a Manger'. 'The First Noël'. 'Good King Wenceslas'. The piano hadn't been used in so long that some of the keys stuck when I pressed them. It took a few weeks of playing before they righted themselves naturally – it was kind of a drunken instrument, broken teeth and a sense of melody that lurched from one pitch to another. Still, I persevered, I think I kind of liked its errant nature. One night I heard a floorboard creak behind me and when I turned around my father was there, a pencil behind his ear.

'You've found something for yourself,' he said.

'I have,' I said.

'Good, then.'

A week later a piano tuner arrived. A small man with huge round glasses, like the ones Dennis Taylor, the snooker player, wore. He carried a leather doctor's bag and the whole thing was a kind of medical procedure, prodding and poking and tweaking and listening, his ear hovering over the strings.

I was surprised by my father's intervention, it wasn't like him to cultivate or encourage an interest in any particular subject. But then a few evenings later it made sense. There was a knock on the back door. Brian entered, with Esther in tow. 'A delivery. One music teacher,' he said, a rare smile creasing his face. I wasn't sure if it was because he was delighted with the notion of my playing the piano or he couldn't help being amused at the notion that his shy Dutch visitor was to be my tutor.

Brian was in his RUC uniform, which wasn't unusual, he had been in uniform plenty of times in our house. But he also wore a canvas-green bulletproof bib. My father found it disconcerting and his discomfort quickly spread to the rest of us. The bib filled the room. Brian cottoned on and started backing out of the door, speaking as he left.

'Right, then. I'll leave yous to it. Good luck, Esther. Don't be afraid to rap his knuckles with a ruler.'

She looked at me, puzzled. I didn't know how to reply. I was as confused as she was, no one had said anything to me.

With Brian gone, my father took over. He stood and gestured for her coat. Esther took a step back.

'Is it that cold?' he asked.

She looked abandoned. Mrs O'Gorman – the housekeeper my father had recently taken on – took pity on her. 'Let the child alone, Peter. It's all new here.'

Mrs O'Gorman offered her a cup of tea, but she shook her head. My father tapped his pockets and told us he'd leave us to it and stepped out into the yard.

Esther and I walked down the long corridor and sat at the piano. I turned on all the lights, so that she could understand her surroundings. The room was freezing. I don't think we'd had a guest in there since my mother's funeral. I didn't know where to look or what to say. Even though I was fifteen years old, I'd never talked to a foreigner before. No one travelled to Fermanagh if they didn't have to. I don't think I'd ever even been alone in a room with a girl who was only a couple of years older than me. I waited for her to speak first – since she was older, a tutor, in a position of responsibility – but she didn't.

'Do you have brothers?' I said. I don't know why I said that. I think I wanted to know if I was as alien to her as she was to me. I think I wanted to fill the awkwardness between us.

She looked straight at me. I think she was surprised by the directness of my question. She nodded towards the piano. 'What can you play?' she said.

I played 'Silent Night'. When I played the final note and turned towards her to get her response, she was smiling – but inwardly, not outwardly – and shaking her head.

'Is that it?' she said.

I was kind of offended by that. A tutor was supposed to be encouraging.

'I have other carols,' I said.

'You have other carols. What age are you?'

'Fifteen.'

She stood up and looked around the room.

'Do you have many horses?'

'No, we don't have any.'

'Why do you have all of these pictures of horses?'

'They used to be here, before I was born.'

'Were they famous or something?'

'No. There was a famous greyhound in Kesh. He belonged to the vicar. He won the Champion Derby.'

'So you don't know who these horses are?'

'No.'

There were a lot of them. I'd never really noticed it before. She picked up things and put them down. On the mantelpiece, on either side of my father's clock, were two large glass domes that contained stuffed animals frozen in a scene – a pheasant standing ceremoniously and a blackbird alert to a sudden noise.

'This is a blackbird, yes?'

'Your English is better than I thought it would be.'

She didn't respond.

My parents' wedding photo was on the top shelf of the bookcase. Esther pulled over a chair and stood on it and took the photo down. My father and mother were surrounded by nurses and dock workers. The contrast was stark. Sober men in ill-fitting suits and a bunch of women all dressed up to the nines.

She turned the photo around and pointed at my mother. 'This is your mother, yes?'

'Yes.'

'There are no old people in the photo? Where did everyone go?'

'They were married in a registry office.'

'Registry?'

'A legal office.'

'And?'

'Aye, well, my grandparents didn't think it counted. It wasn't in a church.'

'Okay.' She nodded, putting it all together. 'Trudy told me about your mother. Are you still sad?'

I looked down at the keyboard.

'Of course you are. Look at this place.'

I looked around the room. The fire wasn't lit, the fireplace remained empty. The furniture was from the fifties and had given up. The piano had two metal candlesticks poking out from its front, and was dotted with woodworm. Most of the photographs were of horses. I had never really seen it before. That fucking clock. The fucking stuffed animals. And it was cold enough to see my breath.

Mrs O'Gorman strode into the room, flinging back the door. 'Are ye both warm enough? We could light the fire.'

'We're fine, thanks, Mrs O'Gorman.'

'You're not playing yet, child? Quit your faffin now.'

'Esther was just telling me what the notes were.' She was still standing on the chair, looking at the photograph. Mrs O'Gorman stood and waited at the door until Esther was back in position beside the piano.

'Okay, Simon, play again,' Esther said.

I played 'Silent Night' once more. Mrs O'Gorman stepped away after I'd finished the first verse.

'*Kutwijf!* That woman is like Mien Dobbelsteen.'

'Who's Mien Dobbelsteen?'

'She's from the TV at home. A doctor's secretary who is always sticking her nose in.' She raised her voice and directed it towards the door. 'Although she did a better job of cleaning!'

I played it again after Esther left, aware for the first time of the weight and density of the notes under my fingertips, and how I could make them sound different by how heavily or lightly I pressed the keys. *Forte. Pianissimo.*

Sex didn't exist for us then. Nor did computers. Even though it was near the end of the 1980s, we were closer – in terms of lifestyle and morality – to the post-war years than to the new millennium. Sex didn't even hold the allure of that which was denied. It was what the bullocks in our fields did, jumping on each other's backs. It was as perfunctory as the artificial insemination man – the AI man – arriving to neighbouring farms.

The only access to pornography I had as a teenager was when Stephen Flanagan stood on someone's shoulders and climbed into the attic above the podium in our school hall and came out with two magazines from the 1970s. There was a lot of body hair and tangled limbs and not much by way of art direction. It was hard to see what was appealing about them. Still, the images burned into my mind and came back to me at night while I lay cocooned underneath my layers of blankets.

Around the time that my piano lessons began, the images fell away and my body found a form of expression that confused me in daylight. My pleasure emerged from somewhere other; it didn't have to be elicited by images. Because of this, the crushing shame I had felt also relented. My body was just doing what it did. The act itself felt cleansing and full of light and I couldn't understand how the sensation related to the AI man or cattle rushing each other. I matched and turned these thoughts together all the time. It felt like I was trying to put together a jigsaw that had no edge pieces and no picture on the box. Shape and colour were all that I could go by.

Esther arrived twice a week. I went to the music shop in town and bought the only two books they had for beginners. *The Beatles Songbook* and *Learning Piano*. After that first evening she didn't talk too much. I was at such a pitch when she arrived, so heightened by her presence, that I couldn't guess her temperament during our lessons. When she leaned beside me to correct a phrase, she smelled earthy – there was soil under her fingernails and cigarettes on her breath. Sometimes she'd stretch my fingers into position on a difficult phrase or hold my wrist and tell me to release the tension so that she could show me how to do a drop-lift. What I felt towards her, under her touch, was not as focused as desire – it was a stab of vitality. A feminine presence had entered the house again – Mrs O'Gorman didn't count – and it cut through the gloom. She brought me a lucidity for as long as she was under the roof. It caused me to wonder what my mother had been like when she was Esther's age. It made me think again about the stories that she had told me. She must have had evenings by the fire with a boyfriend, or read books on the sofa with her feet over its back, or gone horse riding on the weekends.

Two months passed. My summer holidays were nearing and I was doing my summer exams before school finished. I'd sit at my desk working out quadratic equations and thinking of Esther. 'Why are you here?' I asked her one evening, finally working up the courage. 'How do you know the Irvines?'

'They're friends of my parents.'

'Where are your parents?'

'In Holland.'

'They're still alive, then?'

She laughed. '*Natuurlijk*. Yes, they're still alive.'

'There's no *natuurlijk* about it.'

'Sorry. Okay. Yes, Simon, they're both still alive.'

'Why don't they visit?'

'They can't, but they write to me.'

I didn't want to practise any more, I turned away from the keys.

'Why can't your family come and visit you? It's not very far. I could ask my father to pick them up from the airport.'

'It's a long story, you wouldn't understand.'

'I might.'

A wave of something came over her. She put her elbows on her legs and leaned her face on her upraised hands, raking her fingers down from her forehead to her chin. Then she leaned forward and pressed her head into the side of my arm. I reached over and put my right hand on it.

She sat up again, assessing me. She slapped her hands decisively on her knees. 'Where do you keep your music?'

I was confused. Both music books were already on the stand.

'No, for that thing.'

She pointed at a record player in the corner. It wasn't quite a gramophone, but it was still pretty old. It was inside a wooden cabinet whose front fell down when you lifted up the lid. How, I wondered, did she know it was there?

'You think I can't listen and do something else at the same time?'

She rolled her eyes at the disappointment on my face.

'*Helaas*, don't be a baby. You weren't boring me. But it's okay if I never hear another Beatles song for as long as I live.'

We kept the records in a section of the cabinet. They were all classical albums. There were about twenty of them. Many were the same piece, played by a different orchestra. My father liked a few standard tunes, but he listened to music so rarely that he would buy a new album with a different recording, forgetting he already owned one. At least I think this was the case – maybe I'm doing him a disservice, maybe his ear was attuned enough that he could make out the subtle differences in the recordings, maybe he liked to compare and contrast, savouring the variations on those evenings when I wasn't around.

Esther flipped through them and selected one called *Piano Favourites*. She handed it to me and I put it on the player and dropped the needle down on it.

'Okay. Maybe Mien Dobbelsteen will think I play like a concert pianist.'

'Maybe she'll think I've gotten better.'

Esther shot out a laugh. 'If you got that much better that quickly, Ireland has found the next Mozart.'

She sat on the sofa and lit a cigarette.

'What if she comes in?'

'Well, then, I lose my job. A pity, I almost have enough money to buy a Ferrari.'

I stayed standing.

'You're very sarcastic, Esther.'

'Sarcastic?'

'Everything is a joke.'

She threw the spent match into the fireplace. She blew out some smoke and she nodded.

'You're right. I'm sorry. It's because I've no one to talk to.'

'You can talk to me.'

'You're sweet. But I need advice.'

'I can give advice.'

'Adult advice.'

'Well, I can listen.'

'This is serious, Simon. You can't understand. And I don't want to talk about it.'

'You just said you did.'

'Fine. I want to talk about it *and* I don't want to talk about it. I can feel two things at the same time, no?'

'Yes.'

'Okay.' She blew out some smoke to punctuate her point. 'Now you want a cigarette?'

'No.'

'You have never tried one?'

'No.'

'Are you not curious?'

'No.'

'Why not?'

I looked at the fireplace.

'Your mother. Yes, of course. I forgot that she had the cancer.'

She threw the cigarette on the grate: its smoke wisped up the chimney, caught by the draught. 'I'm sorry,' she said.

I nodded in acceptance.

She patted the sofa. 'Come here. Sit beside me.'

I sat down beside her.

She pointed to her knees. 'Put your head here.'

'What about Mien Dobbelsteen?'

'Simon, sometime soon you will need to learn to tell people to fuck off.' She pointed at her knees again. I lay down and put my head on her lap.

We listened to the music and she ran her hand through my hair. I didn't look up at her; I was turned towards the armchair where my mother used to sit. The music was soft and light. It wavered a little bit in places as though it were trying to find its balance.

Esther started talking. She spoke in Dutch, so I couldn't really understand, but it seemed that she was telling me about why she had come to Fermanagh and why her parents didn't want her around and why she wasn't in school or at university. She wasn't sad. Things just were as they were. She talked and ran her hand through my hair and while listening to her I thought, inevitably, of canals and bicycles and flat fields with no hedges. Dutch seemed to me like a soft language, a little slurred, with a few hard edges, like a fishing line whirring out and then ticking as it hit the water, like a game of dominoes, like semaphore, spoken out loud.

Then I felt something, a churning inside her. A charge went through me, like I had just licked the points on a battery. I sat up.

'You're pregnant,' I said.

'Yes,' she said. She didn't elaborate. I suppose she had just told me everything and didn't feel the need to repeat it in English.

I didn't know what else to say. There were too many questions running through my head. Who was the father? Why didn't he come with her? How did she decide to run to Fermanagh of all places? Eventually I asked, 'Do you know what you'll name it? Do you have a name for a boy and one for a girl?'

She smiled at me, a kind smile rather than a happy one and then shook her head. 'I'm not the one who'll get to name it.'

'Oh.' I took this in. 'Well, do you know where it will go?'

'No. I have made the decision not to ask.'

'Why not?'

'Simon, no more questions, okay?' She whispered this sentence. I nodded and lay again on her knees and looked into the empty fireplace and wondered where my mother was at that moment, wondered if she could look down on me and see everything that was happening to me.

8

I slept again and, when I woke, it was late afternoon. The sky outside was dark. On the computer in the hotel lobby, I checked my emails. There was a chain of twenty-two messages from Camille. Some of them also included our friends in France. She had caught a flight to Paris. She would stay with her parents until I came to my senses.

I called my office and spoke to Perry, the company manager. I needed to explain the charges on the company card. I kept it as brief as possible.

Finally, I brought up the website for the Chinatown gallery. Esther had an exhibition about to open and there was a public interview scheduled. The inevitabilities lining up, one after another. I sent an email to the gallery owner, introduced myself, asked her to let Esther know I'd be there.

When Friday came, I took the M train to Delancey. The gallery was on Forsyth Street, adjacent to a park, just a few blocks down from Houston Street. I was in my purple hoodie, body warmer, jeans, aqua combat boots. I thought about going to a shop, buying something more respectable, but couldn't face it. I probably looked like I'd arrived from a long painting session in my frigid studio – at least that's what I told myself.

I was early, so I waited outside, watched a game of roller hockey in progress. I wanted to walk into a crowded room. Few people there meant that I'd have to talk to Esther when she would be nervous and distracted – better to do it after the interview. I didn't want to be a ghost from the past, weighing on her success.

The hockey players were going full bore, no effort spared: they pushed and grappled and jabbed with their elbows. I enjoyed watching them. Full commitment, no quarter given. I liked New York for this, how unapologetic people were in their desires.

I wanted a cigarette but resisted – I'd stink of smoke. We'd embrace, hopefully, and I didn't want her first feeling to be one of revulsion. Did I want something else to happen? I had no idea. I was there, open, ready to make amends with another life.

I looked behind me. A crowd had gathered: the window was full of chattering people. I unzipped my jacket and walked inside. There were large canvases on the wall, refined people staring and talking, drinking wine from plastic cups. At the end of the room was a rostrum with two stools and a table with some water.

I stood, self-consciously, and took in the canvases, each one about twelve feet by six. They were enormous portraits, intricately detailed, but threatening to spill over into incoherency at any moment. I was wary of how I should act around them, thinking that I was being observed, aware of Esther's presence somewhere in the building.

The faces in the portraits looked South American to

me, people of the Andes or the rainforest. She had framed each portrait to erase all context. There were no clothes or background details. Just a face, staring intently back at me.

And then after a few moments of looking, they were not just faces. The pores and wrinkles and moles and sunsplatter began to cohere into something else. And I saw that each portrait was also a blend of topographic map and aerial landscape photo. An estuary dappled around the corner of an eye. A nostril became an inlet. The faces seemed to ease into the broader landscape with such power that I had to struggle to return to a sense of the initial image. The colours wrestled with each other, skin pigments shot through with the red of burnished soil, the wan grey of a meandering river streaking across a lip, the landscapes and the facial details conflicting with each other before finding a peaceful coherence, becoming both.

I looked around the room and saw a petite Asian woman who was attracting a lot of attention. I guessed this was Hing Lin, the gallery owner. She had glossy black hair the same tone as her clothes – a sweater and a long skirt, which were woollen and looked soft to touch. She caught my glance and gave me a sweeping wave, a large gesture that made me feel instantly welcome. She approached me, carelessly bumping into others, her hand outstretched. Her handshake had the firmness of someone who was used to doing business.

'So. You're the rugged Irishman.'

'That's definitely not how she described me.'

'Well, she said you were Irish. I may have extrapolated from there.'

She kept my hand in her grasp, softened it as she continued. 'Esther's excited to see you.'

'Me too. I have to admit I'm pretty nervous.'

She took in my face. A curious, searching look. 'You're older, older than I thought you'd be. I found some photos online. But you're different.'

I didn't know how to respond. I said, 'Wiser too, I hope.'

She smiled, a lopsided grin. 'Well, we'll soon see.'

Esther emerged from a backroom and leaned against the door frame, one hand gripping a coffee cup. People approached her, but she managed to wave shyly with her free hand before greeting them, looking a little uneasy maybe, or maybe that was just me.

She was thinner, looser, less robust. She was willowy and tanned. Her skin had been doused in sun. Still the same long hair, but gone somewhat brittle, the blonde more muted, shot through with plenty of grey. It hung in great drifts down to her waist. She wore feathery earrings and a collection of necklaces, simple threads and strings that ended in ceramic pendants that hung around her chest. She had heavy leather boots on her feet. She had changed, but not completely. I fidgeted and looked at the floor. I never know how to act around artists. She indicated, with flick of her head, that I should go into the backroom. Hing guided me there, an office with a kitchenette.

When Esther entered, I could see her shake off her

public self; she seemed to construct a private sphere with a quietening of her body, a quality I recognized.

'It's really you,' she said.

'It's really me.'

'You look —'

'Old, according to Hing.'

'Oh, you think that's direct? She keeps telling me I'm getting fat. One day we were on the phone and she told me I *sound* fat.'

Hing smirked with pride.

'She's right, you do sound fat.'

Esther laughed at that, her shotgun laugh. 'Fuck you, Hanlon.' And the years immediately rolled away. We embraced and then she stepped back to take me in.

'Simon has become a solid citizen, I see. Votes, volunteers maybe, has an accountant and a lawyer. Maybe he even *is* an accountant or a lawyer.'

'An architect.'

'That makes sense. Serious people following you with checklists. Not like whatever it is that I do.' She accompanied the comment with a circular gesture, as if her canvases came together as a haphazard afterthought.

She was openly appraising me, serious now, and I felt exposed, naked to the turn of the years, wondering if she could perceive a truth that had been hidden to me, some essential quality, or failure.

From the gallery space, I could hear someone giving an introduction. People began to settle.

'So this is where the years went?' I said.

'Some of them, yes.'

I paused. The past seemed so daunting, now that I stood on its rim.

'Are you surprised that this is what I've been doing with myself?'

I shook my head. 'No. It makes sense. Just don't ask me to explain why.'

She squeezed my arm then and there was a softening between us — something surged within me, her touch had lost none of its vitality. She stepped back into the gallery, to warm applause. I followed when the attention settled, made my way towards the back and leaned against the window frame.

The interviewer was a Brazilian art critic. The canvases were from Esther's life in Ecuador, post-divorce, when she began spending time with indigenous Amazonian tribes. She talked about place and identity, how the tribes she met didn't have a fixed settlement. She talked about travel, exile, migration, how what we think of as home doesn't have to be a fixed point but can move in many directions.

The interviewer invited questions from the audience and Esther answered them carefully, her words fluid and composed, decades of consideration lying beneath her answers.

Afterwards, she walked through the room, spent a moment with people. I could tell she was used to it. She was witty and deft, lighting people up. I waited by the window. I spoke to a few people, but mostly I enjoyed watching Esther again, still that kid in that chestnut tree.

We went for dinner afterwards, just she and I. I told her I didn't intend to monopolize her evening, but she waved away my statement. We stepped into a windowless room that was hot and loud, cutlery clanking off plates, bursts of laughter, some cheesy jazz floating in the background. As we took our table, I was aware that I was sweating. Colour, texture, sound, everything seemed heightened. I could hear strands of other conversations, anxiety and aggression in people's voices, bemoaning their lot.

I was conscious of how badly I was dressed. Although Esther's attire didn't fit with the sleek look of those around us, her easy confidence carried her through. She conversed easily with the waiters, chose authoritatively from the wine list, compensated for my uneasiness by giving long lingering answers to my questions, continuing where she left off at the gallery. I listened but couldn't reciprocate; we could both feel her words were disappearing into the ether. She came to a halt and held my hand and said, 'What's wrong?', so slowly and gently that it caused everything to spill out of me. I told her of my marriage to Camille, of the constant tension, the unending rumbling flux of the relationship, all of it building, in both subject and momentum, towards the incident on the highway.

She listened intently, holding back responses, not wanting to break my flow. I found myself breathless by the end, the words tumbling out. When I was through, we both leaned back, looked at our food gone cold, looked at each other. She gestured to the waiter for another bottle of wine, 'I think we might need it,' she said. We both started laughing then, giggling helplessly at the scale of the drama and the ridiculousness of my offloading all of this on a person I hadn't seen in more than thirty years.

I was hungry, all of a sudden. I started eating quickly and she filled our glasses and lifted hers and I paused my eating to raise mine in response. We clinked them together, giggling again. 'To survival,' she said. I thanked her and apologized and she waved it away.

She spoke then of her own failed marriage to an Ecuadorian businessman, a charming man who had offered the alluring combination of financial security and the excitement of life on a different continent, a place where lives flowed through the wide bureaucratic gaps. As she talked, I was aware of the natural intimacies of youth, the easy fusion that happens between those who have not yet solidified into societal roles, and how the openness of young friendships cannot be replicated in later life.

I said, 'I didn't just forget about you. After you went away and had the baby. I'm sorry I was never in touch.'

'I'm the one who should apologize. I wanted to make contact with you, after the bombing. I saw the news of course, it was all so shocking. I should have written to you but I think I wanted to leave that place behind me. It was too painful, too raw to think about. I needed to move on, to start my life over. And also, maybe there was a possibility you were being watched. I didn't know if a letter from me would put you in danger. I thought it was best if I just left you alone.'

Her words confused me. 'Who would be watch-ing me?'

'That man from the island. I thought that maybe he'd be paying attention to your actions.'

'What man?' I said.

'That night on the island.' She waited for a response, and when she realized I wasn't going to speak she looked deeper into me, searching, curious, scanning my expres-sion. 'You really don't remember?'

'Remember what?' Her stare made me uneasy.

'How can you not remember?'

And then it returned. The memory came fully formed, I could see it with such clarity that I felt a constriction in my chest that made it hard to breathe.

On the weekends of that summer before the bombing, for the only time in my youth, I took advantage of the freedom my situation afforded me.

Brian and myself still went fishing twice a week. It was harder to get a catch in the warm weather: the eels sank right down into the cool mud. Esther came with us some nights, and any time she did she brought sand-wiches and tea and a bar of chocolate with her. I let the chocolate sit on my tongue, savouring it. It seemed a great indulgence in that place. She managed to coax things out of Brian that I never would have asked. He told us about his life in theology school. The early morn-ings and the earnestness, how they had to make their beds like military men, sheets crisp and folded over. Bible classes that involved no discussion. He confessed that he left because he couldn't bring himself to speak in front of a congregation. Any time he tried it, he dried up, could only squeeze out a few words. He shrugged his shoulders. 'It wasn't meant to be and that's the end of it. I couldn't speak because I don't think I really believed what I was saying.' Neither of us asked him about his work in the barracks. We didn't want to break the spell of peace that surrounded us.

When I finished my day's work with Liam Hayes, the hay contractor, I dropped over to help Esther in the garden in the evenings. I volunteered to do any of the heavy work. I weeded the beds and mixed cowshit together with hay and shook it on to the soil. The lettuces came up quickly. And there were small radishes that I could pluck from the ground and wipe off and put straight into my mouth; they were so tart and juicy that they made my eyes water. A few hens arrived at the beginning of July and took up residence in the repaired henhouse. I liked to watch them stuttering about. Esther named them after the Seven Dwarfs, and each had characteristics to match. I'd go to check on them in the mornings before breakfast, and, if Esther hadn't already been, I'd set aside a few eggs for our house and leave the rest in a basket by the back door – I didn't like to knock as I knew Brian would be sleeping after his shift. One of the hens laid green eggs and they were the nicest ones, their consistency thicker and richer than that of the others.

Every Saturday afternoon, I packed up my tent and a sleeping bag, along with a rod, some food and water, some kindling and a book, and I walked to the rowboat and took it out alone. Most of the islands were too small and barren to be inhabited, so for a day and a night I was released into an alternate world where the only traces of human existence were the painted markings on the sheep that studiously ignored me. Books gave me their companionship. In those summer months, I lost myself in the smoke of conjured words; I allowed my imagination to unspool under the solace of the moon, inhabiting lands and customs that were not inherited but devised. Sometimes I even read aloud, let my voice twist and run in tune to the water swirling in the small coves.

The night on the island came on a Saturday in early August. That afternoon, I had finished with Liam Hayes around lunchtime. My father had ordered a delivery of lime that week. The soil in our area was very acidic and so, once every couple of years, my father spread lime over it to balance the pH levels. He had offered some to Esther, to use in the garden. When I got back to the house, she was in our yard. She had pulled back the tarpaulin cover and was shovelling the slake into a bin liner. There was a light breeze that day which caught the dust and was spreading it in clouds around her. Our yard was covered in a skin of grey. Esther was wearing her beekeeper's overalls; they had lost their colour with her work. She looked haunted, her eyes streamed red.

'Is there no one to help you? Where is everyone?' I asked.

'Trudy's visiting her sister. Brian is covering a shift in the station. I'm not sure where your father is.'

'You shouldn't be doing heavy work. I'll get the tractor. We'll have it done in no time.'

She nodded her assent, glad of the offer. I told her to run water over her face while I started up the Massey and attached the back loader. I reversed into the pile and then drove it out our front gate and up the Irvines' lane. By the time I reached their garden, Esther was waiting with the shovel.

I swapped places with her and showed her how to put the tractor into a low gear and pointed at the clutch and the accelerator and she puttered along beside the beds, stopping every few yards for me to cut into the pile with the shovel and spread it on to the soil. When we were finished, I insisted that she be the one to drive the tractor back and park it in our shed. She did so and I rode along in the emptied loader.

She offered to make me lunch, to show her gratitude, and I accepted. She left her overalls in the back kitchen and went into the shower. By the time I had finished my own shower, there was soup and a salad on the table.

'You're going out on the boat now?' she asked.

'I am,' I said.

'Can I come with you?'

I must have looked doubtful.

'Please, Simon. I feel like one of the chickens. I need to get out from that place, for one night at least. It's not like I can just go to the pub.'

'What if something happens?'

'What, like I could go into labour?'

'Exactly.'

'Don't worry. It won't happen. I'm not due for another six weeks. The doctor has said that everything is fine.'

'I don't know.'

'Oh, come on. Please. I'm losing my mind. It's so calm there. It'll be good for me. Or maybe you don't want a woman coming along to your secret spot.'

'It's not a good idea.'

'It is a good idea. Please. Just one night, you can take me. We'll be back in the morning.'

I relented. She went back to the Irvines' to get some warm clothes while I dug out an extra sleeping bag. We walked down the jetty at Aughinver. The afternoon was bright and warm. Esther was in such good spirits that I relaxed. I asked her about her piano playing and she told me about her grandmother's house in Utrecht. Her grandmother was a teacher, and Esther spent most of her afternoons there after school, before her parents came home from work. Her grandmother gave her some lessons, but mostly left her to it. Her parents argued a lot. Her home was tense, so she loved the peacefulness of those few hours. The piano gave her permission not to think about anything. The notes did their own talking.

On the boat, she kept her eyes closed most of the way and enjoyed the warmth of the air.

When we got there, I set up my small tent and dragged over a dead branch for us to sit on. We read our books in peace.

As the sky darkened, we fried sausages by dangling them on sticks over the fire that I made. I ate my sausages straight from the stick. Esther opted to take hers off it, blowing on them to cool them down, cursing and laughing before she ate them. A sly satisfaction on her face when she had finished. I remember I could see her as a girl then, full of mischief, so alive to the world.

The fire died, the moon came out. We shared my little tent. We faced each other in our sleeping bags. Close enough that I could feel her breath on my face. I fell asleep satisfied, reassured by her closeness, her presence there confirming to me that I wasn't just an incidental figure in her life.

I woke in the middle of the night – I heard a buzzing sound. At first I thought it was some creature, a moth, a bird, something trapped in the folds of the tent maybe. As I lay awake and listened, the sound established itself. It was an engine. I checked my watch: it was past two.

Sounds magnify in a tent, on a still night. I told myself I was imagining things, but, no, it came closer, and there was no doubt. From its strength and direction, I surmised that it was pulling into a cove on the western end of the island. I ran through the possibilities in my head. They were fishermen who had lost their way. They were hunters, readying themselves for the morning. I discounted both possibilities. There was nothing there to hunt. And fishermen rarely used an engine – they'd scare away their catch, and it was wildly unlikely that they'd dock there, at that time of night.

I was running through other possibilities, because I didn't want to admit the conclusion I'd already reached. There was talk of the islands occasionally being used by paramilitaries. But, because of my fishing trips with Brian, I had dismissed it as conjecture. He wouldn't have put me in harm's way, nor would my father have given me free rein to explore the territories on my weekend trips.

Voices carried through the air. The island was only about five hundred yards in length. A group of men. I could almost, but not quite, make out their words. I heard instructions being issued. They were unloading something. I heard some grunts of effort and footsteps overlapping. I could hear the crackle of every trodden branch. A water hen cooed and received a response.

I should have stayed where I was, settled back down, waited for whatever was happening to pass. But I didn't. Maybe it was a sense of protectiveness towards Esther, or just the natural curiosity of a boy who was only beginning to emerge into manhood. A tent is a lonely outpost, offering scant fortification from any outside threats. I had to see what was happening. I slid the zip down on my bag and quietly slipped outside, careful not to wake Esther. I put my runners on and walked as lightly as I could towards the stirrings.

Through a copse of trees, I could make out the silhouettes of four men moving unsteadily, each carrying a box, obviously heavy, moving it somewhere inland, away from the cove.

I felt a chill run through me. Paramilitary activity had

always been something on the news, something abstract. People talked about it, but I'd never met anyone directly involved, had never met a family who had been victims of the violence. And then it was in front of me, real, in motion.

A rustle to my left. I turned, terrified: someone had seen me. There was a figure there. I felt the impulse to run but my legs couldn't bring themselves to do so. I don't know if it was wit or cowardice that made me stay put. The moon was bright enough for him to make out my face, but I couldn't see him, just his outline.

He said, 'What's your name, son?' He said this in a low, breathy whisper. He was being careful not to let his voice carry, but his words were emphatic. They sounded almost like a hiss.

'Simon,' I said.

'Simon what?'

I hesitated to answer, but I was in no position to be elusive.

'Hanlon,' I said.

'You're Peter's young lad?'

I hesitated. 'Aye, that's right.'

'What the fuck are you doing out here?'

'I'm camping,' I said.

'Aye, well you picked a bad spot for it. Are you alone?'

Again I hesitated. I didn't want to involve Esther if I didn't have to.

'Tell the truth now. If I have to go looking, I'll have to call the others.'

'There's a girl with me. Her name is Esther.'

'You've the wee Dutch girl in there.'

'Aye.'

'She's pregnant, aye?'

'Aye.'

'Ach, for fuck sake, man. You're lucky it was me who found you. Go back to your tent now. Don't make a sound. Don't shift until the morning. And if you breathe a word of this, son, I don't need to tell you.'

'No.'

'Go on now. Quick. And be sure you're quiet.'

Esther was awake when I got back. I whispered to her to be quiet, not to move a muscle. I told her I'd explain in the morning. She didn't question me; she could probably feel the fear pulsating from me. We lay there, side by side, for an eternity. Even when we heard the engine depart we didn't speak.

When the sky began to lighten I talked her through what had happened. She didn't ask any questions, just listened intently. We packed up the tent and I rowed us back. Even allowing for the weak light, Esther looked gaunt, so drained that her skin was almost translucent.

When we arrived at the jetty at Aughinver and disembarked, we held each other tight. A long, relieving embrace. I left her at Irvine's gate. It was the last time I saw her.

The waiter came with the bill and I returned to the stifling room with the conversational hum all around us. I was stunned. Images of that night flooded through me. I looked over at Esther, she too had gone to some other place – her eyes had softened.

'Are you all right?' I asked.

'It's . . . you being here, you know. It brings everything back.' She sighed. The sentence extended into meaning.

She told me how she had become pregnant. It was an older married man, a neighbour. Her parents were too devout to consent to an abortion. Their rector had attended the same theology school as Brian Irvine. She agreed to go away because it gave her space and time in which to decide if she wanted to keep the baby or not; she couldn't stay in Utrecht, not with all that had happened, and she didn't have anywhere else that would take her in.

'You haven't made contact with him?'

'No,' she said. 'I'm prepared for the day that an email will come and open everything up.'

'You think maybe I'm a precursor?'

'It had crossed my mind. These things come in waves, don't they?'

'Yes, they do.'

We sat in silence for a while, exhausted. We had so much more to talk about, but neither of us could summon the energy to do so. I paid the bill. I owed her that much. I walked to the bathroom down a narrow alcove. I was unsteady on my feet, still sweating. I wanted to splash cold water on my face, get away from people, take a minute to recompose myself.

It was when I passed the waiters' station that I could feel someone approach. I heard a voice behind me, a familiar, long-absent voice, that voice from my distant past asking me a question, a whispered question.

'What's your name, son?'
Then a void.

When I came to, I found myself sitting on a tiled floor, my back against a wall. There was a woman holding my hand. She was speaking to me, speaking softly. Her face was blurred. Her skin was warm. The light above her ebbed and pulsed. My shoulders were burning. My neck too. Streams of heat ran from the base of my skull down my neck, down my shoulders, down my spine. She was speaking to me. The sound of her voice was so soothing. She was repeating a word. Her face began to cohere. Eyes. Nose. Lips. I tried to make out what she was saying.

'Simon,' she said. She said it again: 'Simon.' Simon was my name. How did she know my name? I looked at her. 'Simon. Do you know where you are?' Her skin was tanned. Brown eyes, long grey/blonde hair, feathery earrings. 'Simon, it's Esther. Do you remember me?'

9

I woke the next morning in a strange room. Street sounds washed in from the large sash window to my right. I realized where I was – Hing's parents' apartment; they lived near the restaurant and were away for a few days. I remembered Esther helping me to bed. She had taken off my boots for me and given me a set of Hing's father's pyjamas. They were cotton, blue paisley, comforting.

My body ached. I could hardly tell one part from another. Someone, a busker I presumed, was playing an erhu. I lay there and thought that the instrument sounded exactly like its component parts should. A bow being drawn over a thin strand of wire.

I was embarrassed and consumed by a feeling of dread. It had been so many years since I'd had a seizure. I tried to put it down to exhaustion and emotional distress, all very plausible, but I couldn't shake the feeling that it wouldn't be an isolated incident, that I had stepped into another phase of my life.

I lay there in bed, still stunned at how I could have blanked out a moment as important as that night on the island. I looked out of the window to the cross-hatching of the fire escapes across the street. I gazed at the dust motes that moved across the glass and felt that everything was being propelled by its own momentum, moving unpredictably but with a kind of inevitability. I was returning to something I had deliberately erased.

I recalled the weeks after the incident. The years flooded back, and I submerged myself in my past life.

I stopped going round to help Esther in the garden. I kept my distance. I didn't know how to talk about what had happened. I didn't want her trying to convince me that we should speak to Brian Irvine about it. I think I believed that any words I spoke aloud carried implications. The man on the island had told me to be quiet, and the only influence I had over our situation was to be sure to follow his instructions.

September came, and I returned to school. The weather turned. It rained hard. It was an exam year – my GCSEs lay ahead – and in each class the teacher laid out what the curriculum had in store for us. In my bedroom, I laid out my books in separate piles on the floor and prepared myself for the long haul. In retrospect, I was doing what I always did, still do, when threatened by the outside world: I retreated into solitude and books. I didn't know how to help Esther. She was someone beyond my reach. The only thing I could do to protect her was to stay away from her.

As I was walking down our lane from the bus one evening, Brian pulled up beside me in the car, uniformed, on his way to work.

'We haven't seen you about in a bit. There's nothing doin' on the water. I don't think they'll bite unless you're there.'

'Aye, well, school has started. I won't be able to go out again for a bit.'

'Good wee man. You're hitting the books.' I could see the disappointment in his eyes, but he managed to keep it out of his voice.

'I am,' I said.

'There's brains in you Stewarts. Not that your da is short of a few cards either.'

'No,' I said. Compliments weren't something that any of us knew how to deal with. I thought Brian might take the opportunity to end the exchange and be on his way, but he stayed put. The engine ticked over. There was something he wanted to say. I could feel my body constrict. Had Esther told him?

Eventually he spoke. 'Esther's away, lad. I wasn't sure if you knew.'

'Away where?' I said.

'She's in the hospital in Belfast.'

'Oh,' I said. 'Is something wrong?'

'No, no, it's all tickety-boo. A wee bit early, but no problems, thank God.'

'She's had the baby already?' I tried to take the urgency out of my voice, but couldn't manage it. Brian heard it and was softly reassuring in his reply.

'She did, Simon. A lovely wee fella. Don't be worrying yourself now. He's a good head of hair on him and a fine set of lungs. He's on the small side because he couldn't stay in there, but he'll be grand.'

I didn't know how to react. My chest closed up. I could

only breathe from the top of my lungs. I was aware of the chill of the air.

'And Esther?'

'They're fine, lad, trust me, the two of them are mighty.'

He said these lines as if he were talking about a calf. There was no sense of regret for her situation or worry for her future.

'Is she on her own?'

'No, God, no. Trudy's up there with her. She's staying with her sister for a bit to keep an eye on things.'

'Why did they go to Belfast?'

'Well, the wee man is being passed along, you know that. So Belfast is the place for that.'

'Could I come and visit her?'

He shook his head. He was rarely definitive with me; normally he let me tease out my own answers to a problem. But not that time.

'No, Simon. She's been through a lot now. Leave the lassie be.'

I walked back to an empty house. Mrs O'Gorman had taken another job. Maybe she found the place too crushing. And she, unlike me, didn't know how to be a background presence.

I made my dinner, lamb chops and potatoes, and ate it alone, with no hope of rescue. My summer job had ended. School, I told myself, was my only way out of here. I would use it to dig a channel through my books that would allow the river of learning to carry me somewhere else, sweep me towards an estuary.

My father was hardly ever around. It was harvest season. There was a rush to get the crops in before the weather ruined them. Although he no longer had any tillage, he spent his evenings on the neighbouring farms, helping out. I would see him briefly over breakfast, and that was it, I'd be in bed by the time he arrived back home.

I couldn't erase the image of Esther lying in a hospital ward, her baby a few rooms away, and she not being allowed to see him. Or, worse, their taking him off her and her realizing it was their last moment together. I could imagine Trudy by the bed, all cold impracticality. Telling her it was for the best. That she'd get over it in time. Esther wearing a shapeless gown. The smell of overcooked vegetables in the corridors.

I rose, groggily, still wearing Hing's father's pyjamas, opened the door and shuffled my way into the kitchen. I was surprised to see that it held a small bathtub set into the wall, over which there were wet clothes hanging from a rack. Hing was at the table, working on her laptop. She cooked me some eggs. She told me Esther would be along as soon as she could.

I ate quickly, readily. I asked her if she'd grown up in that apartment, and she nodded. She explained that she and Esther lived upstate – Esther hated the city. She said she'd tried to convince her parents to move to a bigger place, but it was their home; it held good memories for them and provided easy access to their daughter's gallery, and, besides, all their friends lived within three blocks.

A lot of people her parents' age had followed their kids out to the suburbs, usually to Jersey, and then moved back to Chinatown after a couple of years. They couldn't handle the monotony of detached homes and wide lawns and the banality of shopping malls.

She answered emails while I drank my coffee. I gave her an apology for keeping her from her work, but she waved it away, told me she was getting more done here – in the gallery there was a distraction every five minutes.

I went back to the bedroom to dress. When I re-emerged, Esther was talking to Hing in low tones at the table. They asked me about my living situation. I told them about our apartment in Clinton Hill, how I couldn't face going back there. They asked me about my seizure, if it was something that had happened before. I told them about the bombing and the episodes that had followed. They encouraged me to see a specialist.

'Let's see what happens,' I said. 'It's been a rough week. It might just be a one-off.'

Esther rolled her eyes. 'It's been over a quarter of a century since you've had a seizure, Simon. You don't think it's significant?'

I had no answer to that. I nodded, relenting.

She wasn't finished. 'You're going to need someone to watch over you. You need people nearby. We've been talking. There's a room upstairs. It was an old lace factory, but it hasn't been used for a while – Hing's father is waiting for the paperwork to come through to turn it into a residential apartment. You should stay there. We can at least keep an eye on you.'

'I don't want to be any trouble.'

'Like a true Irish martyr.'

I laughed. 'We can't help it, we were raised on it.'

'Well, my father would go toe-to-toe with you on that,' Hing said. 'Enough. You're staying.'

Esther led me upstairs. When we reached the top floor, she gave me the keys with a ceremonial flourish and I opened the door. It was near midday, so the sunlight arrived almost directly into the front window of the cupola. The light was warm – it filled the space, gave it a cadmium hue. The space was broken by three steel columns, painted white, arranged in no order I could make any sense of. At the north wall, there was a small room defined by metal frames from which, it was clear, the plate glass had been removed. I presumed it was once a manager's office. Next to it was a grey steel door that housed a toilet and a sink.

The casement windows were set into a rebate frame. When I walked over to them and turned the crank arm, they opened only a couple of inches. I ran my hands along the casing and could feel thin streams of air seeping in. There were low radiators running above the skirting boards. The place was as cold as a metal bar.

At the window of the cupola I took in the city. The room looked directly down on to a small plaza, its lights extinguished overnight, so now it was netted inside a mesh of black electrical cables and bordered by hotels and currency exchanges and a Chinese bakery where men moved about a loading bay, pushing racks of empty steel trays. From the east window, I saw a large scrum of soccer balls tied up in a net and realized eventually that they were cabbages. Next to them was a flat surface of tiny blue dots: a pallet of water bottles – I was looking directly down on their lids. From this height, everything becomes something else, an aspect I've gotten to know well in the six months that I've lived here.

'It's perfect,' I said. 'It's simple.'

Esther smiled, with an eye roll and a curve of her lips.

'It's something. *Simple* is not the word that springs to mind.'

'The view is beautiful.'

'You mean the trains right outside your window?'

'Among other things, yes.'

She stepped over to the cupola and looked out on to the river. I joined her.

'You're right,' she said. 'It has a quality to it. Just get some furniture and some plants.'

'And a cooker.'

'And a fridge. And a heater. And a good mattress. Until you get yourself a decent mattress and some bedsheets, you're staying downstairs. *No* isn't an option.'

I turned from the window and looked at her.

'Thank you,' I said, 'for all of this.'

She smiled warmly, ran her hand on my cheek. 'You're welcome. You've been through a lot. Seeing you last night, on the floor. I felt so helpless, so sorry for you.'

'It'll pass.'

'I'm sure it will. But in the meantime, I'm very glad I can help.'

'I am too.'

She took out her phone. 'Is there someone I can call, I should have asked earlier. You don't have a phone, right?'

'Right. Or anyone to call.'

She smiled, 'You really put yourself on a limb out here, didn't you.'

I shrugged, 'Isn't that why people move to New York.'

'I guess you're right.'

I asked her about how she moved here and she told me a story about meeting Hing at an exhibition in Mexico. When Hing offered her a showing in her gallery she took it as an opportunity to start again. I found it hard to follow what she was saying, my concentration was scattered from what had happened the night before. I sat on the floor. Despite the cold, I wanted to get acquainted with my new surroundings. But mostly I wanted to talk.

She asked, 'What is it? Do you need something, some water?'

I shook my head. 'There's something I didn't mention,' I said, 'about my seizures.'

I told her about the voice, the question. I had a creeping certainty that the voice was from that encounter on the island.

'You heard it before? When you had your seizures?'

'Yes. But I hadn't connected it. Or at least I don't think I had, I don't remember.'

'Why do you think you hear it?'

'I suppose, on some level, I'm connecting it to the bombing.'

'You think he was involved.'

'I have no idea. But yes, I suppose I believe he was.'

'Did you ever tell anyone?'

'About the voice? No. I didn't think there was any point.'

'And about the island? You must have thought about telling your father?'

'I suppose I didn't want to worry him. And he would have had to follow it up, which might have put us all in danger. We were living precariously enough as it was.'

She nodded. We were quiet for a while. No sound in the room other than the ticking of the radiators.

'Where do you think he is?' I asked eventually. 'Your son.'

'I call him Jonas. It was my grandfather's name. Not officially, it's not on any documents or anything. It's just my name for him.'

'What age would he be?'

'He's thirty-four now. He's probably in Ireland, but I can't imagine him there – I can't really remember much of the place. Instead, I see him in Utrecht. I see him walking home from work, wearing a suit, arriving at a house with large windows. I know he's married with children. I don't know what he works at, but I know it's a good job, he's respected. He's a good husband, a good father.'

'Why wouldn't you find out? Why not just call a lawyer?'

'I don't want to bring all that chaos into his world. It would be selfish of me to arrive out of the blue and turn everything upside down. He's made his own life. It's not fair to come crashing into it now.'

'Maybe he wants that?'

'He doesn't.'

'How can you know?'

'I just do.'

She said this with such definition that I let the matter rest.

10

Hing helped me to clean out my stuff from Clinton Hill. Anything jointly owned went into storage. I've sublet the place, which brings in enough to cover my expenses. I've taken a leave of absence from work, but I don't know if I'll return.

My operation is scheduled to happen a month from now. Esther will accompany me. She comes to see me every second Sunday. She apologizes that it's not more often, but I appreciate her making the trip. If Hing is staying with her parents for the evening – usually when there's an exhibition she needs to see – she'll come and spend some time up here. I like having her close, it's much more casual with her now. She's picked me up off the floor, helped me to change my trousers. Once those lines are crossed, there's not much people can't say to each other. We're like an old married couple. She treats this apartment as if it's her own. She scrolls through her phone and sends emails, gives me an account of her day.

I cooked her dinner tonight. I always cook her dinner. I insist on it. 'You don't owe me anything, Simon,' she says. 'You don't have to be a host or anything.'

'I know that,' I say. In truth, though, I do feel like I owe her. Although mostly I cook for her because it makes me feel normal and because it's something my mother taught me to do.

I keep thinking of my mother. I long for her hand on my neck, some reassuring words. I long for that strength she embodied, that peaceful acceptance that she developed in tandem with her illness. I keep thinking about her last moments. I keep wondering if she was afraid, when the end came. She was devout, she had real faith, it wasn't just an obligation for her. It must have made a difference. I'm sorry I never asked her straight out, on those soft afternoons when we sat by the fire: *What do you believe in?* She must have wanted to talk about it and I can't see my father managing to gather up enough wherewithal to broach the subject.

She died on the third floor of the Erne Hospital. It was the same building she had nursed in for fourteen years and where, until the moment of her passing, she was still a registered employee. The staff treated me like I was one of their own. The porter at the main door always nodded to me respectfully when I arrived – wearing my school uniform – and asked me to pass along his regards. The woman in the tuck shop refused to take my money whenever I tried to buy something. It happened enough times that I stopped offering payment and would simply pick something off the shelf and then walk out of the shop, waving in gratitude. There were days when I would walk into my mother's room to find one of the nurses sitting by her bedside, holding her hand, with their eyes glazed over.

When her final moment came, I was asleep, slumped against the wall near the door. She passed away late at night. I'd been curled up in a chair in the corridor. I woke and found that I was alone and pushed open the door of the room. My father and Reverend McKay were gathered around the bed along with my aunt Jackie, some of my mother's cousins and two former neighbours who had made the trip from Liverpool. It was a circle that I felt no part of, or, more accurately it was a circle that warded me away. It felt natural to them all, or so I suppose, to offset any sorrow that they had by transforming it into a protectiveness towards me. They probably believed that they were sparing me from something that I was deemed too young to witness. This is, of course, speculation. All I do know is that no one opened the circle to include me in it. Instead, I took my position against the wall and the intonation of my father's prayers lulled me back into a drowsy stupor.

I don't think I spent any time alone with her corpse after her passing. I remember being woken and everyone filtering out of the room, into the lounge. My father said, 'Well, I'm a widower now,' and, while we were all nodding in tacit agreement, one of the nurses brought us tea and biscuits. She sat beside my father and held his wrist and told us that we could see the body in a few minutes: the others just needed some time to set things to rights. I remember she used the word 'body' and not 'corpse', acknowledging that the life, my mother's life, still hadn't completely drained from it, still held its resonances. She had seen all of this so many times before and yet she still made us feel like we were the only family to have ever experienced a death. I remember this woman as being Mrs Johnston, who, along with her husband, Kit, a retired ambulance driver, was subsequently killed in the bombing. She was from Kesh, just down the road from us. She was a dignified woman, good at music. I can see her so vividly, the way she reassured my father, holding him by the wrist as though she were taking his pulse.

Looking back over the records of that time, though, I realize this couldn't have been the case. When I read through reports of the bombing in the *Impartial Reporter*, I found that Mrs Johnston retired in 1986. She wouldn't have been present, and in uniform, when my mother died in February 1987.

When I stumbled on this fact, it was in such stark contrast to my memory of that night that I took it as a personal insult. I wanted to call the editor and tell him that his journalistic standards weren't worth a shit. But it's backed up by other sources.

Confabulate. I looked it up after the Wada test. *To fabricate imaginary experiences as a compensation for loss of memory*.

The definition is short-sighted and dumb. The notion of memory and imagination being two separate entities is as absurd as a newspaper claiming impartiality. And we don't fabricate imaginary experiences. They come to us; it's not a production process. And nothing compensates for the loss of memory. Just as nothing compensates for the loss of a loved one.

I'm frightened. I don't mind admitting it. It's not death that scares me, it's the threat of permanent isolation. No matter how much the medical staff try to reassure me, try to play up the familiarity of the procedure, the expertise of the surgeon, I am facing brain surgery. One wrong move, a fraction of an inch too far here or there, and I could be cut adrift, abandoned inside my body. My mind would be rendered a place without seasons or tides, inaccessible to visitors, inescapable.

A seahorse and an almond, shapes innocent enough to appear on a child's wallchart.

With this threat, this possibility, looming over me, the notion of veracity, of historical fact, seems crucial to me now. On the other hand, I'm coming to understand that there's no such thing. We are all composites of relative truth. Even this moment, this moment when I'm writing, running a pen along my notebook, has a million different shadings. The now that we think we live in is never *now*. The sunlight we see when we stare at a sunset originated eight minutes beforehand. We look at the Plough in the night sky, but there never was a moment in time when the stars in a constellation were in relation to each other as we experience them. Their light arises from different eras.

In everyday perception, there's a time lapse of around 20 to 300 milliseconds between what we see and the moment the perception is available for us to act upon it. Usually this is explained away by saying our conscious perception is delayed with respect to its external cause. But it can equally be said that our experiences have already happened before our brains react to them. The present is greater than a construct of the mind: it is the world manifesting itself as you, even before your brain is made aware of it. The moment that we think of as *now* is already over. The moment we think of as *then* never really happened – it wasn't a single moment but rather a conflux of different events.

To say that we confabulate is part of that attempt to draw our experiences into easily digestible facts. The notion of confabulation also endows scientists with considerable power. It enables them to tell us that our perceptions are radically separated from the external world, bound inside our skulls, and consequently that we all live in error and need the authority of science to tell us what reality is actually like.

We are taught to oppose the physical and the imaginary. One is truthful, the other a lie. It's a false conflict. Adeline Ravoux said it herself: as a ten-year-old girl, she didn't recognize herself in her portrait. It took a lifetime for her to understand the imaginative truth beneath its surface. Van Gogh didn't paint by observation; he painted by identification, concentrating on the equilibrium between himself and the subject to reveal a deeper comprehension.

According to the *Impartial Reporter*, Mrs Johnston couldn't have been present at my mother's death. But it doesn't change my memory of the evening. And the memory creates its own reality.

Who is this shadow, this man who haunts me daily, whispers into my ear, sends me into convulsions? I can only surmise that, on some instinctual level, I believe him to be one of the bombers. This may not be factually true, but it is true to me. And so instead of thinking of him as a figure from my past, a figure who haunts me, perhaps I should see him as someone active, someone still present, replete with possibility.

Why did he do it? I'd like to ask him that question face to face, to have an honest conversation across his kitchen table, if such a thing exists. He didn't have to protect Esther and me. He might well have saved our lives. And then, a few weeks later, he bombed his own community, slaughtered the people who lined up on a Sunday morning to remember their dead. How do we hold such contradictions in our hands?

I wonder if he is filled with regret, if peace has changed his perspective, or if he clings to his justifications with the ferocity of a drowning man?

No matter. That conversation will never happen. He and I will never meet. Even if we did, I would have no awareness of who he is. A shadow has no resemblance.

The *now* that we experience is a relative now. For something to be present, it only needs to be causally present, affecting my senses even if it's not in my vicinity.

Every day, the man on the island exerts an effect on my body. He's the most influential person in my life. He turns around and around in my consciousness, like a twig trapped in an eddy. And perhaps his – and my – only hope of escape is if I ease the currents of my rational mind and dream him into being, let him slip into the flow of my lived experiences.

Nothing erases division like communal work. My father farmed crops of wheat and barley when I was small, and the happiest, most peaceful times of my childhood were the harvest evenings when my mother and I would bring a nest of sandwiches to himself and the men who had hardly left the cabins of their machines since morning. The late-summer day had played itself out, and we stood in the shed in near-darkness. At that time of year, sunset is still as late as nine o'clock, so it must have been almost ten before they had finished everything up.

Though these men were from various religious backgrounds, they were all the same, all tired, all weary from their toil. I remember many of them being covered in hydraulic grease, great black wads of it across their foreheads, and, as they dug into the sandwiches and passed around some cigarettes, the sense of satisfaction they gave off made me impatient to grow up, to join them in their labour. And when they were finished with their tea, they flung away the dregs, and I watched the liquid spray against the concrete floor, an action that held a simple kind of anarchy for me, as it was something that my mother would never allow in the house.

Those gatherings that I witnessed in our barn might well have been the last of their kind. Our continued collaboration, though I didn't know it at the time, was its own form of resistance, a quiet protest against the partitions that we were all encouraged to uphold.

When I try to put a face on the bomber, I see these men. He obviously knew me, or knew of me. He knew my father. So it's not too much of a stretch to say that he could have been amongst us, one of those weary faces that ate our sandwiches and drank our tea, quietly satisfied with his work under a late-summer sun.

I can picture him clearly now when I close my eyes. I see brief snapshots of him that extend into longer moments. I see him as a young boy, about twelve years old, on an evening in the Fermanagh countryside. He wears grey jeans and a thin brown jumper. I imagine it to be the early 1970s, around the time my mother and father came back from Liverpool. The Troubles have just begun. Soldiers have arrived and taken up residence in a barracks in the town. There are checkpoints where the roads cross the border with signs that say: DON'T BLAME US, BLAME THE TERRORISTS. They raid houses, unannounced, kick in doors. Young Catholic men are placed in internment camps, held without trial.

I watch him step into his small garage and roll out the lawnmower from its spot in the corner. He trundles it to his back garden, releases the choke and pulls the ripcord that ignites the starter, the engine roaring into life. I can see his movements so clearly. How he tilts up the front wheels of the mower when he reaches the edge of the flowerbeds. How methodical he is, cutting the lawn into exacting stripes, like a groundskeeper. I can feel the soft light of the waning sun, hear the thrum of the mower's engine, smell the cut grass clinging to his wellington boots.

Afterwards, he eats his dinner, watches some TV and then goes to bed, reluctantly, when his mother tells him to. I can hear the weariness in her voice. She is tired of giving orders, tired of being the one who has to put some shape on his days.

Now I see him wake in his bedroom. I can see it so clearly, it's a small room at the top of the house. It's painted light grey. The ceiling is so sloped that he can stand up fully only on one side of the room. He has posters of tractors and cars tacked to the ceiling. There's a stack of car magazines at the end of his bed. On his shelf are the machinery catalogues that he collected from the salesmen at the Ploughing Championships, which he goes to with his father every September. I know he likes those days. The Ploughing Championships might well be the highlight of his year. His father spends the day at a bar inside a tent, and the boy collects catalogues as evidence of their fruitful activities.

He is slight and milky pale, except for his face, which has kept some sun from the summer. His hair is cut tight to his head. When his mother used to cut it, it was longer. Since he started going to the barber in town, he looks like all the other boys in his class.

I watch as the boy throws off his blankets and puts on

his clothes, which lie rumpled on the floor. After breakfast, he'll change into his school uniform, but it's early yet. This is his time: there's no one awake to instruct him; early morning carries freedom. He stands to pull his jeans up to his waist. Just below the knees are clippings of cut grass that have gathered there from the lawnmowing; his wellingtons didn't reach high enough to protect him fully. He wipes the grass clippings off. Better to leave them on the floor of his room than to scatter them around the house. He ties his runners and slips into the kitchen, where he wakes their dog, Fluther, giving him warning of his movements – he doesn't want the dog to wake the house. Fluther is named after a character in *The Plough and the Stars*, which is an old play that his ma likes. Fluther is good-natured and doesn't mind the interruption in his sleep. His tongue drops out of the side of his mouth as he watches the boy step outside the back door, closing it gently. Through the glass, the boy presses down the air with his hand as a signal to Fluther that he should stay in his basket. Fluther rests his head on his paws, someone else will be along soon.

The boy steps quietly into the yard, clambers upon the oil tank in the back garden and up on to the flat roof of the garage, then scuttles up the wavering tiles of the house; his parents' room is at the opposite end.

He has started secondary school, and he likes it, though he would be slow to admit it to anyone. There are mornings when he is pressed against the radiator, waiting for classes to begin, when he feels an easy belonging. The casual talk of nothingness. There is nowhere in the world he'd rather be. Everyone lives nearby. There are no buses to the school, no lifts from parents. On wet mornings, they congregate around the radiators, boys and girls both, and the smell in the air is of damp and singed fabric, the same smell as when his ma does the ironing. On the classroom wall there are pieces of paper cut into triangles: isosceles, equilateral, scalene, acute, obtuse. Above them is a map of Europe. The countries are brightly coloured until they reach East Germany. From then on, they turn grey. The rest of the continent hides behind an iron curtain. The boy wonders if this curtain is chainmail or a solid partition that can be slid open on rails, like the door to a garage. The border between Northern Ireland and the South squiggles around like a varicose vein.

He's only just about still a boy. Cigarettes are helping him to shed that state. At school lunchbreaks, he meets the other boys in the orchard at the bottom of their playing fields. They can see the school from there but are obscured by the branches, so no teacher can catch them unawares. Still, they shade the end of the cigarettes with their palms, pinching the butt between the thumb and forefinger, forming a claw, the lit cigarette turned inwards.

Recently he has taken to smoking before school. He likes the smell of his fingers afterwards, like kippers or cured meat.

I see him sit on his roof, embracing the silence of that late-summer morning. An indistinct sun. Trees shifting. Some horses gliding across a field.

He likes the autonomy he feels when holding a cigarette and looking out over the countryside from a height. Here he is answerable to no one.

The rasp of a lighter. The burn of tobacco on his lungs. How the exhalation hangs in the cold air, almost a solid form. Bats flit above his head. He has never been able to make out any pattern in the bats' movements. The way they crash through the air, without plan or purpose, and yet never collide with each other, navigating by the echo of their cores.

The buildings in the landscape around him take no shape or pattern, as if someone had scattered the houses out of a helicopter.

A car's headlights crest the hill in front of him, throwing shades of yellow on to the day. It's moving slowly. It will bend right and then left – he will lose it momentarily behind a large oak tree and then watch it come to a sudden halt before the next crossroads. He can tell this because the ditch has begun to move, a squadron of paratroopers emerging on to the road with measured stealth.

The car slows. The squad leader leans in against the side window, rifle pointed. Already, they know the names of the owner and licensed drivers of the car. Someone in a watch post has had their sights trained on it for a couple of miles. The registration number has already been filed. The squad leader takes the papers, steps away, radios in the details, a crescent of gun barrels still focused on the driver. The squad leader returns to the window, hands the papers back, bangs his fist on the roof to punctuate the end of the exchange, and the car continues on its slow crawl, weaving its way through the loom of the hills, until it dips out of sight.

He is both the watcher and the watched. He is sure that someone is observing him also, from a long way away. They must find his behaviour strange, sitting on the roof of his house as the day breaks around him. They know his name, they know that his da is a cattle dealer, driving livestock over and back from the South. They know that his da's truck is slatted on the sides with orange boards and that the left tail light hasn't worked in years. They know that the boy himself is in the import/export business. Twice a month the boy moves tea and butter to Murray's shop across the border, and occasionally there are other incidentals: shampoo, firelighters – which they buy at a much cheaper rate than they can get at the wholesaler's in the South.

Every second Sunday, Neil Murray writes down the stock inventory in a ledger, then takes a roll of notes from an old film canister, licks his thumb, peels the notes from the stack and plants them on the mantelpiece. The boy lifts them and counts them. Any mistakes, there's only himself to blame. Half the notes he stuffs into an envelope that slides into his back pocket; half the notes he returns to Neil Murray as a reinvestment, buying cartons of cigarettes and boxes of Mitchelstown cheese to sell to the Flanagans, who have a shop and petrol pump in his town.

'The boy giveth,' Neil Murray always says to his wife after the boy has departed, 'and the boy taketh away.'

He moves in the evenings through the fields and the side roads. His enterprise is too small for any soldier to care. When it's raining, he makes sure to use the clear plastic cover that he's scavenged from a pallet of feed. If he's stopped, he'll usually hand over a few cartons of cigarettes. 'Tell them they fell off the back of a pram.' He switches routes at random. Everybody has learned to resist routine. Routine can get you killed.

The boy has a sister, Una, a few years younger than him. He has a brother, Joe, who serves with the Irish Rangers, a regiment of the British Army. Joe signed up in the mid 1960s — not all that unusual a thing for Catholic boy to do at that time. It has since become a problem for the family. He knows people whisper about Joe's involvement. He gets looks when he's in town.

Joe was stationed in Oman for five years. The boy can still name some of its provinces. Dhofar, where Joe had fought. Muscat. Musandam, which sounded, to his ears, like a blessing. When he says the word in front of the mirror, he joins his hands together and bows. Musandam. A leather camel stands on the shelves over his bed, a memento.

On his passage across the border, pushing his cart of illegal goods, the boy has talked to many of the soldiers. They're often young, only a few years older than the boy himself. He knows that if he comes across one alone, away from his platoon, he must be even more wary, more measured in his speech. Their hands often shake. They seem so exposed, so foreign — they're still trying to place themselves in this environment, as though they signed up in a recruiting office and turned a corner and found themselves here, alone, holding a gun in a landscape that on first glance is familiar, knowable, comfortable, and yet is constantly shape-shifting, erratic, like a violent parent. They're anything but independent. The boy wonders if they could even make their way back to base if their radio packed up.

He slips Joe's name into the conversation as quickly as possible, mentions *the Rangers*. They're always wary at first — his surname runs contrary to their expectations — but then the boy lists off Dhofar and Muscat and Musandam. A gleam of recognition, solidarity. In exchange, they trade their own English place names. Doncaster. Leicester. Tooting. His favourite so far is Weston-super-Mare. It sounds like a name from a comic book. Maybe someday he'll visit.

The boy knows where to get the best fried cod in Felixstowe. If he ever has a yearning to travel to Newcastle to watch Sunderland FC in action, he knows to go to turnstile Number Three in Roker Park and ask for Archie.

They stop him on the boreens or sometimes in the middle of a field. He made the small cart himself. He found an old cupboard, bolted four pram wheels into the sides and sawed a broom handle in half for a handle. He painted his name on one side. He did this carefully, in an ornate font. He did it to show he has nothing to hide, to reassure the soldiers that he wouldn't try to make a run for it or anything. He approached Frank Hickey, who did a bit of signwriting, one day and asked him for some tips, and Frank agreed to the proposition if the boy would help him with a few small heifers that he was bottle-feeding for scour. The boy did so. Frank was impressed with the swiftness of the boy, how he could catch a skipping heifer with his arm around the neck, back it into the corner of the shed and throw his leg over it in a few broad, fluid motions.

'Your da has you well trained,' Frank noted when they were finished.

The boy didn't reply, just nodded. Frank took him into his work shed and showed him how to outline a few letters in pencil and then chose some old brushes for him and a few cans of paint that he no longer had any use for and let the boy practise steadying his hand against a mahlstick when he was filling in the letters. Afterwards the boy took an old sack from the corner of the shed and wiped his hands and asked Frank Hickey if he owed him anything and Frank replied, 'No, we're all square now, you did a good job there with the heifers,' and the boy shook Frank's hand and then turned on his heel and left.

At twelve years old, he has become aware of the interplay of nature and language. There are things that people conceal with words and there are things that have words hidden in them, compressed down, ready to flourish at any moment.

He no longer reads the car magazines beside his bed. Instead he takes used copies of the *Farmer's Journal* from the stack beside the fireplace. He knows by now that he'll never own a flashy car. The pictures in the car magazines are from a different place, a different people. The *Farmer's Journal* tells him about his own life. Inside it are the things his da talks about to other men. Whatever he gleans from its pages will bring him respect. He's old enough to know that even his schoolbooks don't wield the same power. So he reads about lungworm and liver fluke and black scour and redwater. All of the curiosities of the body, its wastes and vulnerabilities. This thirst for knowledge doesn't yet transfer to his own flesh. He is still dormant. He is vaguely aware of this, although he doesn't know what effects the alternative will bring.

The third stomach in a ruminant is called a *psalterium*. It's also the word for the Book of Psalms. The body is an instrument of hymns unsung.

His ma is a teacher in the primary school down the road, a two-room building heated by a stove in each class that sits beside the teacher's desk. His ma is responsible for the younger pupils, three different years of them, one column of desks for each. The total number of pupils in her care is usually between twenty and twenty-five. When she assigns them exercises, it gives her time to put some logs into the fire. The children like her. She's slow to scold. She keeps discipline with a stare and a threat to speak to their parents, an eventuality which never comes about, but is a distinct possibility nonetheless.

Because of her position, the older neighbours come to their house in the evenings to ask her to read a letter from America, Australia, England, and to write a reply. He hears them talking at night, their voices rising through the floorboards. The incoming letters tell of strangeness, of unfamiliarity, a misunderstanding at their job, an apartment that fell through, a neighbour that plays an instrument in the wee hours. He has listened enough that he can tell from the words how long someone has been away – the shift in confidence becomes apparent as they begin to master their new world. The letters turn from necessities – apartments and jobs – to talk of clothes and cars and weddings.

The reply is always a collaborative act. His ma selects some threads from the weave of local events and encourages them to put the news in their own words. They tell of cattle prices, funerals, days out at the arcades in Bundoran, a dance in the parish hall, the arrival of a baby. His ma writes in the way that she writes on the board at school. The letters lean forward impatiently, but they hold their shape nonetheless, are always proportionate, the lower case exactly half the height of the capitals. When he writes, the words seem to jolt against each other and slide off the page, but his ma's sentences stay level and even.

There are times when the visitor breaks the rhythm of call and response. They come to the door with some urgent news. In these cases, his ma becomes merely an amanuensis: she does not suggest, she merely encourages and transcribes. The boy listens just as closely to the hesitations of the speaker as he does to their words. He can imagine the letter being opened by a nurse in London, in front of Buckingham Palace. In New York, on the street outside the Empire State Building, a waitress in an apron scans the lines, being jostled by people in suits. A man slides his finger under the flap of the envelope outside a shack in the bushlands of New South Wales, his face mottled with dust.

Some nights, after the letter-writing has finished and the conversation begun, he joins them. He selects his nights wisely. He can sense the occasions when his ma will let him sit for a while before sending him back upstairs. He edges his way from his bedroom to the top of the stairs.

One night his uncle Seamus, his ma's brother, is in the kitchen. The boy sees Seamus's cap on the hook by the door, the crown of it worn out. The boy knows that this a result of Seamus carrying tiles. He is a hodsman. He carries the tiles on his head, up ladders, and a new cap only lasts him a couple of months.

Something has been stirring over the past few days. The UDR are about. He doesn't know much about them, only that they're all Protestants and they're part time, not real soldiers like Joe. They dress in camouflage jackets, with green berets and a harp on their badge. One of the lads in school said they didn't need a uniform, you could tell them by their stink. The boy saw them on the TV news, bulldozing into a march, batons flying.

He steps quietly into the kitchen, takes a chair near the door. Seamus had come from the town. Something had happened outside the convent. A group had gathered around it because they were afraid of its being raided.

The boy couldn't make out why they'd bother. He'd been inside the building a few times, carrying a message from school. Nothing there but pictures and candles and statues of Our Lady – looking like she'd been jammed in the arse by a poker.

Seamus had driven through the town. The place was filled with the UDR. Lines of cars on both sides of the street. 'Hundreds of the beret-wearing bastards, wee little gulpins the lot of them,' he says. Seamus runs through the names of the ones he recognized. The boy knows them. One of the lads from the cement factory. Another, a labourer for the McGuigans. 'All of them carrying them long black rifles with their polished wooden butts,' he says.

'Imagine,' the boy's mother says.

'You don't need to be imagining, hai,' Seamus says. Seamus's voice is softened by drink and his sentences are loose, flabby around the edges. There's a bottle of Powers on the table. Seamus pours himself a good slug. The boy's ma is at the cooker.

'Ah, himself is here,' says Seamus. 'Tell me now,' says Seamus, 'are you growing a vocation for yourself?'

'I'm not,' the boy says.

'Well, listen to me now, start in the morning. Plant that seed, hai. Them boys have it rightly sewn up. You'll get yourself a big house and a nice wee housekeeper and all the wine from here to Fatima. What do you think, Maureen?'

The boy's ma puts some black pudding and buttered bread in front of Seamus.

'Eat that for soakage,' she says.

Her eyes are soft, but not like when she tucks him into bed. His ma has had a glass or two herself.

Seamus stands and wields his knife like a conductor.

'The history of all hitherto existing society,' he announces, 'is the history of class struggles.'

'Pipe down now like a good man,' she says to Seamus. 'Show's over.'

His ma douses him with holy water every time he leaves the house. There are vats of it on the shelf over the bath that she brings back from her pilgrimage to Knock each summer. The plastic vats are the same ones that they use to hold turpentine in the hardware shop. The boy reckons that turpentine has more potency.

His da is known for his temper. His da used to work in the colliery in Castlecomer. His ma often says that his da is still stuck down that hole. When they fight, his da punches the walls. The sound his fist makes against the wall is like wood rubbing against glass. His da's hands never bleed. It's as if he himself is made of coal.

'I'm living with the shaggin' Pope,' his da says, time and time again.

His da is a pigeon fancier. He doesn't keep racing pigeons, he's unnerved by competition. Instead he keeps exhibition birds: rollers, tipplers, tumblers. Every morning, after breakfast, his da turns over the engine on his truck. He has to nurture it to get it started. He leaves the engine ticking over while he greets his birds. His da's favourite bird is an Orlik. It's small and rusty red, with white tips on its wings. In flight, it looks like an eagle. It flies straight up from the coop, never in a circular motion, so full of intent. It can fly more than half a mile up in the air. The boy loves that, despite such freedom, the pigeons always return home.

When his da speaks to the birds, he does so in a gentle voice. He clasps them lightly in his hands. The boy can't manage this, can't get them to settle in his grasp. But his da has a way with them, wraps his index finger and thumb around their necks. Hard to believe he could be so gentle with those hands of his. But he is. The birds look back at him, docile, unquestioning, poking their necks about.

In the evenings, when the weather is good, the boy watches his da watching his birds doing barrel rolls above the house. He says there is no more noble an animal. He says that the Ancient Greeks worshipped them as messengers from the gods and that the Greeks knew a fair bit about gods.

His da feeds the birds with rice soaked in honey and then dissolved in water. They drink the water that his ma saves after she boils vegetables. It helps keep their blood purified. Disease, his da tells him, would spread through the coop like a lit match in a haystack.

A year or so passes. He's old enough to own his time. He helps his father on some of his cattle runs, and this confers authority upon him. Since he does the work of a man, they don't treat him like a child any more.

His ma's cousin Bridie comes into their kitchen one Sunday afternoon. His da is away. The boy is in his windowless room but can recognize the engine of every car that comes into their yard with any regularity. Bridie lives alone in a house over the hill and drives a blue Morris Minor that she trades in every couple of years at the dealership in Fivemiletown. The colour is always blue. The boy never wonders why Bridie has never married — it's obvious she's not the marrying type. She wears a housecoat with flowers on it and another grey coat over it when she leaves the house. He can't tell what age she is. On Saturdays, she goes to the convent near Belcoo and takes the nuns out for a drive. God only knows where she goes with them. Or what they talk about. Every week she visits the hairdresser in the hospital to get her hair done. She doesn't like the idea of going to any of the salons in town, his ma says. The boy reckons she is afraid of the magazines they read there.

Bridie is excitable without ever getting excited. Everything, every act, every thought, any glimpse of modernity is instantly urgent, dreadful, awful, to be feared. Her reactions to these threats come only in the form of words, though. To a deaf man, Bridie would probably seem as contented as a monk.

From his bedroom, the pitch of her voice draws his attention. Bridie never breaks from monotone. Something has happened. He listens more closely. A shooting at a peace rally in Derry. The army opened fire on a crowd. He comes down to the kitchen and tells his ma he's going out. She hardly hears him, she is so stunned.

Bridie reminds him to bless himself from the font before he makes his way out of the door.

He cycles to two neighbouring houses and within half an hour there are three boys wandering around the sleepy town. Then there are many more, all with the same impulse, looking for something to push against. They walk down Main Street towards the barracks at the far end. 'The longer it is,' says Dunner, 'the mainer it gets.'

Fats is the first to throw a stone. He doesn't see Fats pick it up. Fats is usually the quiet one. The older boys in the front turn around. Fats has broken the display window of a photography shop. The photographer won't do any Catholic events. Serves him right, the boy thinks. If he had some Communion photos out front, there wouldn't have been a problem.

Another window goes. An accountant's. A stirring at the end of the street.

Another window and a few RUC men start shouting and running towards them. They don't even have their caps on. Their ties hang loose. They look like they had to put their shoes on to come outside. They have to run about fifty yards to reach the boys, and after the first ten they are red and panting. They don't get any nearer than another ten. A barrage of stones drives them backwards. They pull the metal gate closed to great cheers from the boys.

By the time the metal gate is pulled back again, there aren't just boys on the street. People are dragging out sacks of coal from their sheds. Firewood. A few of the resourceful ones have filled up dustbins with rocks specifically for an occasion like this. They clang their dustbin lids on the road in anticipation. The RUC have made their own preparations. They are clad in their shells. Helmets, riot shields, batons, gasmasks. The boy is on the front line. They began the riot, so they have the honour of leading it. He and his friends start to pelt lumps of coal and blocks of wood at the RUC men, but don't get any reaction. The RUC stay where they are, in front of the gate, letting it happen. The RUC start firing gas grenades and the air becomes white. His eyes sting. He feels nauseous. He starts to retch. The crowd surges forward around him and then relents. Someone drags him backwards. He turns around and sees another riot squad stationed at the opposite end of the street. They are trying to pincer them. The crowd pours into a side street. A few men push a car in front of the entrance. One of them takes off the cap of the petrol tank. Another one lights a rag and signals for everyone to move back.

Turning around, the boy sees that men behind him are pulling up the pavement flagstones.

His ma eyes him when he returns. She can tell, he knows it. When he was younger and she arrived home late and came in to check on him and he was supposed to be sleeping, she could always tell when he was faking it. He's surprised she hasn't clocked the smoking, as of yet. Or maybe she's turning a blind eye to it. He avoids looking at her, busies himself making a sandwich.

'Where were you?'

'I was out.'

'Out with who?'

'A few of the lads.'

'Do these lads have names?'

'You wouldn't know them. Dunner was there. You'd only know Dunner.'

Dunner's parents don't give a shite about anything. There'd be no trouble if his ma called them.

'There was a riot in the town.'

'Aye, right.'

'Where were you?'

He stops and looks at her. His eyes, he knows, are screaming red. They are still streaming. He doesn't want her to mistake them for tears.

'If you already know the answer, then why are you asking?'

She looks stricken. He has never talked to her like this before. He is a dutiful boy, always respectful. He was a dutiful boy. He was a boy. He doesn't feel like one any more.

His ma is flustered; she searches for the appropriate response.

'Your father will be in to talk to you.'

'I won't hold my breath.'

His da is in Longford. He won't be home till all hours.

They visit Drogheda. He likes going south. He can breathe there. They cross the border and everything seems more relaxed. His da says, 'Now we're in the real thing, none of your poky Sabbath towns here.' They're

149

in town for the shopping and they make a visit to the church to see Archbishop Oliver Plunkett's head. The boy knows all about him from his history lessons. Archbishop Oliver Plunkett was hanged, drawn and quartered by the English for promoting the Catholic faith. The Pope beatified him. This means he has God's ear. Anything you ask of Archbishop Oliver Plunkett will go straight to the top.

Archbishop Oliver Plunkett's head looks like it's made from leather. He looks a bit like one of the orang-utans on the nature programmes. His mouth is half open in a grimace. The boy can see Archbishop Oliver Plunkett's teeth. It's the same expression his da holds when he listens to horse races on the radio. The boy wonders if all the dead look like this. If his grandpop, the republican hero up in the cemetery, looks like this, his leathered face grimacing under all of that topsoil.

His ma kneels before it, says her prayers. His da waits outside, smoking a fag. Una is dressed in a summer dress, one that she wore at Padhraig Keogh's wedding the year before. Her shoes have a clasp on them. He elbows Una as she prays, but she takes no notice. She had her Confirmation a few months ago and since then has turned fierce holy. She gets great praise for it. When Bridie visits, she gives Una a prayer card and some money. None of it ever comes his way. He takes this to mean that he's already a lost cause.

He's asleep when they crash down the front door. He'd recognize the engine of a pigwagon a mile away, but he's sleeping deeply. The soldiers are halfway up their stairs before the boy opens his eyes. His da is shouting. Fluther is barking. Now his ma is screaming. And Una. He's still in bed when they stampede into his room. They rip the bedclothes off him. One of them plants his boot on the pillow beside his head and jams the muzzle of his rifle into the boy's mouth. It happens so quickly that the boy can feel that one of his bottom teeth has been chipped. The boy is flat against the mattress, looking up at the soldier. He can see nothing else. The jowly red face blocks out everything. There is a smell of drink on his breath. The boy wants to move, to pull the gun away, but his body doesn't respond. There is a voice in his head: it comes warm and so clear that he could be listening to the radio. *This will be over in a few minutes. Stay calm. Don't move unless they tell you to.*

'*Will I* blow your fucking brains out? Will I? Blow your *fucking* brains out?'

The soldier is from the north of England – he can recognize the accent, the words coming out flat and round. The boy has bypassed fear. He is aware of every micromovement on the soldier's face. The soldier's eyebrows are blond. The soldier is afraid. It's the same lost look they have when they're alone on the roads but magnified, intensified. The boy thinks of the blue flame that he isn't supposed to look at when his da is welding.

His ma from down the hall. 'Where's my son? Where's Una?'

Una is screeching. An animal wail that he can feel in his teeth.

They launch him down the stairs. His ma is in her nightdress in the middle of the living room, shivering, unsteady as a new-born calf. From behind his right shoulder Una rebounds against the wall, knocking all the pictures off it. When she turns, she is wiping blood out of her eyes. He and his da are wearing matching pyjamas. His da has been replaced by a different man. He is older. Meek. Frail. Scruffy. The boy has to stare at his da to understand that it's actually his da. His ma calls for Joe. Does she think Joe still lives here? Or is she trying to tell them that her son is in *the Rangers*? Does she think Joe is amongst them?

His da is very contained. He's barely reacting, doing what he's told. The boy doesn't know whether to admire or despise this.

There seem to be twenty people inside the living room. They club their rifles into everything in sight. Breakages all around them. The grandfather clock tips over and smashes on to the floor. It happens in slow motion. The boy steps left to avoid its crashing against his legs. A gurning sound of coils unsprung.

Fluther howls and runs in circles and snaps at the soldiers. Two of them wrestle him to the ground and tie a rope around his snout and head and drag him outside. The boy has to be held down while this is happening. They hear a shot. The boy screams, Una screams. His ma tucks her head into her armpit, like one of the pigeons.

They take the boy and his da outside where the pig-wagons are parked. His da finally loses it. 'He's only a

152

boy.' He keeps repeating this. 'He's a little Fenian fuck, is what he is,' the commander says. They put the boy and his da in the same Jeep and tell them to lie face down on the floor. The engine starts. They pummel the two of them with their rifle butts. Pain explodes on the boy's arms, legs, back. They spit on his head. They take his da by the hair and smash his forehead a few times against the radio on the floor of the Jeep. It's about the size of a petrol can, but heavy, and it hardly budges with the impact.

One of them puts a revolver to his da's head and clicks off the safety catch and orders his da to sing 'The Sash'. His da says he only knows one verse. 'Good enough,' says the soldier. The boy's face is still rammed to the floor. He has to close one eye to focus on his da. His da sings. The boy has never heard his da sing before. His da takes big gulping breaths between the lines, like when a small child sings.

The smell of drink is powerful off them. The boy knows it's possible he and his da won't make it to the barracks. He remembers one evening when he was small: they were around the dinner table, him, Joe, his ma, Una, his da, all of them, and Una was in her high chair, mouth wide open, crying her lungs out, so loudly and for so long that none of them could think. And his da picked her up and carried her outside and dunked her in the rainwater barrel. The boy followed them out, ahead of his ma and Joe. The rage on his da's face and the frigid fear that took over Una's whole body. He looks at his da now and sees that same grip that overcame Una, that stuttering shock, only now his da is the one paralysed by fright.

The soldiers make the both of them sing 'God Save the Queen'. The words drive the men into a fever. They stamp their feet and keep time with their rifle butts against the boy's back.

At the barracks they drag the boy and his da by their hair down some stairs and into a basement room. There are ranks of bunk beds on each side, full of other soldiers who punch and kick them as they pass. The boy can see that the bottoms of his da's pyjamas are torn on one side and his arse and thigh are showing. His da's ear is caked with blood. They shove his da into a cell. When he realizes the boy isn't following him, he bursts out. It takes four men to push him back inside. He keeps bellowing the boy's name. The boy looks to him as he is shoved onwards down the corridor. His mouth is open so wide the boy can see the back of his throat.

They don't put the boy in a cell. They take him to a caravan out the back. The night is freezing, but the boy doesn't feel it. There's a man in a red jumper and beige trousers sitting at a camping table. The boy has to stand up straight. He feels so tired that it seems like only the arrangement of his bones is keeping him upright. If he slumps or wavers, a soldier screams in his ear. The man tells the boy his da has been carrying explosives over the border. The boy says that he doesn't believe him. The man tells him the sniffer dogs were all over his da's truck. 'We're doing forensics on it right now. You'll believe me when you see the results.' The man is very calm. He never raises his voice. His hair is well brushed. He asks the boy question after question. Everything about where his da goes. How long he goes for. What routes he takes. Whom he buys cattle for. The boy answers honestly, tells them whatever he knows. His da is hard but straight as a die. His da can't stand the IRA. He often says they couldn't organize a piss-up in a brewery.

The man doesn't ask about the riot. The boy is waiting for him to ask about Neil Murray. But he doesn't ask. They know everything already.

They swab his hands for forensics and photograph him and then take him to a cell. There is only a wooden bench there with a blanket and a pillow with no case. The pillow is covered in brown stains. The boy throws them both on the floor. He'll be right enough without them.

He has no chance of sleep. When he goes to the toilet, a soldier stands behind him as he pisses. It takes an age to get anything out.

In the morning, he's brought to an interrogation room upstairs. Two men tell him they are detectives. A Union Jack covers the wall behind them. He is still in his pyjamas. They ask the same questions as the man the night before. They are as calm as he was, but their calmness is, he can tell, from a lack of enthusiasm. They don't want to be there either.

The forensic tests come back in the afternoon. The dogs were going wild over creosote, not explosives. A soldier brings in a pair of jeans and a green jumper and a pair of runners and tells the boy to put them on: he's been released, his da too. He says it in a way that makes it sound like the two of them have been wasting the time and resources of Her Majesty's Government. The clothes are miles too big for him. The runners are minging – their insides feel like they're coated in butter.

He meets his da in the courtyard. His da is rightly shook. His da puts his arm around the boy's shoulder. His da's hand is vibrating. 'Good man,' his da says to him.

Cecil Cox is waiting outside the gate. He's their nearest neighbour. He used to be a minister, but gave it up to work the land. He's in the RUC, a part-time reservist. The boy's da often says that Cecil Cox is a failed minister, a nearly failed farmer, a policeman in a failed force, but no question he's a good neighbour.

His da is cold with Cecil. He doesn't fancy speaking to someone on the other side.

'It's a terrible thing,' says Cecil. 'I'd no idea they were on the lookout for you.'

'Aye, well, your friends are just doing their job, I suppose.'

'I've no side, you know that as well as I do. I'm just trying to pay some bills. I'm sorry, Con, I had no idea.'

'Aye, you've said that already. What about Maureen and Una?'

'They're fine. They're in Bridie's.'

'We're going there so?'

'Bridie asked me not to. She gave them something to help them sleep. They need their rest.'

'Bridie doesn't want to be seen to be involved.'

'You can stay at ours. Gwen will have the dinner on the table. You'll get some rest.'

'Ach, talk fuckin' sense, man. Bad enough I'm seen getting into your car. Now take me to my wife and child.'

Bridie gives them a cold welcome. The boy's ma holds him close. Presses his head hard into her. She is distant from his da. Una is like a shepherd who has lost her sheep.

The soldiers were in the house all night. The boy's ma and Una had rifles in their faces the whole time. They tore the place up. Ripped up the floorboards. Drilled into the bricked-up fireplace. They even intercepted the postman in the morning and went through their letters. There was a line of troops in the field, combing every blade of grass. The boy wonders if the pigeons are still alive.

12

When I picture him again, the boy is no longer a boy. He lies in his bed, looking out of a window into a narrow garden. His hair is long and splays over his pillow; he has thick woolly sideburns.

The window he looks at is coated with a film of condensation, through which he can see the outlines of trees.

He lives in a small town, not unlike Enniskillen, but far enough away for him to be able to live his own life, be his own man – Newry maybe.

It's winter, thick bare lines break the soft blue of the mottled sky.

There are brown water stains that run from the ceiling to the floor. The ceiling leaks so much that there are nights when he has to move his bed away from the wall. The paper above the window has peeled off, but not all the way. When he first arrived, the wall was dry and flat and newly papered. A few weeks ago a large bubble, like a bladder, appeared after a storm. It took a couple of days to burst and when it did it happened in the middle of the night, while he was sleeping. He was already standing by the side of his bed by the time he woke up. He thought someone had thrown a bucket of water over his head. It brought back other memories. He was relieved when he realized it was just the fucking wallpaper.

He looks about twenty-one. The year, I think, is 1980.

His room is on the second floor of a terraced house on the Camlough Road, two miles out from the centre of Newry.

He's been there for the guts of a year.

He has a good job, as a cutter in a meat factory.

He tried university but it wasn't for him. He studied engineering but country schooling didn't prepare him for the rigours of calculus, physics. The equations melted in his head: he couldn't transfer them from the textbook to the page, and the problems were beyond him. He didn't tell anyone that he'd left, but simply found work on a building site. Eventually the university accommodation kicked him out and phoned his ma into the bargain.

His landlady is called Mrs Donnelly. She has a soft Dublin accent, and he doesn't know how she ended up where she did.

He hasn't told her about the leak. He tells himself he doesn't want to bother her, but really he doesn't want to give her the excuse to come into his room. And, besides, then there'd be the bother of builders and plastering. What harm is a leak, really? He avoids Mrs Donnelly as much as he can. She's a decent-enough skin, in dire need of conversation. Her flat is in the basement. Whenever he goes to give her his rent, she insists on bringing him a cup of tea, then sits by her three-bar electric fire with nothing to say to him. They end up watching the BBC together. She likes *Steptoe and Son*. The wizened old *Steptoe* da is always bathing himself in the kitchen sink. She

159

laughs when this happens. Some people can't be tamed, she says. Her accent is all flat vowels. She says 'Peeeple'. She says 'Taaamed'. She's not much older than his ma. He doesn't like to think of his ma living in the same way, stuck in front of the TV with nothing to say for herself.

Every morning he rides his bike five miles to work. He likes the cycle, even in winter, even in the rain. He is grateful for the sense of space that the surrounding fields offer him. There are only two things he really misses from the farm in Fermanagh, fields and open fires.

The meat factory is a hulk of a building, built in the late 1950s, concrete blocks and concrete slabs. He got the job by pull. His da delivers cattle to the meat factory in Enniskillen and so knows someone who knows Mr McCarthy, the floor manager here. He is the youngest cutter by far. The others resented him at first – word got around that he'd got the job by connections with the IRA. Little did they know. He got the job because someone felt sorry for his father. A few years beforehand his da had given an IRA man a cheque that bounced – his father was never one for being tight on the bookkeeping – and the IRA took half his herd in reparation. That killed it for him, took all the pleasure out of farming for him. His da never said it, but it was Joe's army service that was the real reason. His ma pleaded with Joe to come home, give it all up. He would have too, but they couldn't raise enough for the discharge. The house became like a morgue for a couple of years. His da hardly left his bed. The curtains in the upstairs room were always drawn; visitors stopped coming. His da got back in the lorry eventually, limping his way from mart to mart, jowly, drink-sodden.

The rest of the cutters are bald and have bludgeoned their thumbs down to a nub. It hasn't impaired their ability to slice a carcass, but each of them has to ask someone else to tie their shoelaces before they leave the changing room in the evenings. There are showers that they use after their shift. The hot water lasts for about ten minutes in total. It is always tepid by the time he gets there. He brings his own soap but it makes no difference: the smell of blood is impossible to wash off.

He likes working. He's never shied away from hard work, a lesson his da taught him. He likes the routine and the hollow feeling in his legs and arms when he lies down on his bed in the evening. He won't do it forever, though. Already his hands are draped with a latticework of scars, and his knuckles are so swollen that he can't close his fingers together without making a fist. He won't be one of those men. He won't be broken like his da. The secret to life is to have a job at a desk. His plan, as far as it goes, is to meet a girl who understands how the world works and has his best interests at heart.

He gets a ten-minute break every hour and a half while the apprentices push rubber blades along the floor, channelling the stagnant blood into four-inch holes. Through these it runs into barrels in the basement to be mixed with preservative and sent to the cannery, where it will be funnelled back into the tins before sealing.

Nothing is wasted here other than effort. The heads and feet of the cattle are transformed into glue, horns are whittled into combs and buttons. Bone char is used to whiten sugar. Knuckles and sinews are broken down into gelatine, shoe polish, violin strings.

At lunchtime on Saturday he queues for his wage envelope. They all make sure to shower before they join the queue. It makes no sense to have an envelope of money sitting around the changing room. As Mr McCarthy hands over the pay packet, he asks him if he's all right. He nods back, *Aye, fine.*

He's paid sixty pounds per week. He pays twenty to Mrs Donnelly, sends twenty home, saves another ten and has ten left for himself.

When he goes to the post office on Saturday afternoons he likes to check the balance in his savings account, likes to watch how the number climbs slowly and steadily. He has few possessions but the number that appears in front of him is his and his alone. Money in the bank is freedom, independence. Have enough of it and you can live a life of your choosing.

Each hour, an average of 450 cattle are slaughtered in the killing beds. He has two minutes to bleed fifteen bullocks. They dangle around him all day, suspended by shackles that grip their hind legs, their necks twisting at the height of his shoulder. His skill with a blade is apparent even to the casual visitors that occasionally stand in the viewing galleries above him.

The beasts pedal their forelegs wearily, as if trying to gain purchase on the floor just beyond their reach. Their eyes rotate around the rim of their sockets, disorientated by the blow of a bolt gun that has been dispatched to their heads in the crush pen. They buckle on to their bellies with the shock of the blow, and the side gates are raised and the shackles are locked around their ankles. Under the eaves of the roof, the hoisters set the winches in motion, running back and forth along their gangway, stooped over so low and for so long that they have all lost the ability to raise their arms above their shoulders. Sometimes a bullock isn't struck properly and comes to before the chainers have had time to clamp the shackles, and then in its panic it runs amuck around the cavernous space, its bellows resounding against all the metal surfaces. When this happens, the beast claims temporary ownership of the slaughter line. The men run towards the side walls and once in safety they watch with quiet respect as the animal careens into gates and columns, butts its head into the giant cast-iron door, railing against fate and circumstance, the vigour of its protests equal to the injustices enacted upon it. They squat down against the blockwork, grateful for the unexpected pause, and watch Mr McCarthy emerge from his office overhead; they know that someone will lose his job today and they wait until the beast runs itself into exhaustion, snorting its heavy breaths, eyeing everything as its enemy, and then the chainers throw a loop over its neck, twisting it to the floor, and the doomed worker wields a sledgehammer, finishing what he started.

When things go as they should, the physiology of the cattle follows the uniform procedures of the plant. The creatures swing in their lines and he steps forward and slices a thin crease across their throats, which only becomes visible as the bleeding gains momentum, ribboning downwards after he has paced another ten feet along the line.

His room contains a bed, a wardrobe, a desk, all white, all sturdy. His mattress sags in the middle and is filled with horsehair; it leaks out in tufts. To touch, it feels like wire wool, but it's jet black, and when he squeezes it in his fist it returns to its shape. In the corner is a two-ring hob. Underneath it is a shelf with pots and pans and a bowl, a plate, a spoon, a knife and fork, and some utensils. Next to it is a small fridge. When he needs water he has to walk to the communal bathroom next door. He hates doing this, so once a week he fills up a few large plastic 7-Up bottles that he keeps in the fridge. He never cooks. He eats a dinner in the canteen in work. On Sundays he eats battered cod from the chip shop on the corner. One big meal a day is enough for him.

On the cycle back from the meat factory he dreads the evenings that stretch out long and dark and empty ahead of him. Too wet to go for a walk or to the dogs. He goes to the cinema but is usually drenched on the way there and has to sit in his own damp. Condensation rises above all of the seats, mixing with the cigarette smoke so that the picture, like everything else in this town, takes place behind a veil of obscurity. On Saturday nights he goes drinking with the other men from the meat factory. On

Sunday he lies sick until long into the afternoon. Once he woke up with such a screaming headache that he shuffled into the bathroom to see if there were any pills in the cabinet. All he could find were sleeping pills. He took two and woke up late for work on Monday. A sickly, groggy feeling ran through his veins all day.

There are two other men on his floor of the house. They pass each other sometimes on the stairwell. Mrs Donnelly doesn't say much about them. All he knows is that one of them is from Glasgow and the other is from Sligo. They both work in the feed mill. He sees their hairs in the bathtub. One set is frizzy and dark, the other blond. They go through toilet paper like there's no tomorrow, so he keeps his own stock in his room. He never washes there, not even his teeth. He spits the toothpaste out of the window and rinses his mouth with the water from the 7-Up bottle. A couple live upstairs. As far as he can tell they have the whole floor to themselves. They work odd hours, so he never sees them, but he can hear them riding some nights and some Sunday mornings.

He's still a virgin, a secret he holds close. Women give him glances but there's something too shuttered in him to allow him to approach them. He doesn't know why — other lads manage it. Before he came here he'd never even heard the sound of sex. When he first woke to the sound of their headboard knocking against the wall, he thought that someone was pounding on the door outside. Then the moaning began and he realized what it was. It disturbed him, a kind of savagery that he didn't expect. He had never thought of sex as being so raw. He thought it was something muffled, contained, secret, as with all forbidden things. The man grunts irregularly, but the woman wails like a banshee. He had heard before, probably in a sermon, that sex was a power. He took this to mean that the man exerted his influence, but now he thinks differently. When he lies in his bed, looking at the stained colours of his window pane, listening to the woman, he hears the sound of a power being unleashed. He was certain at first that Mrs Donnelly couldn't hear it from the basement, but now he thinks that maybe she might. She too, after all, had left home for some reason, left things, thoughts, beliefs behind her. He wonders, when the time comes, if the time comes, if he'll be ready, capable. He has to admit that he's shy of the whole thing. Or at least he would admit this, if he had someone to admit it to.

An opportunity presents itself without warning. Ten of the factory workers go to Belfast for a match. Cliftonville are playing Shamrock Rovers in a friendly. They stay in a house in Ardoyne – someone's cousin, floor space only. No one brings a sleeping bag or even a change of clothes: they don't want to be carrying bags with them, don't want to look like outsiders.

They thought Newry was heavy, but Belfast is the epicentre. The place is basically a prison. They're used to the sight of Saracen troop carriers: they'd often see one on patrol. But here they're parked up every few blocks, squat and plated like a rhino, eyes watching him from behind the armour. There are command towers dotted all over the place, dripping with barbed wire. Most streets have at least one collapsed house. The black shells of burnt-out cars are cast about like litter. The place smells of sulphur, but it tastes like it too, a bitterness in the air. There's a sharpness, a clarity to everything. Nothing feels offhand, trite, accidental. Even the dogs cautiously pace the pavements.

The kids in Ardoyne eye them suspiciously. Hardly out of short pants, they've no problem interrogating the new faces. *Where yous from? How comes yous are around here? Any fags?*

Cliftonville get hammered, but it makes no odds, they're already five beers deep by the time the final whistle goes. Outside the ground they follow the river of supporters until they end up in a social club around the corner from their digs. The place is jammed to the rafters, a haven. Bare floorboards, high stools, spirits in their racks, rich amber hues. The curl of cigarette smoke. Deadheaded pints. Hoddies, brickies, sparkies, delivery men, mechanics, grocers, hairdressers, cleaners, canteen ladies, sequins and stilettos, purses on laps, check shirts, football jerseys, unpolished boots. There's a singsong in the corner, a few lads playing whistles and banjos and melodeons, wearing Aran jumpers, sweating like nuns in a whorehouse. A thirst on them all, so strong it's a hunger. He isn't drunk yet. He's a few in, his round bought early. He winds his way out the back to the jacks, side-steps a skinhead carrying three full pints. He pushes open the door and finds her by the sink, applying mascara. She wears a green velvet dress. Her hair is made into ringlets which are fastened to her crown and drop down to her shoulders. She stands to attention, her legs neatly together, her stilettos shaping her calves into clean contours. She leans forward towards the mirror, the mascara brush in her right hand, her pinkie raised.

She turns to him, turns back to the mirror, takes another look, runs a finger around her eye socket, turns back to him again.

'Well?' she says.

Does he know her? He takes in her face. Flat, wide cheekbones, full lips, deep brown eyes. Her features are almost too large for her face but composed, still, unyielding.

She speaks again. 'Is? It? Smudged?' She has to separate the words, she's clearly talking to a simpleton.

'Oh,' he says. 'No, no, all good. You look grand.'

'Grand? Don't fall over yourself with all the compliments.'

She turns back to the mirror.

'This light is shit. No wonder men don't wear make-up.'

He's in the right toilet after all. He was about to ask.

'Maybe if they did, they'd get better lighting.'

She gives him a side glance while she takes out her lipstick. 'Maybe you should try it – it'd bring out them nice cheekbones of yours.'

Her accent is upper class, rounded vowels that fit her features. He can't go while she's there. He leans on the next sink, watches her apply her make-up. Pressing her lips against one another, checking her teeth.

'What do you do, then?'

'I slit throats.'

She puts her lipstick away. Reassesses him, eyebrow raised.

'No shortage of work around here so. I've not seen you before, have I?'

He falters, can't keep up his false confidence. 'I came for the match. There's a few of us staying near the gardens.'

'You're not a tout, are you?'

'It'd be a brave man to do that here. You wouldn't make it five steps from the bar.'

'Right enough. They'd be serving you in their ham toasties by tomorrow lunch.'

'I work in the meat factory in Newry.'

'Do you now,' she says, smiling at his formality. 'A silent assassin, then. I bet the poor craters never see it coming. I'll have to keep my eye on you so,' she whispers.

She checks herself in the mirror again. He is frozen, unsure what to do next.

'What's your name?' she says.

'Brendan.'

'All right, Brendan, let's go,' she says.

'Go where?' he wonders.

He pushes open the door, steps back to let her go first.

'No, you,' she says.

He walks towards the bar.

'Wait,' she snaps. 'Take my hand.'

He takes her hand. She leans near, whispers in his ear, 'Take me out of here.'

They walk together down the corridor and into the bar. He walks quickly, his nerves pushing his pace – he's not sure what to do once they're outside.

A guy steps in his way. Check shirt. Collar done up all the way to a thick neck. Leather jacket. Hair around his ears. 'So, that's it,' he thinks, 'she needed a blockade.'

'Where the hell do you think you're off to, sunshine?'

'He's taking me home,' she says.

The lads from the factory are at a table near the door. Brendan raises his chin and they stand up immediately.

'Like fuck he is,' leather jacket says.

Brendan eyeballs him, buying time. Leather jacket dives towards him but the lads arrive, drag the lanky fucker towards the jacks. There's a parade of bustle, half the bar wants in on the action.

Outside, the street is rainslicked. The blaring conversations inside are reduced to a hum. A black umbrella bobs beneath streetlights, passing cars fan water on to the pavements. They cross ten streets before they find a cab rank. Their jackets are still in the pub. Her ringlets sag from the rain. She leans into the driver's window and asks for the Royal Vic Hospital. The man nods and she gets in the back, closes the door behind her. Her body oozes like a long drip waiting to fall. She winds down her window.

'You're nice,' she says, flashing a smile, 'for an assassin.'

'What's your name?' he says.

'Go straight home now. Don't be out on the streets on your own.'

He takes the next Monday off and stays in the city, tells the lads to make up some excuse. They give him a fierce slagging but he isn't bothered – he needs to see her again. He checks into a B&B near Queen's University. The digs smell like horseshit and he doesn't sleep a wink, too much static in the air, noises in the night.

The owner is full of questions, most of which he dodges politely, well practised as he is with Mrs Donnelly. He tells her he's a Fermanagh man. She lists off a few people in Enniskillen, and she backs off once he establishes his provenance. She's curious that he doesn't have a bag with him. He tells her it got stolen from the luggage rack on the train from Newry.

'You can't be leaving things unattended. You're not out in the country now.'

'Aye,' he says, used to playing the dummy.

He waits outside the Royal Vic. He sits on a bench with a book. The afternoon turns into evening. He stole a set of crutches from one of the corridors, so people don't pay attention to him. He watches the procession of the sick. Hangdog faces, heavy intermittent movements. The doctors move alone, upright, busy, spectacled. The nurses travel in packs. Blue uniforms, flat shoes. He has no chance of meeting her alone. He has no strategy, can't think of anything to say. In the end, it doesn't matter. She is there, out of nowhere. He looks up and she's asking him what he's reading. He hands it over, like he's been caught cheating in class. A Dick Francis thriller he picked up from a rack in a corner shop. Nefarious deeds at a racetrack.

'Horses,' she says. 'Expanding your repertoire, then? I hear they make good burgers.'

She's wearing a tunic with red shoulder tabs. A small watch dangles just below her shoulder, underneath a silver nameplate, SARAH C. HADLEY. A Protestant name. His respect for her jumps a few notches. Not too many Protestant girls would brave a social club in Ardoyne. He wonders what her middle initial stands for. Catherine, he guesses. She has a dappled birthmark on her neck, an aubergine splat.

She hands back the book. The look on her face says she doesn't want to be infected by such drivel. Is she beautiful? Here, now? In the real, in the fading light? He can't decide. He doesn't know his own mind.

'Where did you get the crutches?'

He'd forgotten about them. He reaches for an answer: maybe he should tell her he hurt his leg. But she's a nurse, she'd know. Instead he just shrugs.

'Put them back,' she says.

'I was just borrowing them. You know.'

'I get it. Now put them back.'

He carries them up the steps, leaves them in the corridor, makes sure no one sees him.

She's still there when he steps outside again. When he nears, she jerks her head like she's telling a dog it's time for walkies. He follows her to a food market. The pavement is crowded, so he has to walk a couple of steps behind her. The market is half inside, half outside. Once they're under the canopy, he can take in the trapped smells. Fish and spices. The stallholders are packing up for the evening, hefting boxes into white vans. Lads his age wipe down metal counters. Small mounds of wet newspaper are dotted around the walkways. Stray dogs lick the concrete.

She's formless in her uniform. Hair in a loose bun. Slightly plodding in her soft shoes. She hands over some cash to a man leaning against a van. Then beckons Brendan over with two fingers. He picks up a box sitting inside the van: it's filled with loose vegetables and meat wrapped in greaseproof paper. He follows her across the road. The box is heavy enough for him to wonder how she ever manages to do this on her own. She opens a large blue door to an institutional building, presumably another part of the hospital. A man is sitting behind a glass cubicle reading a newspaper. 'Delivery boy,' she says. The man doesn't even look up. They climb three flights of stairs. Firm, sturdy stairs, like the ones in cop shows on the TV. On the third floor they walk through a corridor. Most of the doors are open. Each room has a bed in it. Women not much older than himself drift about, wearing curlers and dressing gowns. They talk to each other in their bedrooms, smoke, eye him up as he passes. It's only when they reach the communal kitchen and she begins putting the food into a press with her name on it that he realizes that she lives here.

He says, 'The wife of Abraham.'

She stops what she's doing. He feels like an item on a list that needs to be ticked off.

'Who is?' she says.

'Sarah, the wife of Abraham. In the Bible.'

She takes the meat and puts it in a large fridge which is sectioned off into square steel containers. 'Haven't read it,' she says. 'I hear it's a page turner.'

She makes them tea, pours milk into his mug without asking. No suggestion of sugar. She leans back, puts her feet on an adjacent chair, cradles her mug in her hands, embracing its warmth. She asks him a barrage of questions. She doesn't want expansive answers, just his particulars. It's as though he's filling out a police report. Eventually she stands and walks down the corridor. It takes quite a while for him to realize he's meant to follow. She's either too tired to gesture or he's not worth the effort. Either way it's not a good sign.

He can't find her door. There are no names on them.

He stops at an open door. Two women in cardigans are sitting on a bed, smoking. One holds a metal ashtray.

'I'm looking for Sarah.'

'And you are?' says the one with the ashtray.

'I helped her with her deliveries.'

'I bet you did.'

The other one snorts, smoke coming out of her nostrils.

'Sarah! Your boy wants his payment!'

They wait. No answer. They look at him. He is conscious, for the first time, of what he's wearing. Trousers and a jumper and an old raincoat.

'Number Twenty-seven,' says the one with the ashtray. He has a sense that if he were more dressed up she wouldn't have told him.

Sarah Hadley is lying on the bed, shoes still on. She's looking out of the window. She has loosened her hair. It takes on a lustre under the lamplight, shades of honey and mellow browns. She doesn't greet him. He sits on the bed, not too close.

'I just wanted to make sure you're all right.'

'Well, now you know.'

She needs something more, a compliment. He knows the things he should say, knows the lines his workmates use. But they don't come out right from his lips. They sound thin, rehearsed. He says, 'I was waiting there from lunchtime.' It raises a quiet smile.

'How much longer would you have waited?'

He thinks about this. 'Well, I was only on page fifty.'

Her lips move again. She isn't looking at him, she's staring at the ceiling. 'A slow assassin,' she says.

He lies beside her. She doesn't welcome him, doesn't ward him away.

The room, now that he sees it, is filled with good furniture. The bed has brass fittings. The dresser and wardrobe are dark wood. In the corner, a stack of cardboard boxes rises all the way up to the ceiling. There are clothes all over the floor. There's a faint smell of perfume and staleness. A white lace bra hangs from her sink tap. He's never seen a bra before, out in the wild. His mother and Una were always private with their under things. A strange shape to it, cups and two loops.

They lie there for a while, then she kicks off her shoes and leans into him, rests her head on his shoulder. He is aware of his heartbeat. Nurses, so the lore goes, have no hang-ups about sex. They spend their days attending to bodily needs, nothing is beyond them. He can't tell her he's inexperienced, not with all her experience.

She takes his right hand and looks it over. It's thickened over the past year, callused. He's not ashamed to have a working man's hands. She smells it, takes in the scent.

Then her hand is in his pants, matter-of-fact, a routine check to see if everything is in order. They haven't even kissed yet. She holds him, cups him, waits for him. He stiffens. She stands suddenly, walks to the sink, splashes water over her face, then takes off her clothes. No ceremony.

And there she is. Naked. One hand on the sink, the other pulling off her tights. There she is. Real and alive in the lamplight.

Breasts free, unencumbered; light glances off her at all angles. She sweeps a hand down in front of her body like she's selling something at a stall in the market. Here are my wares.

'It's happening,' is all he can think. He is on the verge of the legendary moment, the subject of a thousand daily innuendos, at school and work and in the pub. She is sitting beside him, saying something. He can't take in her words. She smiles again, shakes her head, pulls out a drawer and hands him a condom. A French letter, a johnny, a rubber.

While it is happening, he watches himself from above, watches his motions. He is thinking about it happening and it is also happening. It's like he's seeing himself on TV. He clutches at her skin to make sure this is him and not someone else.

When it ends, she is softened. He can't tell if it's from satisfaction or sympathy. She lies sideways, facing him, wipes the sweat from his brow. Did they make noise? Did the others hear? He lies back on the pillow and she rests her head on his shoulder. His heart is thumping. She reaches down and slides the condom off him. She ties it and throws it into the sink. It lands with a *thwack*. She wipes her hand on his chest, running it through his chest hair.

'Are all Fermanagh men this hairy?'

'Just the Catholic ones.'

She grins. 'You think our side shave themselves all over?'

'They're all trying to be gentlemen, aren't they?'

She snorts a laugh. 'Aye. Right enough. Gentlemen.'

He's back the next weekend. He takes her to the Strand Cinema. He buys them tickets for a French film with subtitles. He doesn't understand the story. People moving in and out of rooms, shaky camerawork. People talking and fighting and fucking. Long, lingering shots of children on a train in springtime. He spends most of the film trying to gauge if she is enjoying it. He tries not to move his head while he does this, tries not to make her aware of it. The couples around them are sophisticated.

He's sure she's been to a film with subtitles before, but maybe not with a man.

'Did you like it?' he says when they settle down over a drink.

'I don't know. Yes, maybe.'

She's reluctant to talk. So much he wants to ask her. He thought that maybe she'd explain the film to him, open up his world. How women see. The secret thoughts of a woman. These are subjects he knows nothing about. He doesn't know how to ask her. He expected her to talk and he would listen. He has heard that this is what women like. He is there to learn, to observe, to understand.

They sip their drinks.

'You're quiet tonight,' he says.

'Am I?'

'Yes.'

'Maybe I'm always quiet.'

'That's not true.'

'No?'

'No.'

'What makes you so sure? You don't know me.'

'A Protestant girl drinking in that club. That takes guts.'

'Guts or stupidity.'

'A fine line.'

'You're not wrong there.'

'Have you talked to him since?'

'No.'

He waits for her to elaborate but she doesn't. Instead, she finishes her gin and tonic. Then she dips two fingers inside the empty glass, fishes out the slice of lemon and eats it, dropping the rind back inside the glass.

'You like eating lemons like that?'

'I like a slice. I like the taste on my tongue.'

The other women step into her room at any time, don't bother to knock. They sit on the bed and smoke and talk. They don't start conversations, they continue them. They show no interest in him; he's as incidental as a lampshade. On her bedstand are thick books by foreign writers. French, German, Russian. She plays classical music on her record player. Their sex becomes slower. She teaches him – by putting her hands on his – that to move slowly is best. She throws a scarf over her lampshade to signal when she's ready to begin. The room blurs into a pink glow. He is learning a language he didn't know existed.

They do ordinary things. She waits in the barber's while he gets his haircut, doesn't care about the men seated around her. He walks to the post office with her. They play cribbage.

He watches her dress. He likes watching her pull up her knickers in the morning. Her sheets smell, she rarely changes them. He likes watching her eat, especially when she's not paying attention, moving a fork around a plate. He thinks this is what she must look like when she's alone. In the bathroom, he learns that there are creams for the night and creams for the day. She puts egg white on to her head when she's washing her hair, rubs it all in. She kisses the scars on his hands. She shows him her own work wounds, a burn mark on her forearm, a scar on her left elbow.

Her parents are divorced. Her father auctions old furniture. Sarah and her father have dinner in a restaurant once a month, like a business meeting, like an affair. How do they come up with subjects to talk about? Protestants really are a different race. She invites him along. He doesn't particularly want to meet her father, but the whole concept proves too tantalizing to resist.

On the way to the restaurant, he buys a new shirt in Marks and Spencer. When he puts it on in the toilets, the shirt has boxy creases. It's obvious it's straight out of the package. They walk down Botanic Avenue. The Christmas lights are up, bringing a gentle cheer. The city needs it, a reminder of what peace feels like. He realizes they're only a couple of minutes away from the B&B he stayed at. He suggests that he could pop in, ask the owner if he could borrow her iron. She kisses him and tells him to stop worrying, it's only a fucking shirt.

When they arrive, her father is waiting at the bar. He reminds Brendan of a history teacher, corduroys and wild hair and thin glasses that drop from a chain around his neck and bounce around on his chest when he moves.

Her father talks furniture to him. At first he thinks the man is just trying to relate to a Catholic, talk to a working man about work. But the more he talks, the more Brendan realizes that the man is speaking out of passion. He tells Brendan about Charles Rennie Mackintosh. He was an architect from Glasgow who made long-back chairs for a tearoom. They give a feeling of enclosure, her father says; the motif of a flying swallow is carved out on their headrests. He talks about them in so much detail that Brendan can picture them in his mind. He would like to visit that tearoom, if it's still there.

Sarah's father shakes his hand enthusiastically outside the restaurant. A friendly innocence to him. His life is so different from the ones in Ardoyne – you need money to be able to be complacent.

After this meeting, he can't bear to talk to his parents on the phone. Weather. People who are sick. People who have died. Una's marks in school. The phone call is like a news bulletin. Joe is stationed in Cyprus. His mother describes the postcards he sends home. Boats in a harbour. *Happy Valley, Episkopi.* Happy Valley right enough, lucky bastard. Why can't his father talk to him like Sarah's father? Brendan asks him about the pigeons, one evening, just to raise some talk from him. His father grunts and hands the phone back to his mother. They keep worrying about the price of a phone call, don't want to keep him on the line for too long. He is grateful for small mercies.

1981 arrives stillborn. By the end of January, the country is paralysed with dread. The republican prisoners in the Maze announce their plans to enact a hunger strike until they are granted political status. A reckoning is approaching, everyone knows it. Unless Thatcher falters, the prisoners will begin refusing food on March the 1st. He goes down to Mrs Donnelly's flat to watch the news on the TV. Bobby Sands, the IRA's commanding officer in the Maze, will be the first to refuse food; others will join every two weeks until everyone dies or their demands are met. Death by voluntary starvation. The raw truth of it leaves no room for ambiguity. A horrific prospect, to resolve to waste away for your beliefs.

Even the newsreaders seem exhausted by the tension. In interviews, in parliament, Thatcher carries an air of utter indifference. A republican's life is not a real life to her. They're not flesh and blood, they're spaces on a roulette wheel. Red or black, live or die. *We do not negotiate with terrorists* – that pompous, strained voice of hers, constant breathy exasperation, as if the prisoners are children who refuse to behave.

Suicide, in her lexicon. She has no capacity to understand courage, despair, the purity of a choice that arrives when there are no other choices. The newsmen keep referring to a battle of wills, a test of resolve for both parties, sentences that cause him physical revulsion. It takes no courage to sit in a house of state and sip tea while she makes pronouncements. Did she think about that over lunch? Did she ever once lose her appetite, look down on her dinner plate and feel gratitude for her abundance?

The tensions in the Maze seep into every crevice of the province. There are nightly riots. Shop assistants and post-office workers have a gloom about them, a heavy mien. People have stopped making eye contact. No one talks about the weather any more. He joins a Saturday-afternoon march on a weekend when he's visiting Sarah. Thousands of people walk around the Divis Flats in the sheeting rain. He walks beside two women, about the same age as him, wearing flimsy cotton dresses. He gives one of them his coat. They giggle in gratitude. He thinks them stupid to have come out in the pouring rain without a decent coat, then looks down at their worn sandals and realizes they probably can't afford one. He keeps an eye on them, not because he wants his coat back, but because of their lightness, fleetness, they leap over potholes and puddles. They aren't riven with anger like most of the people around them. It takes him a while to understand that they believe change is coming. Perhaps they're right. Years of strife coming down to this, such a potent focal point, a man's withering body.

The RUC speed through the area in their armoured Land Rovers. They drive so close to the fringes of the crowd that people have to leap out of the way. The crowd churns and lurches, a single organism, and this only increases their sense of solidarity.

They hear a wailing from one of the flats, so strong and focused it carries above the sound of roaring engines, of the collective chanting. A woman emerges from a doorway wearing a dressing gown and slippers. He is close enough to make out her features. She is crow-like, thin with dark hair down to her waist that's riven through with streaks of silver. She screams about a son of hers who died in custody, another who was shot dead by paratroopers. Her words are so elongated that they contain a kind of musicality, a lament. She is a keener from centuries past. She begins to sway as if ready to faint. The crowd comes to a stop, listening to every word. A man approaches her, tries to lead her away, embarrassed probably at the raw emotion, but she resists, stands where she is, continues her wailing. He's close enough now to see her teeth: they're yellow broken stumps, except for one on the bottom row.

The march flows into Andersonstown, corporation houses with flaking paint. Narrow streets, dogs, kids banging bin lids on the pavements, a tribal rhythm. He sees a lump of raw meat at a kerbstone, a purple heart, a cow's heart, someone's dinner, no steaks for supper here. The body an instrument of hymns unsung.

Back in Newry, he doesn't sleep for more than a couple of hours at a time. Night after night he sits in his bed and stares at his hands and pictures Bobby Sands, pictures Bobby's wild hair around his shoulders, Bobby sitting in a cell with no windows, staring at his own hands. He's heard visitors describing a strange kind of peace emanating from the prisoners. The peace of certainty, of living without contradictions. The peace of resolution. There are some nights – though he would never admit it to another soul – that he's envious of those men.

He dreams, regularly, of Oliver Plunkett. He sees that leathery face, sees that grimace. Hanged, drawn and quartered. He doesn't know exactly what that means. He looks it up. It means they hanged him until he was nearly dead, took him down, put him on a table, ripped out his intestines and then chopped him up into four pieces. He again remembers the grimace on Oliver Plunkett's face.

He starts to read, serious reading. He goes to the library on Tuesday evenings, picks out books and works through them in bed, or early in the morning at the kitchen table. He wants to understand, wants to step inside the minds of the hunger strikers, wants to peer inside the machinations of inequality, how power manifests itself. He reads Marx, he reads Engels, he reads Trotsky.

He buys a blue notebook in the newsagents. If he doesn't understand a word, he writes it down and looks it up later in the dictionary. If he finds a phrase he likes, something that rings true, he writes it down, commits it to memory.

Marx: *The need of a constantly expanding market chases the bourgeoisie over the entire surface of the globe. It must nestle everywhere, establish connections everywhere.*

There's an ad in the paper for a forklift driver in the Warrenpoint docks. Regular hours, much better money than he's on, and he gets to sit down most of the day. May as well take a punt on it – what's there to lose?

He avoids inviting Sarah to Newry. He knows this is a source of conversation amongst the other nurses. Eventually she accuses him of having someone else there. He laughs at the thought, says he couldn't afford it. She doesn't laugh back.

She comes on the train the next weekend. He buys her a nice dinner to prepare the ground. It's late by the time they get back. Mrs Donnelly's light is on. He knows there'll be questions in the morning. Mrs Donnelly will be sure to hear two sets of footsteps on the stairs. He has to resist telling Sarah to tread carefully. He even thinks about asking her to remove her shoes. At last they're on the landing. She looks nervous. She knows – he now realizes – so little about him. When he opens the door, he sees his life from the perspective of a stranger. He sees what a copper would see. White walls. A bed. His fridge. His desk and chair. A wardrobe. It's a monk's cell. There are no personal touches, no posters on the walls. It is a space waiting to be filled, or abandoned.

He knows he's nervous. His chest is held in a web. He sits her on his only chair and pours a whiskey for each of them, a bottle he bought for the occasion.

'What do you do here?' she says.

'I read.'

She rolls her eyes. 'Those horse books?'

She is asking for something to believe in, something that reveals his true self, he knows this. She's been patient long enough.

'History mostly. I get them from the library.'

She joins her hands, rests them on the table.

He takes a book from under his bed. It's a book of the Shackleton expedition to the South Pole. Their ship was crushed in the ice. They camped on the ice floes in the Antarctic for a year and a half. He sits on the end of his bed and reads to her, a letter from one of the men to his wife back home, a letter that could never be sent.

When he's finished, she sits beside him and kisses him.

'You're a strange one,' she says.

'Am I?'

'You are.'

She looks around the room again.

'You've never had a woman in here, have you?'

'No.'

'You could have bought some flowers, to brighten the place up.'

'I wanted you to see how I lived.'

'Oh, I see all right.'

She chuckles to herself, a kind of internal giggle.

'What's so funny?'

'That film. I thought that's what you brought women to.'

'No. I'd never brought a woman anywhere.'

'That was quite a choice.'

'I thought you liked it.'

'I hadn't a clue what the fuck was happening.'

'Oh, right. Neither did I.'

'Well, I know that, stupid. You spent the whole time looking at me.'

He smiles. No point in denying it.

'Not much of an assassin are you?'

'No. I suppose not.'

13

Sarah's pregnant. She tells him while they're watching *Coronation Street*, alone in the common room of the nurses' quarters. The ad break comes on, he stands up to make a brew. When he comes back in with a tray, she has the sound turned down on the TV. He knows instantly, before she's even said the words. It's not even her behaviour that gives it away, it's something in himself, a sense of things building, a sense of culmination, like watching a wave arrive to shore.

He places a hand on her belly. He places another hand on her cheek. She smiles, sheds a tear. His life makes sense. A father is a permanent fixture, so he is now rooted in something, he has assumed an unassailable position. He places both hands on her belly. He's never known her more deeply, more clearly, than in this moment, enlivenment in her eyes. His child will have this look, these eyes. It will carry her vitality, a far more potent force than anything he can endow.

He asks her to marry him. She says *yes*. She says *of course*. He tells her he wants to marry her on White Island on Lough Erne. There's a church from the twelfth century with a Sheela-na-gig on the wall. He describes it for her. A small figurine, a symbol of fertility, potency, a bald woman with her pelvis spread so wide that her knees are parallel with her waist, a wide grin across her face. 'I bet she does,' Sarah says. He tells her that he sees her arriving by boat to the waiting congregation, that she'll step in off the lake and pass amongst them like a blessing. She laughs at him. He tells her he's serious, he'd like to create some beauty amongst all the sorrow. She rubs his cheek, tells him he's a man with notions, but they're fine notions all the same.

The hunger strikes have begun. The tension has exploded into a full-blown fever. Bobby Sands is running for parliament from his deathbed. Brendan's ma tells him every lamp-post in the town has Sands' smiling face on it. He can't tell his ma Sarah's pregnant. They're not married. He can't even tell her about Sarah. He's in love with a Presbyterian – he can't find words for that over the phone. His ma's voice has changed on the phone these past weeks, her sentences are filled with vitriol. He's not surprised – how can you stay neutral when a starving man is smiling down at you from every lamp-post?

A letter comes in the post. He's been given an interview at the port. The better money would definitely come in handy now. He phones in sick to the meat factory and takes a taxi to Warrenpoint. On the way, they pass Narrow Water. He recognizes the castle keep from the newspapers – two years before, the IRA bombed a convoy there. He looks for evidence of the damage, but the grass has all grown back. The driver notices Brendan looking back through the window. 'Aye,' the man says, 'that was the spot all right.' He doesn't say anything more, and Brendan doesn't ask.

The interview happens in a Portakabin at the docks. The foreman is called George, a belly pouring through his check shirt. There's paperwork everywhere, notes tacked up on the walls, stacks of boxes leaning precariously against the walls. The questions are standard, and he can tell George is impressed with his work in the meat factory, solid labour, he's a man who knows how to put in a shift.

When the phone call comes a couple of days later, he asks for a day or two to think it over. Sarah is delighted when he tells her that weekend. They decide she'll come to Newry; she knows one of the consultants in Daisy Hill Hospital. Two good salaries will give them a firm foundation. He'll be a family man. No more living the monastic life.

It all moves so fast. Every week is like six months. They find a flat with two bedrooms, on the Orior Road. It's on the ground floor, and opens out on to a small garden with a patio. Sarah says she'll read there and have her coffee in the mornings, before she goes to work. He laughs at this. He's never known a morning when she's not bustling out the door, having stretched out her sleep for as long as possible. The place needs a paint. The landlord offers them a discount on the rent if they do it themselves. They spend a weekend sanding down skirting boards, scraping off the loose chips, painting, painting and repainting. Her doesn't like her up a ladder, even if it's a stepladder. He tells her as much, but she ignores him. They drink tea and share sandwiches at lunchtime. Her calves hurt from standing on her tiptoes. They're workmates, a different kind of intimacy. She tells him of her weekends as a kid when she followed her dad around at auctions, wandering around country estates which were stuffed with odds and ends, tags on the furniture, the auctioneers and their strange patter, everything seeped in aspic, women in ornate hats, everyone trying to pretend that the twentieth century hadn't happened yet, all of them trying to preserve something long past. He tells her about moving cattle from place to place. How, if you want to gain control over a bullock, you stick your fingers in its snout and lock your grip. She laughs at him, her simple country boy.

There's a day's training in how to drive the forklift. It's counterintuitive, you steer with the back wheels. At the end George hands him a certificate, the first qualification of his life.

He doesn't want to pay movers, so he steals a trolley from the supermarket and loads up his stuff, making trips in the evening while she's still at work. Going back and forth, he's reminded of the locks on Ballinamore Canal: one apartment drains, another fills. They allow her da to bring over some of his furniture. The new place is more suited to it. He buys a painting from a stall in the Cathedral Quarter. It's of Ophelia, Hamlet's girlfriend. She's pictured floating, drowned in a river, her dress billowing out, flowers in her still hands, reeds by her side. He's not sure what to think of it, but he reckons

Sarah will like it. She does. He feels older, giving it to her. It's a present that a man would give, a man with a career and a suit and an appreciation for the finer things. She puts it on the kitchen wall. Her mother asks her to move it somewhere else – too much drama to be displayed in plain sight. Sarah slides it under the spare bed. He expected her to put up a fight. He wonders if this means something, indicates something about the woman she'll become. He is, he realizes, a safe rebellion for Sarah. With a domineering mother, his religion gives Sarah something to hide behind. Catholics are a strange breed to her mother. She can't be seen to be directly resistant, and has trouble finding day-to-day cracks she can exploit. Her mother is intimidated by him. It's an odd realization, and not unsatisfying.

At the docks there's bustle, a constant flow of movement – ships coming in, containers being unloaded, crates, cranes, the smells of oil and water. At lunchtimes they sometimes play football in a storage yard, boxes for goalposts. They jostle and shoulder and pause to take smoke breaks. Occasionally the customs men join them, stripping off their uniforms down to their undervests. Status becomes – temporarily – irrelevant. They do it to feel like kids again. The game matters and it doesn't matter. He likes this too, it's been a while since he's felt the surge of competition.

Sarah comes home exhausted. He surprised to find that he envies her a little bit, he misses the satisfaction of hard labour running through his body. She soaks her feet in front of the TV. He admires her too. She could easily take the softer route. 'Pity the rich,' his ma used to say, 'they can't live under the illusion that money brings happiness.' Sarah knows this innately. She's never needed anyone's pity. He loves her wisdom, her practicality, her steadfastness.

They get married in Belfast City Hall. The room is a greenhouse. Shrubs and greenery everywhere. She doesn't buy a new dress for the occasion. She wears a white ball gown, adjusted by a seamstress. It's simple, it doesn't billow around. She has small yellow flowers in her hair. The girls from the Royal Vic are there. They can't contain their surprise: didn't think he had it in him, thought of him as a temporary fixture. He doesn't invite his family, no point, they wouldn't recognize a civil service, he'd just have to hear arguments to the contrary.

Mrs Hadley thinks it all very strange. He thought about inviting Mrs Donnelly, just to have someone in his corner, but he decided against it. The Hadleys leave early. The nurses colonize a bar. He and Sarah are tucked up at home by eleven. He goes to work the next morning.

He paints the nursery in magnolia. A nice, non-committal colour. When he steps back and looks at it, he thinks of the music they play in lifts or in large shops. Sarah's da brings them a wooden cot. It's like something a doll would sleep in, high sides, both ends bent into an arch. He paints it turquoise, her favourite colour. He doesn't tell her. She sees it when she goes in to measure for curtains. She comes back out and kisses him on the neck. This is life, life progressing.

He buys a car, an old Datsun Sunny, from a dealer in Poyntzpass. He wants to have a mode of transport for when Sarah goes into labour, and it's time to stop taking the bus to work. The dealership doesn't have an office, it's just the man's bungalow with ranks of cars parked outside, threading all the way down the nearby laneways. The car is red, but the bonnet is light blue. 'Not exactly a beauty,' the man says. 'But she'll get ya from A to B.'

'And back?' he says.

The man enjoys that. 'Oh, surely, back as well, as long as you have something to come back to,' he says, chuckling full-bodied.

Brendan pays him in cash and the man signs the registration forms.

'Now, would it be your first car?' he says.

'It would all right.'

He puts the forms in an envelope, hands it over, and Brendan slips it into his pocket. Then the man plants the keys firmly in Brendan's left palm, a ritual significance to the act, clasps his right hand and squeezes it.

'It's no small thing, a man's first car. You won't know yourself. I wish you well wearing.'

Brendan thanks him, can't stifle a grin as he sits behind the wheel, another small milestone, another sign that he's an independent man in the world.

14

The weeks slow as the hunger strikes continue. The football games stop.

Eventually it happens: Bobby Sands dies. When it's announced, the place is consumed in an inferno of rage. Riots combust all over the province. A teenage girl is shot dead by the army with a rubber bullet. A crowd on the Antrim Road in North Belfast stone a milk lorry; the milkman panics and crashes into a lamp-post, killing himself and his fourteen-year-old son. A military sniper takes out a lad in the Divis Flats.

The tide of anger encroaches. Andrew, one of the customs agents, tells him over a cigarette that the IRA have blown up a Saracen in Bessbrook, only a couple of miles from Newry. It throws him. Ray McCreesh from Camlough joined the hunger strike eight weeks ago. It's obvious that the incident is connected, a show of solidarity. Bessbrook is close to the lad's home.

It all feels more real, more present somehow, with this news. He can't concentrate; he bangs the forklift into a stack of pallets, scatters them. He leaves early. He wants to get home before Sarah arrives, straighten the place out, have a dinner in the oven. Normality is something to cling to, calm within the chaos.

The nearer he gets to home, the heavier the military

presence. He leaves his car in town; the traffic is packed up. Choppers criss-cross overhead. There are troops everywhere. He has to pass three checkpoints just to get into his street. The soldiers speak robotically, ask questions with a steeliness in their gaze, no humanity in their voices, easy to see how a man can turn into a machine. His neighbours stand in their doorways, unspeaking, some nod their head at him. There are none of the usual joyous bleats of kids at play.

He turns the key in the front door, opens it, closes it behind him and then leans against it, pressing his back to it, taking deep breaths. The world, finally, is out there, not in here. He can't help but think of the McCreeshes sitting at home, a ten-minute drive away. How can you function, eat, breathe, shower, do normal things while your son is voluntarily wasting away? He looks anew at the life that he and Sarah are building, looks at the sprays of dried flowers in small vases, the coasters on the coffee table, the throw rug on the back of the sofa, the lamp with green tassels dangling from its shade. Pink fridge magnets in the shape of elephants. All of it drains of meaning. The protections that domesticity offer are laid bare as an illusion. What kind of place are they bringing a child into?

He opens the fridge, ready to cook for Sarah, but he feels a repulsion when he looks at its contents. He can't help but picture Ray McCreesh, emaciated, buckled on a bed. He sits at the kitchen table. Rain ticks against the windows. He sits, looks and listens, feeling like he's intruded upon his own life, feeling like he's a foreigner in his own land.

He hears the door close, hears Sarah put down her bag, take off her coat. She's exhausted. She slumps in a chair and asks him to put the kettle on.

They sit, cradling their mugs.

'We shouldn't have come here,' she says.

'Where else would we go?' he says.

'We could go down south, start again.'

'And what then? We'd forget about what's happening here? We can't just block it out.'

She starts to cry, sharp silent tears. He holds her, puts his hands on her belly. He can feel the child moving inside her. It's hard to believe that a human will emerge from there. Because of him, but also not. Attuned to him, but also not. He feels incidental, if he's honest. A mother grows the child; a father offers protection. How can he possibly fulfil his side of the deal?

In bed, they make love with floodlights streaming through their curtains, throwing strange shadows around the room.

After that evening, work feels different. He hates rising in the morning. At the breakfast table, he dreads the day ahead of him. He doesn't want to be out and about, doesn't want to have to deal with people, take orders.

The drivers come to him for favours. Occasionally they ask him to stash some boxes out of the way. They clip some cash to the back of his clipboard to make sure things go more smoothly. He's no hesitation in accepting, all of them working a system that none of them devised.

Engels: *The appropriation of unpaid labour is the basis of the capitalist mode of production and of the exploitation of the worker that occurs under it.*

Life turns eventually, orientating him towards the conflict. He can't stay on the sidelines forever.

Now that the football games are done, he spends his lunchtimes in a park by the harbour – when the weather permits. He reads and watches squirrels and listens to the sounds around him, looks at whoever is lolling on the grass in front of him. Snatches of conversation float his way. The park has its own rhythm. People sit in the same areas. He begins to write down his observations, lays them on to the back pages of whatever book he's reading.

The bus arrives from Rostrevor; its left indicator light is broken.

A woman searches through her handbag, lays out its contents on to the grass.

A man struggles with a black umbrella.

Sarah may well come across them and think he's losing it. No matter. Take comfort in the simple things.

He's immersed in this activity the day that Joe shows up. His brother sits on the bench beside him, waits for Brendan to notice his presence. Nothing. Eventually he starts speaking.

'That's a quare lot of scribbling you're doing. Is it an epistle you're writing?'

Brendan bolts upright, covers his pages. It takes him a moment to confirm that it's Joe, dropping in out of nowhere.

'What are you doing here? How the fuck did you find me?'

'Una told me about your job.'

Joe's aged, thinned, greyed. It's like he's looking at a younger version of his father, like he's watching a photograph being enacted in the present.

'You're on leave? Ma never said.'

'I'm out.'

'How do you mean out?'

'Done. I paid up my discharge.'

'What? When did this happen?'

'A few weeks ago.'

'You haven't been home? Ma never said anything.'

'That hasn't been my home in a long time. I've a few things to square up before I chat to her. But, aye, I'm back, no fucking way I can wear that uniform again, not with all that's been going on.'

'Where are you staying?'

'I've a mate in Dundalk. I'm on his sofa for now.'

'You're being careful? There's plenty who'd be interested in your whereabouts.'

'Aye. I've made official contact.'

'They pulled you in?'

'Well, I did it voluntarily, but, aye, they dragged me over the coals.'

He gives Joe a pause, gives him some space to fill in those words, but his brother looks back at him blankly, well practised in giving nothing away.

'I'm sure they did. And now?'

Joe looks around, looks at his watch. 'What time does your shift end?'

'Five.'

'Right, pints after?'

Brendan shrugs. 'Can't really say no, can I?'

Joe slaps him on the shoulder. 'Good man.'

They meet in a pub on the esplanade. Joe is sitting in a snug when he walks in, reading the paper. Brendan buys two fresh pints and carries them over. Joe smiles, a lopsided grin. Something worn about him, something embittered. He's missing a few bottom teeth. Brendan wonders if it was a fight or just wild living.

'Baby brother buys the drinks.'

'Who said one's for you?'

So much to talk about, too much. Joe is, and has always been, a stranger, a rumour. They sup their pints. Joe talks about his wee brother's smuggling practice, the barrow with his name on it, pushing it across fields and down boreens. Brendan smiles, despite himself, at the precociousness of it. Kind of remarkable really, in retrospect, that they let him do it.

'You always were a sharp wee hoor. I bet you're still doing it, crates going missing here and there.'

Does Joe know something? 'It's all straight as a die,' he says.

'Aye, I bet. Be careful with that.'

Brendan drills him with a look. 'You're fucking kidding me. Are you really going to lecture me about morality?'

'Take it as brotherly advice.'

'Right, cheers. It's great you coming here to dole it out, can't believe what I missed out on.'

They have another pint, they talk football, giving themselves some breathing space. Brendan waits for Joe to turn the subject around, but he doesn't. He realizes his brother is nervous. He looks around the place, to make sure they're not overheard. He lowers his voice. 'What are you doing here, Joe?'

'The fight has changed. We've got to take a side. I can't ignore it any more.'

'You've already taken your side. It's way too late to change it now.'

'Look, Brendan, you were too young to remember, but when I joined up I was a mess, I needed to get out of home. I didn't have any skills, and joining the Rangers wasn't a big deal – plenty of lads did it. I was glad of it, if I'm honest, I needed the routine.'

'What was the model of the gun they had you carry?'

Joe answers softly, aware where this is going, 'You know what it was.'

'I think I might need a reminder.'

'An L1A1.'

'Right, aye, I know it. I had it pointed in my fucking face when I was lying in bed one night. Maybe that'd have been the time to think about leaving? When your comrades beat the shit out of me and Da? I thought we were done for, so did he. But don't worry about it, I'm sure you were all just doin' your job.'

'I didn't know the extent of it. You know how Ma and Da are – they didn't elaborate much. I knew Da had been arrested. I didn't know they'd brought you in. I didn't know about the raid, any of it, really. I only found out properly a year or two ago, when Una told me all about it.'

'There's a smell of bullshit here, Joe. Anyway, you could have left then.'

'I thought I was better inside, that having an Irish battalion would keep them honest, keep us respected.'

'Don't fucking give me that.'

'It's what I was telling myself. I'm not saying it was right. And, aye, fine, I'll admit it, I liked being a soldier. Actually, no, I loved it – you carry a gun and wear a uniform and you're fucking invincible. And I was pissed off with this place, I didn't want to know.'

'And now, all of a sudden, you do.'

'Aye. That's how it is.' Joe sups his pint again. 'I'm sorry you went through that, I'm sorry I wasn't there. But I'm out now. And it's time to make amends.'

'With who?'

'With anyone who's angry with me. You're not wrong. I left yous all, took the shilling, didn't give a shit. And now I've got to live with that. I have to make my reparations.'

The place begins to fill; the barman stops cleaning glasses. Joe looks around him, scanning faces. When he speaks again, it's in a whisper, but casual, careful not to draw attention.

'I was friendly with Martin Hurson as a kid, did you know that?'

Eight of the hunger strikers are dead by now. Martin Hurson was the sixth one to go. Brendan stares hard at Joe: his face says he's telling the truth.

'They had a wee farm. I'd meet him the odd time when I went with Da to the mart in Dungannon. We'd knock around together a bit while the trading was going on, kick a football around. He was only a year or two older than yourself.'

'He only died a month ago. That's not why you left.'

'He died of fucking dehydration, you know that? He didn't die of hunger, he died of fucking thirst: his body couldn't hold down water. Think about that. That wee lad I kicked a football with.'

Brendan rises, definitively. 'Enough. Jesus wept. You chose your fate, Joe. You can't just switch it around. I hardly even fucking know you – all you are is a postcard. Do whatever you have to do but don't be bothering me about it.'

He strides out into the street, good to feel the air on his face, rounds a few corners, reaches his car. He looks at his watch. It's pushing nine. He really shouldn't drive with a feed of pints on him, but the bus would mean he wouldn't be back till all hours. He decides to sit inside, have a wee bit of shut-eye, he can decide in a half-hour.

He's only just tilted his seat back when there's a tap on the window. Joe.

For fuck's sake.

He winds down the window.

'What about a lift, hai?'

'To Dundalk? Aye, great idea. Crossing the border half fucking cut. Sure, that's all I need.'

Joe sits in, starts to light a cigarette. Brendan tells him to open a window. He puts the smoke back in its box. Then he just sits there, staring out on to the street. Brendan gets impatient, puts the key in the ignition. Joe starts speaking; Brendan doesn't turn the key.

'So you're signed up?' Brendan says. 'Got the Green Book and all?'

'I had to. There's no other choice. It would have put everyone in too much danger if I hadn't.'

'Don't bullshit, Joe. Don't make it about us. You just want to keep carrying a gun, pretending you're a big man.'

'It's not what you think. It's a lot more structured than you'd imagine. It's not flying columns hitting an RUC barracks any more. It's refined. They've learned from international activities.'

'There you go with *they* again.'

'Fine. We.'

'Good. Aye. At least that's clear.'

Joe shakes his head, looks about him. 'Grow up, hai. This extends way past Belfast or Derry. There's a movement happening here, an international groundswell. There's a brotherhood and sisterhood of struggle. Lebanon. Palestine. Look at Baader–Meinhof, how they've rattled Germany. The Red Brigades took out the Italian Prime Minister. We're learning from each other. Anything is possible right now. Don't be so fucking small. We're talking about democracy serving the workers.'

'All right, speech over. It's got nothing to do with me.'

'We're all involved. The hunger strikes have changed everything. Deny it if you want, but you know I'm right.'

His brother leaves and walks into the night. And still Brendan can't help but find himself half impressed by the swagger of Joe, the one who always somehow manages to have the last fucking word.

He stares in the mirror in the mornings and wonders if he also looks like his father. He tries to see a resemblance to Joe. There's something there in the hunched eyebrows, in the tightness of his mouth. It's an eerie sensation, time catching up with him. He tries to grow a beard but it doesn't take: it's wispy and curly, patches of red and black in it. Sarah threatens to shave it off him in his sleep.

He's restless. Autumn descends. The hunger strikes keep going, no end in sight. The rain makes him impatient. Sarah's shift work gets him down, she's not around on weekends. He avoids pubs, he doesn't want to hear the talk that goes on in them. He goes for walks along the Albert Basin, throws bread to the ducks, spends proper time in the library. He sees a rower on the river, wonders if he should take up rowing. He watches the smoothness of the man's motion, oars skimming back and forth, propulsion and momentum, gliding freely along the surface of his life.

Joe comes round for dinner, brings flowers for Sarah. He says the right things, remarks on the furnishings, compliments their choice of home, talks about the dedication of the nurses in the military hospitals. He offers Sarah snippets of Brendan's childhood, the stuff he himself had forgotten, how he'd twisted his ankle in a rabbit hole, how he'd had a set of Dracula fangs that he carried in his pocket for years, how he'd been a model altar boy, always chosen to serve the Christmas Mass, sitting at Sunday dinner smelling of incense. He can see his wife listening intently to his brother. Maybe he needs to be grateful for Joe's presence – at last a semblance of family life emerging.

Sarah reaches her final trimester. She can't sleep great. Her movements in the night cause him to wake, startled. In the drowsy moments between sleep and waking he sees a rifle pointed directly at him. '*Will I* blow your fucking brains out?'

At checkpoints he eyeballs the soldiers. They don't look away – they're trained to engage. He looks and they look. He's careful not to be aggressive, he's just letting them know they're not welcome here.

His da never did really recover from that night when they were hauled in. It wasn't that his nerves were shot: it was more the humiliation of how he'd been treated in front of his own kids. His speech dropped off a bit afterwards: he started to mumble, started to second guess himself. Small things. He'd stall the truck a lot or be hesitant taking a turn. It's the small things they take, with their guns and their arrogance.

It could be him, in twelve years. Him dragged into a cell with his wee boy following. Him made to sing 'The

Sash' from the bottom of a troop wagon while soldiers lay boots into his son's back. There's no end in sight. And maybe he needs to think about what he'll tell his boy when he's grown up. He thinks of Ulrike Meinhof: *Protest is when I say I don't like this. Resistance is when I put an end to what I don't like.*

15

Joe rents a place in Carlingford. Brendan gives him the deposit, taking a certain satisfaction in his elder brother asking him sheepishly for a loan, and drives him to auctions over a few weekends, tying furniture to the roof rack of the Datsun.

The talking gets easier. Joe doesn't try to persuade, just outlines his thinking. The older brother still carries an authority that holds Brendan in his thrall.

One night, he phones the house and asks Brendan to drive to Carlingford. He has something he needs to discuss. Brendan can tell from his tone it's not a casual meeting.

He pours boiling water and Epsom salts into an enamel tub. He uses a towel to carry it to the living room, places it on the ground in front of Sarah. He takes off her shoes and socks, rubs her feet, works his thumbs into her soles. She ignores the TV and leans back into the headrest, stares at the ceiling, some soft moans. He tests the temperature of the water and, satisfied, places each foot in. She smiles groggily at him, half escaped from herself. He stands and kisses her on the forehead and moves towards the door.

'You're going out?'

'Aye. Joe needs me. I won't be long.'

She knows he's hiding something. She's near full term. 'What if my waters break?'

'You have his number. It's only a few hours. I'll be back by bedtime.'

'I've heard that one before.'

'I'll put on the electric blanket before I head out, just in case.'

'You think that'll soften me up?'

'When has it not?'

A small grin – hard to be angry with your feet planted in a basin of warm water.

Joe is sitting with another man in his living room. The man is not much older than Brendan himself. He's dressed in a denim shirt, denim jeans, large black boots. The hems of his jeans are rolled up, the shirt is free of creases. His hair is jet black and sleek, tucked behind his ears. He's clean-shaven, bright, easy with his movements.

Joe introduces them, first names only. The man is called Cathal. He offers his hand. 'How's about ye?'

A Donegal accent, feather-soft. The handshake is firm but not so strong that he's trying to make a statement. University educated, Brendan guesses. Engineering maybe. That kind of cautious pace about him, that kind of logical mind. Despite his relative youth, Brendan gets the impression he's been in the IRA a long time. A scholarship kid maybe. A chemist maybe. A bombmaker maybe.

Cathal has a proposition. There's a UDR major, Tom Warwick, who works in the customs office at the port. They've been watching him for a while.

Brendan looks at Joe. 'What are you asking here?'

Cathal says, 'We'd like you keep an eye out, make a note of any details, even small ones. Anything regarding his routines would be particularly useful.'

'I'll not sign up for anything.'

'We're not looking for any commitment, just a nudge in the right direction.'

'I'll think about it,' Brendan says. Cathal doesn't labour the point. It's clear Brendan's answer is no more than he expected; he'll leave the rest of it to Joe. He stands, shakes their hands, leaves.

Joe lights a smoke, puts the kettle on. 'You could have told me,' Brendan says.

'Don't give me that. You wanted to come.'

He brings back two steaming mugs and a jug of milk.

'Where's this headed?'

'Where do you think?'

Brendan drinks his tea, takes a minute. 'You'll not use local men, if it comes to it?' The operation in Newry has a reputation for being ham-fisted. The tales that lurch from pub to pub are of botched operations, inefficiencies.

Joe nods. 'They'll be experienced. There'll not be any loose ends.'

'You can't guarantee that, though, can you? What sway do you hold?'

'None, but Cathal does.'

'He's not local?'

'Don't be asking questions I can't answer.'

Sarah's asleep on the sofa when he gets home. He doesn't want to wake her, but he wants to be near her.

He lies on the floor beside the sofa. He hears her moaning in the night, a pleasant noise, a kind of satisfied purr, light and bouncy. He feels essentialized, lying there, floorboards under his back, connected to something greater than himself.

He gets a call at work the next day: it's the hospital. Sarah's in the delivery room – a complication has arisen. He jumps in the car, drives back to Newry. He's forgotten to change, and feels self-conscious striding through the hospital in his work clothes. At the nurses' station he's told to take a seat. When he asks them how it's going, they reply that Mr Fitzpatrick will fill him in when he gets a minute.

He knows nurses well enough to be worried when they get taciturn.

He sits. He cries into his hands. He can't tell why. It's like someone took a sledgehammer to a rusty tap in his chest. A nurse takes pity on him, tells him that Sarah's blood pressure rose to concerning levels, so they brought her down for a C-section. She tells him Mr Fitzpatrick wasn't concerned: he's experienced, and the procedure is more a precaution than a necessity. She says to just sit tight and wait, they'll have news soon. He nods through the tears; he can't think what he must look like.

Time passes, he's not sure how long. The nurse comes back, brings him a cup of tea and a biscuit. They know Sarah works here, so he's probably getting preferential treatment.

'It's all fine. I talked to the theatre nurse – it all went

fine. You've a wee boy. Have your tea there and rest yourself and you can go in and see him in a few minutes. Sarah is still under, but I'll let you know when she's come around.'

The softness of her voice sets him off again. He puts the tea and saucer on the floor, under the chair, and walks to the window to distract himself, compose himself. A breeze ripples through the trees outside, leaves turning over. This is what they talk about when people have told him everything will change. Now that his child is here, the world feels different. Life feels different. Continuous. Essential. Simple. Repetitive. Life feels beautiful. Life feels delicate.

In the neonatal ward, the boy is in an incubator, delicate as a twig. Jet-black hair pasted on his forehead, tiny fists, fingers shaped like miniature bananas. A range of expressions already. The baby clamps his face into a grimace, then opens his eyes wide. His mouth opens, lips form around a perfect black circle of fascination, then a full-blown cry, a wail. Moods like weather, storm fronts rolling in from some invisible bay. So reassuring to watch, these unconsidered impulses.

There he is, clamping his fists, consumed with rage, already preparing for what lies ahead.

16

He starts noticing things around work, just small things. He jots them down. Tom Warwick drives a Vauxhall Cavalier, powder-blue, registration VYY 179. He's in his early fifties. His hair is thinning on top and combed behind the ears. He's about five foot ten, weighs about a hundred and seventy pounds. He still looks sturdy, looks like he could pack a punch.

He stops skimming boxes from the loads.

One by one, he tells the lorry drivers that he has a wee boy at home; he can't take the risk any more.

He tries to get a sense of Warwick's routines, but, as a supervisor, the man can change shifts at will. He seems friendly, though, the way he deals with people, the way he speaks to the lorry drivers. A loner more by choice, by caution, Brendan suspects, than by natural inclination.

Eventually, there's a weakness. One morning Warwick walks from his car carrying a cake with chocolate icing; it looks homemade. Brendan is having a smoke with Andrew when he passes.

He asks Andrew, 'What's the big occasion? Did I miss your birthday?'

'Aye, as if. Dunno if he even knows my name.'

'Is he tryin' to suck up to someone?'

'All of us, I suppose. We call it *Warwick's Elevenses*.' First Friday of every month, he brings in a cake. I suppose he thinks that his missus's baking is tasty enough to keep us from skimming off the top.'

'Aye. And does it work?'

Andrew flicks away his smoke, a glint in his eye. 'It'd need to have wee dancing girls leapin' out of it.'

He contacts Joe. He drives out to Carlingford that evening. Brendan tells him everything he knows and hands over his notebook. Joe leafs through it. 'Aye, there should be plenty here.'

The hunger strikes end. There's no victory, no jubilation on the streets. It's been trickling to a halt for a few weeks now. After Paddy Quinn's parents insisted on medical intervention when he lost consciousness, the other families began to follow suit. The Bishop called for a cessation. Sinn Féin went into negotiations with the Northern Secretary. The will of the thing had been broken. It's hard to become vitalized by neglect. Everyone looks drained, fraught, in need of a good holiday, a jump in the sea. There are kids out on the streets with fireworks. But that's it. No one else feels like marking the occasion. There's no sense of relief on the radio, in the newspapers, in passing conversation. It feels like the last few months, all that rancour, all that brave talk, have been pointless, water poured down a drain.

A couple of weeks of domestic peace. They've decided to name the child Malachy, after Brendan's grandfather on his da's side. The man died while Brendan was small, but he remembers his kindness. He was a machine-fitter for Cadbury's in Dublin. He remembers that when they visited his granda Malachy's house he'd ask his granda to show him his shop and his granda would take him into his shed and show him his tools and his leftover buckets of paint and Brendan would be delighted, captivated at the range of accoutrements a working man possessed. Malachy sleeps in a basket in the corner of the bedroom. Brendan wakes some nights to see his wife breastfeeding his child. The room, filled with maternal care, feels like a womb to him too. He lays his head on her when she returns to bed and she accepts him, nurtures him. She's older, experienced. Now that she has a child, there's a gravitas to her, a depth of knowledge that he can't possibly fathom. He's reluctant to leave in the mornings, he wants only this, only this tranquillity.

They christen Malachy in Enniskillen. His ma and da are delighted with this concession. Sarah's parents come along too. Una is the godmother. Sarah's brother Craig, the godfather. He can tell it's the first time Craig has seen the inside of a Catholic church: he stares like he's just walked into the Sistine Chapel. The baby cries blue murder when the priest pours cold water on his forehead. 'Fine set of lungs on him,' the priest says. Brendan knows he's said this about every single baby, at every single christening, and yet he still smiles, proud of the way his boy doesn't take any shit.

They go for lunch after, in the hotel in Killyhevlin. Una is up from Dublin for a few days. She won't look at him. No doubt she has talked to Joe, has suspicions regarding their carry-on. She has a job as a legal secretary, plans to study for the bar. She's groomed and poised, demanding respect by what she wears, how she moves. The kind of woman that Sarah can relate to, using her brains to make her way through the world. Sarah and Una sit in the lobby and talk while the others are having a pre-dinner drink, searching desperately for points of commonality. Sarah's da talks furniture, at first out of nervousness, but then warms to his theme. The others placidly listen along, grateful that he's filling the silences. As he speaks, Brendan thinks that maybe his da should find an interest of his own, something to shake him from his slumber. The pigeons are long gone.

Sarah's conversation with Una changes things. His sister probably didn't say anything outright, but implied some truths, the way women talk.

Sarah stops feeding Malachy in the bedroom. Instead she goes into the living room and sits by the radiator, listening to the BBC. Through the wall, he can hear the plummy voices: dispatches from Egypt, discussions on Greek philosophy, the migratory habits of Arctic birds.

Now that she's not working, she brings a book with her everywhere, even to the dinner table. She sits on the front steps when it's not raining, head down in one of her books, Malachy in a basket on the bottom step. Malachy is content with all the stillness. The neighbours wave, yell, 'It must be a good one, can't keep your nose out of it.' She ignores them. They stop yelling.

He sits beside her on the step, lights a cigarette and asks her what she'd be in a different life.

'I'd be still in Belfast,' she says.

He laughs that laugh of his, half-snicker, half-grimace, air blown out of his nose. 'Not exactly exotic, is it? You wouldn't go for Honolulu or somewhere?'

'It's where I'm from. It's where I belong.'

'You don't think you belong here?'

She doesn't look up from her book. She turns a page with a snap, one of her minute ways of protesting. He smokes with his right hand. With his left he tickles Malachy's neck, and the child gurgles in response.

He asks it again. 'You don't think this is your home?'

'No. I don't.'

'Why do you say such a thing?'

She ignores his question.

He puts his hand over her pages so she can't continue reading. She keeps her head down anyway. The smoke from the cigarette dances into her face.

'How can this not be your home? You child is here, I'm here.'

She doesn't answer. It's like they've walked backwards down a path and ended up back at the nurses' quarters of the Royal Vic. That indifference that she's cultivated throughout her life. It was alluring then. Now it makes him want to smash up some furniture.

'We could move to Belfast if that's what you want.'

'Aye, I'm sure we could. You and Joe would work it all out.'

'What does that mean?'

She stares at him, says, as blankly as if she's asking him to put on the dinner, 'Get that cigarette out of my face before I stab you in the eye with it.'

His car packs it in at the end of October. No protest from the engine. It doesn't even stutter, just sits lifeless. He attaches jump leads to his neighbour's car and tries to start the thing but to no avail. He calls a mechanic, who scratches his head, tells him they'll have to tow it to the garage and give it a good going-over. He's back to riding the bus again.

He sits at the bus stop on a Friday evening, the last Friday of the month. He's not looking forward to the weekend: two whole days of monotony and Sarah blanking him. It starts to pour down. He's no umbrella, no anorak. He left them at the docks – things like that have been happening recently, his head full of distractions. It makes sense: he's so used to doing without things that he has trouble remembering any new possessions. The roof of the bus shelter leaks. He moves about to avoid getting wet, but the rain gets him eventually, darkening his shoulders, matting his hair on to his head. He stands and waits, unbothered, the only one there.

A powder-blue Vauxhall reverses towards him. He hadn't noticed it pass. It pulls to a stop, then reverses beside him. Warwick leans over and rolls down the window.

'You work on the docks, don't you?'

'Aye, that's right.'

'You live in Newry. I think I've seen you there before.'

He's about to deny it, but Warwick could look at his personnel file and wonder why he'd lied.

'Aye,' he says.

'Hop in. I'm headed that way.'

Brendan hesitates, but it doesn't feel like he can refuse, especially since the man reversed for him. He opens the door and sits, closes it again. The quiet is instantaneous, unnerving.

'Thanks so much.'

'You could spend all evening there.'

'Aye.'

'The girls at the office call it *the phantom bus*.'

'It comes all right. Just never when it says it would.'

'You'll need to get yourself a car.'

'I did. It's on sick leave.'

'Typical, right. Never rains but it pours.'

'Often rains, usually pours.'

Warwick laughs at that. 'Where your destination?'

'The Orior Road. I'm sure it's out of your way. If you just drop me off in town, I'd be very grateful.'

'Nonsense. Not on an evening like this.' He speaks into the mirror: 'Just going to take a little detour. That's all right, isn't it?'

Brendan hadn't noticed a passenger. He turns around to see a girl in a duffel coat with a pink tutu underneath. About seven years old, he guesses.

'We're off to ballet class,' Warwick says.

He can't remember the last time he was around a child her age. He doesn't want to stare, but feels compelled, for some reason, to take her in. Brown hair, flattened tight on her head, probably in a bun. Large brown eyes. She looks at him curiously, openly, doesn't smile, doesn't need approval, a confident kid, used to strangers.

He turns around again. Not a daughter. A grand-daughter probably. He doesn't want to know anything about her, doesn't want Warwick talking about her; he must steer the course of the conversation.

Brendan says, 'They're stopping telegrams, you heard that?'

'Who?'

'BT.'

'No more telegrams? Is that what you're saying?'

'Aye, that's it. BT Says It Will Stop Telegrams Stop.'

Warwick laughs at that. Warwick says, 'I got one from my mother when I was a kid. She was visiting my aunt in Glasgow. She was letting us know she was coming back the next day; we were to pick her up off the train. We had no telephone, you know, it was just after the war. The man came to the door and I answered it, took the telegram, read it. The message was: Stop Coming Home Stop. Why would I stop coming home? I couldn't for the life of me figure it out. In the end, I just threw it in the bin.'

'So she didn't get her lift? I bet she was rippin'.'

Warwick smiles at the memory. 'Oh, aye, fit to be tied.'

They pass Abbey Park, where groups of punks are sitting on the grass in the pouring rain, drinking cans, deliberately unconcerned by the weather, their mohawks impermeable.

It's a modest car, now that Brendan thinks about it, for a senior supervisor and a UDR major. Probably frugal with his cash. Probably stashes it away in a savings account for his grandkids.

They could have been friends, in a different life. Warwick has an easy manner to him. Warm, sincere. Brendan respects the precision of the man's movements. Even the way he drives is very efficient.

Chances are, Warwick will be dead in a week. If Cathal is going to act on the information, he'll do so next Friday. The first Friday of November. They won't just sit on it: they'll act or not act. It feels weird, knowing that. The man next to him, soon to be erased, smoothed off the plain of life. It feels like he's not talking to a man but a memory, a story to be told one day. Thrilling too, that kind of power, knowing something so vital to the man's life, so intimate. Those hands on the steering wheel will soon be inert, under soil. It's like seeing Malachy in that incubator, existing so near to the thread of life, the same but opposite. He feels a tenderness towards Warwick, wants to reach over, touch his hand, tell him not to worry, it'll all be quick. Instead he asks, 'You've been with HMRC for a long time?'

'Straight out of school. I count myself very blessed; it meant I got a head start on other people, and I was able to set myself up for the future quite young.'

He's lying. It's unlikely you get to be a major in the UDR without military experience. An understandable lie, though, considering the circumstances, not wise to go around broadcasting your credentials.

'I imagine it was quite a relief,' Brendan says, 'to have all that squared away young. There's enough problems with raising children. No point adding to it with money worries.'

'Aye. Dead on. Once you have a roof over their heads, everything else is icing on the cake.'

They're quiet for a while.

'Do you like the work?' Warwick asks.

'Aye, it's a decent job.'

'Where did you grow up?'

'Fermanagh.'

'Ah, gorgeous spot. I've been fishing on the Erne.'

'Oh, aye, whereabouts?'

'Och, it was a while ago. Somewhere on the northern edge. Me and a few friends stayed in a cottage. The nights were long. We shambled into the boat on a few mornings. I needed a rest when I came home.'

'A break from your break.'

'Exactly.'

He'd like to open up and talk about the waters he's fished in, talk about tackle and rods, but he stops himself. Why does he feel the need to befriend the man? Guilt? No need, he's in the right. This, after all, is about freedom, the entitlement to live in your own country without an occupying force. The right not to be owned. Not to be satisfied with the few scraps thrown from the table. 'What's ours is ours but what's yours is also ours' – the right to overturn that premise.

He looks out of the window to discourage any more chat. Restaurants and taxis, shops and cyclists.

Warwick drops him off at the end of his road. Brendan shakes his hand, thanks him, while still in the car. As he opens the door, the girl in the back seat pipes up, 'Good-bye,' she says. He wishes she'd stayed quiet.

17

Thursday evening, he walks Malachy along the river. The child is strapped to his chest: Sarah borrowed a contraption from the hospital. The child likes it, he does too. The child sleeps while Brendan walks, the fresh air settling both father and child. The boy is still only six weeks old, about the same weight as a bag of carrots. Light has fallen, and his surroundings are reduced to blocks of shaped shadow. The reeds rustle. The water gurgles. A duck calls out in stutters.

These weeks have been a revelation. Bathing his child. Cleaning his child. Watching his wife feed his child from her body. He has a domestic soul – a man of the household who cleans the dishes and takes out the bins. He feels the safety of the house, the barrier that Sarah produces that protects them from the rest of the world. A woman with a child is not to be trifled with. His wife reading under lamplight, an archipelago of skin creams and nappies and soothers cast around her chair. He feels such gratitude for her. She too will come around, eventually, to the cause. She too wants her boy to have the same opportunities as everyone else, to grow up in a country that he can call his own.

Two joggers pass him, going at a decent clip, effort strained on their faces, not talking to each other, just breathing heavily.

He'll tell Sarah this, when he's back home. He'll take her face in his hands, her freckle-dappled winsome face, he'll push the hair from her eyes and tell her that he hopes their boy looks like her, has her mouth, her fire, her honesty. He'll tell her this and dance her around the kitchen, no need for music.

When he gets in the door, he finds Joe in the kitchen, alone, supping on a tea.

'How's about ye?' Joe says.

'Where's herself?'

'Inside, head stuck in a book.'

He walks into the sitting room, removes the child from his chest and lays him down in the wicker basket at Sarah's feet. Her look tells him not to approach any closer, don't even think of reaching in for a kiss.

'You'll get him out of here,' she says.

'Aye.'

'Now?'

'Aye.'

He and Joe step into the wee garden out back. Joe talks in whispers.

'It'll happen in the morning.'

'Should I call in sick?'

'No, best not, just go about your day as normal.'

'You'll be there?'

'No. Haven't earned my stripes yet. Besides, it'd drag you into it if anything happens.'

Silence. Joe has something to say. Brendan waits for it.

'Is she going to be a problem?'

Brendan leans forward. 'What are you fucking asking?'

Joe runs a hand through his raggled hair, his military look well and truly set to rest.

'All right, calm down. It's just, you know.'

'I don't, as it happens.'

After she hears the front door close, Sarah walks into the kitchen.

'What's going on?'

'Nothing.'

'Your brother doesn't even want to see his own nephew?'

'He had to go. It was just a quick call.'

'I bet. Busy man, I hear.'

'Don't start.'

'Start? I'm the one who's starting this? You're starting this. You're starting it, continuing it, finishing it. Am I just supposed to sit back and watch?'

'You're supposed to take care of our son. You've enough to be doing.'

She strides to the phone, picks it up. Dials a number.

'Who are you calling?'

She doesn't answer, just leans against the wall, head tilted upwards, like she's prepared to wait all night.

He rushes towards her, grabs the phone with his left hand. Hits her with his right.

He hit her.

He hit her open-handed, not a slap, not a punch, a kind of hard push against the jaw. Okay, the heel of his hand made proper contact, caught her at the join of the jawbone, just below the ear. Enough force for her to be trying to right herself against the wall, using her hands to push herself up to standing, legs woozy and buckled. One hand on her jaw, the other in the air, finger raised, like she's trying to make a point at some debate.

He opens his mouth to speak, but what's there to say?

He walks to the bedroom, takes his copybooks from the desk and shoves them into a plastic bag. The child has started crying, of course he has. He steps past her in the corridor, her wide, disbelieving eyes. He walks outside into the rain, walks for twenty minutes, until he finds a suitable rubbish bin and stuffs the bag down into it, replaces the lid quietly. There's no one about, other than a fox, which scrutinizes him from across the road.

He wakes on the sofa, goes into the bedroom for his work clothes. Sarah's not asleep, he can tell by her breathing: she has bad sinuses and when asleep she has a slight wheeze in her breath. *A catch*, his mother would call it. He sits on the end of the bed and places a hand on her ankle. He tells her he's sorry. He tells her there's pressure at work and with the child and everything, well, he just doesn't know himself. She doesn't reply. She moves her leg away. Malachy is awake, looking at him from the basket, bobbing his head from side to side.

In the bathroom, he decides he'll run her a bath later. He'll do the ironing too, give her solid, practical proof of his good intentions.

Normal things. Normal thoughts. That's what he reminds himself as he's dressing. Pretend the day is like any other day, a few things going on, that's all. Nothing to see here, nothing to feel here, a straightforward day, he'll go to work, come home, make dinner, run a bath for herself, watch some football while he's ironing, no problem, all straightforward, nothing that can't be salvaged.

On the bus to work he's jumpy, can't help it, he keeps scanning around him, wondering if he's being watched. The bus stalls at the traffic lights on Kilmorey Street. He looks up and down the street, convinced it's a tactic, they're going to be boarded. But nothing happens, everyone just going about their normal day.

He clocks in, puts his lunchbox in his locker, looks at manifests of the ships that have docked. He makes himself a coffee and sees Warwick walk across the car park into the HMRC building. He's carrying a cake. Such a small detail in the expanse of a life.

While he waits for them to inspect the containers, he sits in his forklift and does the crossword. Lorry drivers trickle in, come over for a chat. He keeps his head down, keeps his attention on the newspaper. He wants to tell them to get the fuck out of there quicksharp.

They're unloading a container from Portsmouth, crates of fridges. He starts up and unloads the pallets into their allotted corner of the warehouse, forward and back, up and down, grateful for the repetition.

The crossword clues mangle his brain – all morning and he's only managed three. He looks at the racing page: there's a meet in Newmarket. He scans the names, might have a flutter later, then realizes he won't.

Warwick passes in the yard, on his way to the car park.

Brendan stops what he's doing, steps out of the cab, lights a cigarette, watches the man reverse out of his parking spot, drive towards the exit, exchange some words with the security guard in his booth, then turn left on the road, heading out along the river.

What's he feeling, here, now, when a man's life is about to be extinguished? He feels satisfied. He's been as pragmatic, as single-minded, as Major Warwick. He feels free, unfettered, untrivial. Finally he's taken a stand, taken a side.

The bus takes a detour that evening. From the top deck of the bus he can see Warwick's car, men in white coveralls surrounding it. Army trucks blocking off passage. Journalists flitting around the scene, speaking to people on the street. History already winding its way around the day.

18

July 1987. Nearly six years have passed. He's back in Fermanagh, has been for three years now, since his daughter, Aoife, was born. Three years of regularly intermittent rain, sodden pastures, the free-standing stone walls he would never again take for granted.

His involvement increased after that day in Warrenpoint. But he began to long for the fields of Fermanagh. He's a country boy, down to his very cells, and such things don't change. He told Sarah that he wanted a country life for his boy. When she got pregnant again, he couldn't countenance bringing up another child in the town. He wanted to provide a haven for them, a place far away from the bloodshed. He said this to her over dinner and she laughed openly, called him a hypocrite, called him many other things as well. He told her he was going back to where he had come from and he wanted her to follow, of course he did, but he wasn't going to beg.

He left his wife and child in Newry. He rented a house in Whitehill and waited.

Days like years.

She called at last. He drove back with the truck, packed up their belongings. They didn't discuss it: her decision, his ultimatum. Neither of them wanted to cast it in the light of victory or defeat. She mentioned to his mother, though, over tea, in those early days of her migration, that she understood that the hunger strikes had left no space for compromise. Perhaps all his reasoning had had an effect after all.

He had intended to step aside from the struggle, but the struggle remained, and he felt guilty, felt like he'd abandoned all sense of purpose. Coming back home had been a revelation. To bring a family back here, to present to his children the ways of his own childhood, caused him to recognize the longer patterning of time. Every day, keeping an eye on the few cattle his da kept, walking through the fields near his childhood home, reminded him that it was not just vegetation that grew from the earth but language, culture, the fluency of nature that floods the synapses and gives articulation to every motion, every thought, each word that trickles from brain to tongue. The place, his home, reasserted his sense of belonging, his fidelity to his country. The country of his people.

Now he's one of the commanders of the South Fermanagh Brigade. He doesn't carry a gun. He'll never shoot someone dead, that's been his position from the start. But he does compile case files, acquire information, plan out the procedures. Before he came back home, the South Fermanagh unit was shambolic, but now it runs like clockwork. Tight and disciplined, no outsiders, only men he's known since childhood.

He walks the fields again near his parents' house. Not to check up on the cattle – this time he's walking away from an operation, looking for cover, hoping to lay low. The target had been taken out all right, but there were complications with the exit strategy. He'd had to ditch the getaway car. He'd been waiting in Sarah's Ford Fiesta in an alleyway, waiting for two gunmen to drive up and switch cars, the final manoeuvre in the operation. Just before the gunmen arrived, a removals van had shown up – someone had picked that day to move. Just bad luck. The gunmen were seen loading into his car, sawn-off shotguns crooked in their arms. They drove away, but he had to ditch the Fiesta before they arrived at a road block. They'll meet tomorrow, all going well, for a debrief. He'll have to explain the situation to Sarah. Maybe he'll just tell her the car was stolen. Sometimes she's more willing to accept the obvious lies. First time and all that he'd ever used her car for an operation.

He's given instructions to the lads to dump the guns in a gully near his place. He'll dispose of them later. They're having to improvise, but it's not the first time. They can't just pitch the guns any place. It'll be fine. He'll deal with it later. One thing at a time.

His heartbeat is calming. It'll all be fine. He's resisting the impulse to run. The bottoms of his trousers are wet. When he climbs over a gate and into a fresh field, he can see rabbits bolting, bounding towards privacy, taking refuge, not so unlike what he himself is doing.

In truth, he could have done a better job of scouting out the route. Could have taken a few more weeks or called in help. He's been letting things slip, small things. He's finding it difficult to sustain his intensity, his sense of purpose. Partly, it's fatigue. Three and a half years is a long time to oversee operations, to make sure everything runs smoothly, define targets, scout them out, be a nurse-maid and a shrink to the armed units. Partly it's nerves. He can feel the authorities getting closer, his name becoming more prominent in the RUC files. At a check-point a couple of weeks ago, a squaddie handed back his passport but didn't let go of it. For maybe thirty seconds there was a minute struggle between them, each with a hand on the passport, the soldier looking him dead in the eye. The soldier knew who he was. Said it without saying it. And the way people treat him in brief exchanges. The farmers at marts don't joke with him like they used to, their conversations are stilted, he can see them wanting to make a polite exit as soon as possible. He's become someone to be feared. Not what he'd had in mind but an inevitable consequence of his effectiveness.

Lately he's lost his hunger, his belief in the capacity for change. For him the struggle was never really about a united Ireland. It was about a new way of ruling, a true democracy, run by and for the people. They had the opportunity to create a state free of elites, unbeholden to market forces, a state that had enough agency and will to truly respond to the needs of the people. No such thing as an underclass. No such thing as exploitation of the simple worker. The hunger strikes were about a vision of purity. That's where their potency lay.

But recently he's watched the slow creep of the

movement towards parliamentary politics. He's watched men on podiums soak up the attention, the adulation of the crowds. Constitutional politics inevitably leads to the cult of the individual. And the individuals are inevitably preening men, jacked up on notions of their own importance. At rallies, he can feel the sting has been removed from their sense of purpose. Their leaders are no longer visionaries but used-car salesmen spouting meaningless sentences, their words chosen only for their popularity at the ballot box. And the potent rage of the people, on the streets, has been watered down; the immediacy of sacrifice has waned. The hunger strikers have been fashioned into icons, and all the blood has seeped away from their actions.

He nears his parents' house. He'll have to find some excuse to say why he walked there. If he says the car broke down, his da'll only insist on driving out to it to take a look. The only thing the man knows how to do is to lord it over his son. No matter how far he climbs, his da would still happily snap off a few rungs of the ladder.

His da has retired, passed along the cattle lorry when Brendan moved back. The engine, base, chassis, remain the same, but it looks different, Brendan's made it his own. He tore down the orange slats of the sidings, ripped away the frame. He replaced it with welded grids of box iron and iron sheeting, painted them with Hammerite. It definitely looks better, but now the cattle are reluctant to enter it. They leap uncertainly on to the entrance ramp, then bound in when he thrashes them with a stick. Brendan keeps it parked in his parents' driveway, no space for it in Whitehill. He might have to drive the kids home in it tonight, pick up Sarah in it. She won't exactly be thrilled.

He walks in the door, doesn't need to knock, and finds the kids at the kitchen table, tucking into some black pudding and baked beans. Their hair is wet, they've been out in the garden with their gran for the afternoon. The radio is on, the local station, a match report from Enniskillen, that dramatic convoluted tone GAA men have when recounting a game, like a play that's going on in their head. He kisses both kids on their crowns. He's not usually that affectionate, but he's so relieved to see them, to step back into calm normality.

'You're all right, son?'

'Aye, fine.'

'You look a bit bedraggled.'

'Aye, rushing about trying to get things done while they're not around. They were no bother?'

'Not in the slightest. Great wee workers.'

He moves to put on the kettle. A hot brew is the least he deserves. The broadcast moves to the news headlines. He wants to turn it off but his ma is already there, turns the volume up. A news addict. She watches the six o'clock and the nine o'clock on the TV. It's a moral compulsion for her, another one of her forms of devotion. He respects it. Some people make a decision to stay blind to the events around them, but that wouldn't align with the educator in her.

A Catholic man has been shot in a betting shop in Fivemiletown.

He turns to his ma and gestures towards the kids chomping away. She nods, turns the radio off.

A Catholic man shot in Fivemiletown.

A Catholic man.

'Cup for yourself,' he says.

'Aye, go on, then.'

He roots out some biscuits from the cupboard, puts them on a plate. Scalds a pot, fires some teabags in, pours the water, brings it to the table. He's watching his hands, looking to see if a shake will betray him, but they're steady. He avoids eye contact with his ma, not that it's difficult, it's not something they're accustomed to anyway. He sips his tea and looks out of the window. He turns around and asks Mal about his gardening. The young lad has ketchup on his face. He'll deal with it later. Mal chips away, talks about the contents of his granny's greenhouse. They were weeding and plucking sideshoots off the tomato plants. Mal could talk for Ireland, a characteristic that he's grateful for now – it gives him some time to compose himself.

It's his fault. He knows it immediately. A few weeks ago he'd seen a car in a petrol station in Maguiresbridge, a green Chrysler Alpine. He remembered it from years before, when it used to drop in to their next-door neighbour, Cecil Cox, the RUC reservist. It was a one-of-a-kind car. He followed the Chrysler, just to make sure, and it drove right into the RUC barracks in town. A week or two later he saw it again at the same petrol station – he'd made it his business to return there regularly. He followed it to the bookies that time, a Saturday, figured out the man had a weakness for the horses, a fatal one, not that the man had the first fucking clue.

What kind of Catholic drives into an RUC barracks?

He can't taste the tea, but then tea is tasteless anyway.

He looks around the kitchen, at his ma, feels nothing. A strange house with a strange woman in it, but it's always been that way, hasn't it? He feels empty inside. His body has no reaction. He looks at his kids, feels love, pride, but only theoretically, only as an abstract concept, like it's just something he'd write down on a questionnaire.

He's numb.

The only surprise is that the numbness isn't the result of shock. He's been this way – he realizes now – for a long time.

He's been absent even from himself. The only reason he's noticing now is because he's sure he should feel *something*: regret, revulsion, fear. He thinks of his ma's cousin Bridie, God rest her, so composed, so monotone, not because of some inner peace, that reassuring faith that she so piously espoused, but because she had settled into stone. Repress something long enough and you end up being so condensed that nothing can get in or out. Look at his da. Can't even find the motivation to shove some pieces around a chess board; the garden's piled up with weeds. He hasn't even taken to the bottle just in case he'd let slip some raw emotion. Hard to scrub away the tracks of your upbringing.

'Robin,' Aoife says.

'Aye, tell him about the robin,' his ma says.

His mind turns to practicalities. The guns he's stored in their house will have to be moved. He can't count on people's silence now; there may well be reports. They'll find Sarah's car by this evening. Those removals men will be sourced. Enough about his feelings, there's things to get done. There're hot weapons in a gulley right behind their house. He puts his cup in the sink.

'Right, both of yous, time to hit the road.'

They're not finished. They look up.

'Come on. Now.'

'Leave them be, Brendan.'

'Now.'

He picks up Aoife in his arms; she's still holding a fork. She cries with the sudden change in pace. He plucks the fork from her, has to fight her for it.

'Now,' he says to Malachy, who is less resistant, used to orders.

His ma looks at him, wants to say something but holds her tongue. Parenting young kids is never easy.

They drive the cattle lorry to the hospital to pick up Sarah. They're stopped at a checkpoint along the way. There are probably journalists on the scene by now, asking questions, getting the lay of the land.

The soldier asks him where he's headed.

'Erne Hospital, to pick up their mother.'

'Strange mode of transport you've got.'

'Aye. Other one's in the garage.'

'That a fact?'

The soldier nods to his colleagues, one hand on the butt of his rifle. He indicates that they should check the contents of the truck. They peer in through the slats. Nothing to see. One of them climbs up the sides, scans it. All good. They're waved through. They pass a man having his car stripped down, two soldiers throwing out the contents of his boot, the man leaning against the car, hands on the roof, an abundance of guns.

They wait at the hospital entrance; they're early. The kids are still upset, whining and sobbing beside him. He asks Aoife what a dog says, what a cow says, a cat. She doesn't bite, determined to be annoyed with his behaviour.

When Sarah arrives, they're still restless.

'Where's my car?' she says.

'We had a breakdown.'

'And you couldn't have borrowed your da's?'

'He was using it.'

'Like hell he was. You can't be hauling kids around in this thing, Brendan. Look at their faces, they're pure flustered.'

'We hit a checkpoint. It rattled them.'

She sits inside, puts Aoife on her knee. He starts driving. Traffic is so heavy they're only crawling along, no point in bothering with a seatbelt. Sarah's gestures are huge, full-arm stretches – it's what she does when she's vexed.

'You didn't have to bring them. You could have left them at your folks' place.'

'I've been doing enough toing and froing today.'

'Oh, really? Lord have mercy on you? You got a bit tired today, did you?'

'The lawnmower needed fixing, so I had to go to the garden centre.'

'You heard about Fivemiletown?' she said.

'I did.'

Testing him? He's not sure. He'll just play it straight. She'll not question him in front of the kids.

The spaces in their marriage are taking their toll. He's always out. She has a point. He's not unsympathetic to her position.

They're held up again. A long tailback out of town. He wants to turn on the radio, but doesn't, won't. It'll help no one.

Sarah plays *I Spy* with the two. It calms them, distracts them. He stays silent.

She's resolute, slow to complain, accepting. He doesn't take it for granted. So many other lives she could have lived. She doesn't talk about the smallness of the place, the lack of cultural knowledge, erudition. Her parents visit once every year at most. He knows they look down their noses at the place, even her father, their daughter lost down a boreen – and yet she doesn't grumble. Her work, no doubt, aids him. It's not as easy to wallow in complaints when you work with the sick. She builds people up, he tears them down. He's not unaware of the paradox. Maybe this is what fuels them. Life finding definition in opposites.

At the checkpoint, the soldier sees the nurse's uniform and doesn't even bother to tap on their window.

He thought he'd be the one to provide ease, reassurance. Maybe he will someday, and the roles will change. Isn't this what marriage is, wearing the other's pelt?

When they get home, he takes out the colouring books and they stay out until bathtime. The kids forgive his earlier rashness. He puts them to bed, both of them sharing a room. As the elder, Malachy gets to pick the bedtime reading. Aoife goes along with his selection, reasonable, trusting. Which one of them did she inherit that from? Lights out.

He leaves, lets them fall asleep, then returns after ten minutes to look at them, in the light of the open door. His children's restful breathing the most peaceful sound in existence. He stays there, he doesn't know how long. He could fall asleep leaning against this door jamb.

A Catholic man. *Shane Moore.* He catches the name from the sound of the TV news drifting up from the sitting room. He blocks the rest out, doesn't want to know the particularities.

He doesn't let guilt in, he learned to block it a few years ago. A war has casualties. A war has collateral damage. He didn't wish for any of this to be brought upon his people. He looks at Malachy and knows, someday, his son will ask him to account for his actions and he believes he'll do it with pride. He'll talk about how he defended his people against the occupiers, tell him how a free and fair Ireland was birthed from the pain of others. He'll explain the word 'gerrymandering', tell him his people were once second-class citizens on their own soil. Tell him that nothing comes easy, without sacrifice.

The Moore family have been given an opportunity to become part of a noble purpose. It's a gift, in a way, even if they can't see it right now.

He says this to himself and tries, honestly tries, to believe it. Discipline is all that's needed to forge a new outlook on the world. Discipline and reading, which are the same thing when it comes down to it. Sharpness of body, fleetness of mind.

Enough of the domestics. He needs to get rid of the weapons out back. He has a hard rule: don't panic. Let everyone in the house think things are progressing normally and he'll believe it himself. He washes his hands in the bathroom, then slips out the back door.

It's not dark yet, but he'd be foolish to leave it any longer. Who knows when their door'll be kicked in? He climbs over the stile at the bottom of the garden and into the neighbour's field. The gully is at the end of it. He just hopes the lads found it, didn't get confused. He reaches the place and kneels down, looks around him as he does so, half expecting the countryside to stand to attention, to see ranks of SAS troops rise up in camouflage. He takes a breath. Listens. Nothing.

If he's going to move the guns, he needs to do it now. He rolls up his sleeves and dips his arms into the murky water. Can't feel anything. He keeps his arms down there, fingers touching the soft muck at the bottom, the water cold and slick on his skin, and he shuffles along, bent over, waiting for his catch. He should have told the lads to put down a marker, to save him this hassle, but, then again, that'd be inviting trouble. Five minutes turns into ten. His hands are numb. He's not even certain he'll be able to feel the hard metal at this point. Maybe they stored them in another spot, decided against the gully. He's worried now – he can't call them, can't drop over and ask, their places may well be under surveillance. And then, at last, his fingers land on something hard and slim. One gun. He pulls it out and dumps it on the ground. No ambush at least, that's for sure. They'd already be on him by now if they'd been lying there in wait.

Another gun. He drops it on the ground and slaps his hands to get some circulation back into them, wipes them dry on his trousers.

Light is dropping slowly. He listens again. He's alone.

He walks through the fields to the lake. It takes fifteen minutes, and he feels every one of them. He's so exposed out here. There's no explaining to do if he's caught holding two guns. He arrives at last, stashes the guns in a ditch and makes sure the jetty is clear of people. He comes back for them and drops them into his uncle's boat, pushes it into the water and steps in himself. He rows out to Namafin Island. There's a weapons bunker there. He's tempted to just drop the guns in the water, be done with them. But they've been given strict instructions not to take short cuts. They can't afford to be complacent. The weapons bunker is too valuable for any tracks to be left.

Still, though, he's glad to be out in the air. The stillness of the evening light, it's what he needs. Clear his head. Clean out any blame. He wasn't to know. Of course he should have been more thorough, run the plates through their contact in the tax office, but he was certain. He would have sworn at gunpoint that he recognized the man's face – a situation he may yet find himself in.

He reaches the small cove, ties the boat up. He waits and listens: nothing. He makes his way along the track in the gloaming, arrives, eventually at the ruin, down the staircase he helped to build. Into the bunker. He leans the two guns against the wall. He wonders if he should have brought something to mark them out as unusable, but the mud on them should be enough to show that. Anyway, it's unlikely anyone will come here without notifying him first. Stacks of green metal boxes around the room. Enough artillery here to make a difference if, or when, it comes down to it.

Sarah's asleep when he comes in. He curls up against her. She's too out of it to resist. He is grateful for the warmth of her body.

He tells her early in the morning. He hasn't slept, thinking over his decision, watching the shadows creep and drift on the ceiling. A raid is probably coming, no point denying it, all of his instincts point towards it. She's shocked, angry, no more than he expected. He moves her quickly towards practicality, a language she understands: she and the kids will stay with his parents until it passes. She threatens to go back to Belfast, but he knows she won't. She's had plenty of reason to do it before now.

He brings them to his parents' house – still using the truck – before they've even had breakfast. Malachy will stay in the room Brendan had as a boy, tractor posters still on the ceiling. Aoife will sleep with Sarah, give her company. His da is still in bed. His ma is pottering about the kitchen, still in her dressing gown. When they enter she freezes, a teaspoon in her hand.

He pulls his mother into the hallway.

'Sarah and the kids need to stay here for a few days.'

'What for? What's happening?'

'It looks like we'll be raided.'

The shame on her face punches him in the gut. A look he hasn't seen since childhood. Does she have an entire storeroom of expressions behind those eyes?

Sarah has started cooking eggs; already she's making it into an adventure for the kids. He goes outside to do some jobs in the yard. He doesn't want to eat with them – let them get on with it. He comes back in when it's time for Malachy to leave for school.

The young lad is delighted to sit in a big truck. He leans forward towards the windscreen and looks out over the road, king of all he surveys.

Tommy Devine, his operational commander, is waiting across the road when he emerges from taking Malachy to his classroom. He returns to the truck and follows Devine for a few miles until they reach an old quarry. Devine steps out, comes over to Brendan. The man is in his sixties, built like a shithouse, huge hands, a life on building sites.

'You made a right hash of it, didn't you.'

'I didn't know he was Catholic.'

'You didn't follow up. You got sloppy. I gave you too much rein. How could you have been so fucking stupid? I'm under the cosh now too, you know.'

He's never respected Devine. Too fond of the drink, a loose wire, plans his own operations on a whim. Bloodthirsty, erratic. Brendan has bailed him out enough times.

'You'll go to Dundalk,' Devine says. Dundalk is down south, where Brendan can't be charged.

'I'm not moving my family.'

'It's not a request.'

'Fine. Shoot me so.'

Devine waits, gives it space.

'The others are already there.'

'With their wives and young kids?'

'We'll sort out the arrangements, don't worry about any of that.'

'Aye, I've seen what they look like.'

Devine waits again. Little good it'll do. Does Devine think he'll change his mind based on a minute or two of silence?

He goes back to Whitehill. Waits for the inevitable. He sleeps fully clothed on the sofa: they'll not catch him in a state of undress. The next morning he's supposed to go to the mart in Clones to pick up some cattle. He calls to cancel. The farmer will badmouth him to everyone in the area, complain about his turning down good money. Had to be done. He doesn't want soldiers trooping into his house with him not there. He hates waiting, hates idling. He decides to do up the bedroom, may as well make use of the time. It might even take the edge off when Sarah eventually agrees to come home.

He buys some wallpaper in the hardware shop in town, blue flowers on a cream background. He sponges the walls in their bedroom with hot water, then goes at them with a scraper. He stays away from his parents' house, he doesn't even call, no sense in upsetting the stalemate.

The phone stays silent.

No banging on the door.

No word from the rest of the active service unit or higher up – they're keeping wide of him for the moment, standard procedure. He eats porridge in the morning. He roasts a chicken and picks at it for a few days until it's finished. Then he roasts another one. He finishes the bedroom and starts in on the hallway. He buys a copy of the *Irish News* while he's out paint shopping. A headline: IRA SUSPENDS VOLUNTEERS IN MOORE OPERATION. Hardly a surprise, but they could at least have told him before it leaked. He paints the hall in magnolia. Then the kids' bedrooms.

Another two days, that makes it a full week. An Opel Kadett pulls into the driveway. He can tell the make and model by the sound of its engine. At least now he can get it over with, take his scolding, bring his kids home.

Devine steps out from the back seat; he doesn't recognize the two men in front.

Devine looks at his paint-splattered clothes. 'Hard at it?'

'Aye, keeping busy.'

'Plenty of time to kill.'

'Aye.'

'There's worse ways.'

'Aye. Getting sensible in my old age.'

'We'll be in Dundalk for a few nights. You'd better let herself know.'

A few nights is the least he can expect – a debrief is inevitable.

'Right. You'll give me a minute.'

'Aye, no bother.' He looks at the open door. 'Magnolia, is it? Maura has been at me for the same job, you'll not mind if I take a look.'

The politeness unnerves him. Devine's not one for social niceties. He goes upstairs, changes his clothes, packs a few things in a sportsbag. He writes a note on her good stationery, seals it, leaves it on the dresser. He doesn't say where he's headed, just tells her it'll be a few days. He doesn't write that he loves her; it feels too ingratiating in the circumstances.

He comes back down the stairs. Devine is still in the hallway, arms folded. He walks towards the door.

'You're not going to call her?'

'I left a note.'

'I'll need to see it.'

'You're fucking joking me?'

'I'm not.'

He walks back up the stairs again, brings back the note, doesn't unseal it – let Devine feel bad about it.

He doesn't. He tears back the envelope. Reads it. Puts

the note on the mantelpiece. 'You're some charmer,' he says.

'Fuck right off.'

They drive for a couple of hours, small country roads, no checkpoints. From the few words the men up front say, he reckons they're from Belfast. Probably high up, part of the internal security squad.

They park outside a two-storey house on the outskirts of town. There are no other houses nearby. It's the kind of place where you could make some noise without being heard.

Devine leads him to a room upstairs. It's mid-afternoon, but the curtains are pulled and a sheet has been draped in front of them – a murky light hangs through the room. There's nothing in it but a chair that faces the wall opposite the window. He sits. Two men enter; he can't see their faces, but he can tell from their build that they're different from the ones in the car. It's likely they're ex-prisoners: these are the kind of dirty jobs they give to members who've been flagged. Devine leaves them to it.

How did you decide on the target?

He explains the previous connection with Cox. Talks them through the petrol station, the Chrysler pulling into the RUC depot.

One of them speaks in whispers close to his ear. He tells him that Shane Moore worked for the gas board; he probably went there to check the meter.

He can smell the man's breath, a smoker. Whatever

effect he's trying to achieve, it's not working. He's not intimidated. He's made an error, but it's not a shooting offence.

All Brendan can think is that the man should have refused to enter an RUC depot. It's no place for Catholics. If he was too stupid to understand that, maybe he deserved what he got. He says this out loud, thinks it might make an impression, reassert his commitment to the cause. The men don't respond.

They ask him about his relationship with Cecil Cox. They ask about his da's relationship with Cecil Cox. Cox hasn't lived in Ireland for fifteen years. He tells them as much. A friendship with an RUC man – even a vanished one – is a little too close for comfort. The line of questioning unnerves him; he's on weaker ground than he thought.

Why did you want this man killed? Did you think he knew something?

Tell us again about your da. We heard he sold Cox's cattle after Cox moved to England.

He's been trained to resist interrogation, but that applies only to police questioning. It's harder this way: he can't resort to shutting down, he has to remain open and compliant, can't look like he's screening his words. He talks through his da's history. He talks about Cecil Cox. He tries not to be complimentary about the man, but doesn't talk him down either. He plays it as straight as he can.

What does your da do now, since you have his truck?

He tells them his da is retired.

Plenty of time on his hands, so. Plenty of opportunity for loose talk.

He tells them he's not responsible for his da. If they think he's a grass, they should bring him in for questioning. That shuts them up.

The light on the wall fades away. He can't tell how long they've been at this. They ask him again about the petrol station, he tells it again, tries not to repeat details, which he knows they'd take as a sign of lying. He wants a drink of water but doesn't want to ask. Right now, thirst is a weakness.

They ask about the operation. He gives them the details. They want timelines, trying to figure out if he had the opportunity to meet up with any detectives, spill his guts out.

Over and over. The incident gets replayed but always from the same angle. There is no other angle. There's just what he experienced.

No doubt they've questioned Marco and Dunner, the two gunmen. How loyal, he wonders, will they be?

He wonders if they're putting it on, this concern for Moore. He doesn't share it. The man is a name amongst many names. There are greater concerns. History is always bigger, more powerful, more important than the individual.

A whisper in his ear, *You've placed the movement in a bad light.* Does the man not know that the movement is great enough to withstand any blow? The movement is not a choice, it's an inevitability.

They leave the room. Devine comes back in.

'You're still suspended.'

'Aye. They made that clear enough.'

Things fall back into place. He goes to his parents'. His ma can look at him again. She's fallen into a pattern that he's seen in other mothers: she has no resort other than excuses, lies – what's the alternative? The kids are full of questions. Did he bring them anything from his trip? Did he go to the beach? He shows them his arm, pretends the paint splatters are freckles. Aoife believes him. Mal isn't so gullible. Una is there, up from Dublin for a few days. She won't look at him. She's beyond him now, no sense trying to talk her round to his perspective, she'd pick holes out of every sentence that came from his mouth. His da eats in silence, watches TV. He'd take him out fishing but he has to avoid the lake.

19

August. He begins writing again, at night, at the kitchen table. A memoir of sorts, not that anyone will ever read it. He writes about his aunt Bridie, in her grey housecoat, listening to *Sunday Miscellany* on the radio. Her Morris Minor. He writes about caravan holidays in Bundoran as a kid, playing the slot machines, watching the pennies build up on the edge of the machine, right above the coin drop, tantalizing him and Joe. The crazy-golf course they had there, how he'd be the first to arrive and the last to leave, thinking he could master the thing, treating it like it was a real sport. The girls playing tennis in jumpers and jeans, the way they moved their feet, the way they shimmied around the court, a kind of dance, the way their hips sprang out when they hit the ball, all grunting effort. He doesn't know why he's doing this; it clears him somehow, reminds him of who he was before he became who he is.

Devine sends word that he wants to meet early on Friday evening. When the headlights of Devine's car sweep up the drive, Sarah looks at him, shakes her head, wells up with tears. She thought he was done, out, that the Moore event was the final straw. He didn't say as much but he didn't disabuse her of this opinion either. He hasn't seen her cry in a long time. He's about to say something but stops himself. She looks lost; her hand wobbles on her knee. She resembles a pensioner, arm wavering; she reminds him a little of Mrs Donnelly, way back when. She's paid a price for him, no doubt about it.

He gets in the front seat. Just the two of them. 'No others,' he says.

'No. Not tonight.'

'Where are we off to?'

'Clones.'

'You're not serious.'

'Do I sound like I'm kidding?'

Clones is across the border. It's where they meet the South Armagh Brigade when there's a big operation in the works.

They pull into a farmyard in the middle of nowhere. Bits of machinery scattered all around them, fertilizer bags on pallets, sheets of corrugated iron and old windows stacked up against sheds. A few mangy dogs eye them up suspiciously.

He follows Devine towards the farmhouse, three cars with Northern regs parked outside. He doesn't like the look of it. He still hasn't had an official reconciliation with the leadership. Officially, he's still suspended. This could be a deeper interrogation, one that has a purpose at the end of it: he's brought the movement into disrepute, drawn attention to himself. If they were to take him out, this is the kind of place where it would happen. He wants to run, but then where would he go? Even if he did get away there'd be repercussions for Sarah, maybe Joe and Una.

They step into a smoke-filled kitchen. Five men are playing cards – there's a full ashtray and a half-empty bottle of whiskey in the middle of the table. Joe is one of them. Such a relief he feels like crying. They wouldn't take him out in front of his brother. It's not unheard of to include family members in tests of loyalty, but Joe wouldn't countenance it, even if they tried to put him up to it.

Joe puts down his cards walks up to him. The other men keep talking, an intensity in the air. The brothers stand by the door. They haven't seen each other since Christmas. Joe's put on weight since, looks portly and self-satisfied, doesn't exactly give off the air of a Spartan warrior.

'How are the kids?' Joe says quietly.

'Why are you even fuckin' asking? They hardly know who you are.'

'I've been kind of busy.'

'Aye, surely. We're all busy, Joe.'

Joe glares at him. *Don't start. Not here.*

A man walks over. It's Cathal, Donegal accent, the man he met in Carlingford. He's older, even more authoritative now. He's grown a dark beard, muscled up. Still that same firm stance, firm handshake, none of the whiskey gleam Joe has in his eyes. He carries the assuredness of someone in charge. 'Good to see you again,' he says to Brendan. 'That business with Moore was a mess, but we'll put it behind us.'

Brendan just nods. *Behave*, he tells himself.

Cathal turns to the room and announces that they'll begin. The others down their cards immediately, no complaints, and pass into the living room, sit in a semi-circle by the fire. Cathal stands in front of them, launches into a speech, no preliminaries.

He talks clearly, cogently. He echoes thoughts that Brendan has been running through his head for months. A rot has set in. The IRA are taking a back seat in the struggle. The resources of the republican movement are being directed towards constitutional politics. The Sinn Féin leadership in Belfast are moving towards ending the military campaign either by ineptitude or stealth. They're engaging in gutter politics and look where it's getting them. Thirteen per cent share of the vote in the European elections. A display of weakness like that is making it gradually impossible to manoeuvre the people of the South to get behind their cause. They need a mass movement south of the border which can be channelled into a renewed military campaign. They'd built their campaigns on firm foundations, but the Shinners were turning those foundations into sand.

Brendan's been in similar situations before – review meetings, planning meetings – but he's never seen any-one hold a space like this. Usually there are nervous half-jokes, a smattering of slagging to warm up the group. Not this time.

They need a galvanizing event, Cathal says, some-thing that those on the fence can get behind. What better place than Bobby Sands's own constituency? He outlines a plan they've been discussing, a bombing on

Remembrance Day. How dare they honour British troops in the country they're occupying? Time to remind everyone of the truth of their circumstances.

A vote. The men raise their hands. He raises his hand. It's only after they stand and go back to their card game that he takes in what just happened, it all came about so quickly. Have they really just agreed to bomb a civilian parade?

He's silent in the car on the way home, lets Devine talk. The words wash over him. He doesn't sleep that night. Nor the next night either. He grasps maybe ten hours in the entire week. The face that stares back at him in the mirror is haunted: there's no sense of anyone or anything beneath his features and even these are alien to him. Is his nose really shaped like that? Have his ears always stuck out? He can't tell if he's losing or gaining weight.

At checkpoints he mumbles his replies, can't look the soldiers in the eye, can't muster any indignation when they decide to search his truck. The days move and he moves with them, developments happening of their own accord. He's a bystander who knows where to be, what to say, what to do. The life he's living – the meals and baths and bedtime stories – feels like it's happening retrospectively, a story he's recounting at some future event.

They gather at the jetty near Killadeas, five of them: himself, Joe, Cathal, two other South Armagh lads. Cathal felt that their armoury near Keady was compromised, so he's decided to use Brendan's dump on Namafin. It also holds the advantage of easy access to Enniskillen: they won't have far to travel. They've arrived separately, three of the cars scouting for the other two that contained munitions, SAM-7 missiles, anti-aircraft guns and the bomb. Devine had laid out the route well in advance, and they'd patrolled it continuously over the previous few days, scanning it every few hours for activity. Brendan and Joe had covered the Fermanagh section; the South Armagh lads had taken care of the rest.

Now that they're here, there's already a sense of cautious relief spreading through the group. It's a warm, still August night, the stars are out. No ripples on the lake. They had discussed rowing back and forth, but elected to use an engine. It meant only one trip, and there were never any patrol boats on the lake. It was a perfect blackspot, which is why Brendan had chosen it in the first place. He steps into the boat – his uncle Frank's – and primes the engine while the others load the cargo, taking care to distribute the weight evenly. They spread a tarp over it, tucking it underneath the crates to secure it. Brendan pulls the ripcord as Joe unties the hawsers.

They pull out, the men hunkering down against the sides. The boat slices easily through the still water, separating it into smooth, generous ridges. After a few minutes, despite the risks they're taking, there emerges a generous solidarity that Brendan has seen a thousand times on the water, the boat imbuing them with a common purpose, a sense of expanse. One of the lads hands around a hipflask and a pack of biscuits. They drink and eat and there are a couple of muffled laughs, although Brendan can't make out what's being said. The trip takes fifteen minutes. They pull into a cove on the western end of the island, his usual spot. Devine and Joe jump out, knee deep in water. He throws them two ropes and they wrap them around a tree, using the tension to guide the boat inwards until it touches the pebbled under-surface. They all disembark. Brendan pulls the tarp off, and they unload the crates. The ground around the cove is unsteady: he uses his torch to point out the secure places where they should drop the cargo. They work quickly. He tells Joe to lead them down the trail, while he secures the boat. The men move off, grunting with the weight they're carrying. It'll take a bit of back and forth, but they should be out of there within a half-hour. A quick check of the lake for signs of unusual activity.

A lovely night, a still night. He looks at the stars. He's always felt at home on the lake, a refuge, time moves differently here.

The men come back, load up again. As they walk back down the trail, Brendan hears a rustle to his right, very faint, hears it again. An animal maybe? Definitely not a bird. He walks carefully towards it. It could be nothing: a plastic sheet caught on a branch. Through some bushes he can make out a figure in the moonlight, a teenager, skinny, his white T-shirt almost glowing in the clear night. He looks in the direction of the boat. The others will probably be gone for a few minutes more. He freezes, he thinks about letting the boy be. But it's too great a risk, he can't compromise the location. And if Cathal finds the boy, who knows what he'll do. A few months ago he probably wouldn't have cared, but Shane Moore's death has worked its way into his bones. He strides towards the lad, tries to keep his footsteps as light as possible. The boy turns, and Brendan can see his face now, muddled, terrified. He recognizes the boy. He knows he's seen him in town, but can't quite place him.

'What's your name, son?' he says, trying to sound authoritative with his whisper, not that it matters – the wee buck is practically shivering with fright.

'Simon.'

'Simon what?'

'Hanlon.'

'You're Peter's young lad?'

'Aye, that's right.'

'What the fuck are you doing out here?'

'I'm camping.'

'Aye, well, you picked a bad spot for it. Are you alone?'

A pause. The kid is fifteen, sixteen, maybe. All protective, trying to be a man.

'Tell the truth now. If I have to go looking, I'll have to call the others.'

'There's a girl with me. Her name is Esther.'

'You've the wee Dutch girl in there.'

'Aye.'

'She's pregnant, aye?'

'Aye.'

'Ach, for fuck sake, man. You're lucky it was me who found you. Go back now. Don't make a sound. Don't shift until the morning. And if you breathe a word of this, son. I don't need to tell you.'

'No.'

'Go on. Quick. And be sure you're quiet.'

The others return to collect the rest of the cargo. He joins them and they make their way to the bunker. The lads pop the lids on the metal crates, hand around the munitions, excited as children. They take particular delight in the SAM-7s, long and grey, thick as an eel, Russian-made, Cyrillic writing on the box. They pass them around, take pleasure in the way the light bounces off them, treating them like they're bottles of aged whiskey. The bomb is in a crate of its own. They open the lid but don't take it out, just gaze down on it as if it's a sleeping child. Made by their technician in Ballinamore. He's heard Joe speak of the man: they talk about him with reverence, a chemistry graduate from Queen's. It comes in two plastic tubs, each about twice the size of a lunchbox. Cathal lifts the lids, talks him through the configuration. One is filled with pink ammonium nitrate pills – fertilizer – that have been ground down to increase their potency. In the other are two large freezer bags: one contains gelignite, while the other holds a combination of diesel, sugar and nitro-glycerine. An electronic timer sits to the side, covered in clingfilm, two red leads curled up underneath. All they have to do is add a battery to the timer, set it and connect the leads to the gelignite. The whole thing looks harmless, a novelty, the kind of contraption a teenage boy might put together. It's the timing device that gets him, a small black box, like a wee alarm clock. No room for ambiguity, no turning back once it's set, no control over what happens; they can only set the time and then let chaos reign.

Then again, the Hanlon boy might well report them. He can't deny that part of him hopes he does.

They head back. The lake is still. Out beyond the turbulence of their wee craft, the world is solid, defined, timeless. Trees, islands, a slate-black sky, starlight punctuating the heavens. Simon Hanlon. Fifteen, sixteen. At sixteen Brendan was still in school, ditching classes, smoking behind the bike shed, not the faintest idea what his life held in store.

20

My seizures have stopped. It happened progressively, yet
steadily, a kind of winding down. In the first week of
writing, I had only three episodes. Then the following
week it was one, and the week after that it was none. It's
September now, and I've been without a seizure for
almost two months. The city feels welcoming now, less
threatening, less aggressive; it's taken on that particularly
clear quality of light that arrives in autumn. The air has
cooled, people are less sweaty, less irritable – at least by
New York standards – and everything feels like it's been
cleansed from the muggy humidity of summer. The
block parties and barbecues have ended. The private-
school kids are back in their uniforms, wearing their little
backpacks like intrepid explorers. Rhythms are re-
establishing themselves. In a couple of weeks, Washington
Square Park will be filled with college students poring
over notes, lounging between classes, the music students
using the benches as impromptu rehearsal studios.

I feel like I'm part of a milieu again, part of the great
cascading horde. The empty spaces in my life have gradually begun to fill in, to be populated by people and
practicalities. I go to the office two days a week, gradually easing myself back into my previous role, and I
find reassurance in the sense of a linked grid around me,

the hushed productivity that reverberates around an office space. My colleagues in their casual workwear tap heedlessly away on their keyboards, sending information this way and that, exchanging ideas, tracing lines, rotating brightly coloured shapes in the three-dimensional space behind their screens. There's a sense of order and command, a sturdy chain of action which ordains that a scribbled diagram can eventually become a building, something solid that people will walk through, sit inside, stare out of, the intangible made realized.

When I step into a store, I'm no longer captivated by the vast selection of goods, by shape and colour, branding, packaging. The East River is only a river, the trees in Seward Park are simply trees – they still retain their lines and colour, the leaves continue to sway indolently, but they don't carry the resonances of previous months, they no longer hold the capacity to ignite my nervous system. I suppose all of this is a way of saying that I no longer feel raw.

I came across a Japanese phrase recently: *Mono no aware*. It describes an experience of beauty which is intermingled with a wistful sadness from the awareness of its passing – a kind of bittersweet appreciation of transience. It feels accurate, a perfect summation of my ambient state. I say it out loud sometimes, to no one. I like the feel of the words on my lips, *Mono no aware* – the words confirming the sensation – and I find it so reassuring that a foreign culture, centuries ago, came up with a phrase that feels so apt.

Of course, I'm grateful for the reprieve. There's no

guarantee that I won't be thrown into convulsions at any given minute; it all may flare up again tomorrow, or an hour from now, and a bittersweet appreciation of anything will be the least of my concerns. I remind myself, constantly, to be appreciative that I'm at least temporarily in the clear. No surgeon will tinker with my brain – not in the near-future anyway – and Dr Ptacek has reduced my medication. Yet I can't help but sense that I feel less alive somehow, blind to the constant stream of micro-miracles that unfold all around me, at any given moment of the day.

I met Esther this morning. Last week, I emailed her all of the pages that I've written. I'm not certain why, maybe I wanted her approval. I don't have anyone else to show it to. Maybe I needed her permission to write about her.

She called yesterday, told me she'd take a train down to see me. We arranged to meet on the steps of the Met. She was early. As I walked up Fifth Avenue, I could see her from a distance, spread over the steps, waiting for me. She looked so peaceful, even from fifty yards away. Her arms were behind her, supporting her weight, her head was tilted towards the sky, her eyes closed, her long skirt spread out before her, rendering her legs invisible. She stayed in that position even as I approached and said, 'Hi.' She didn't reply, just smiled in response as I sat beside her. I found that I couldn't share her stillness; my mind was ticking over. I was nervous, I didn't know what she'd make of my rambling pages. I wanted to ask, but didn't want to break her repose. I knew she'd tell me in her own time.

Finally, she opened her eyes. 'Ready?' she asked, as she rose and straightened out her skirt.

When we got through the security line, she picked up a map and looked at it.

'You know where we're going?' I said.

'I do,' she said. She told me that whenever she visited, she'd usually pick a room at random and choose one painting and sit with it. It was the only way she could navigate a place as huge as the Met.

'But not today,' I said.

'No, today we're going to Gallery Two Eighteen.'

So we paid and climbed the main staircase and made our way through the labyrinth of rooms until we came to our destination.

Two-Eighteen was one of the smaller rooms. She didn't have to point me towards her choice. The walls were filled with dull pastoral images – goats frolicking on manicured fields, lute players – with one exception, a painting by Georges de La Tour called *The Penitent Magdalen*. It wasn't a large canvas but it dominated the room; its strength cast all of the other work into irrelevance. I thought Esther might give me some context, explain it to me, but she didn't, she just sat on the bench and began looking. I joined her.

I'd seen it before in an art book somewhere. The painting was very dark. It was a study of Mary Magdalen sitting beside a nightstand. Her red skirt was the only striking colour in it, otherwise it was all muted: whites and browns and golds. On the nightstand, a candle stood in front of a mirror. Mary Magdalen looked like she was prepared for bed: her clothes were loosened, her blouse undone. Her sleek hair seemed recently brushed. On her lap lay a skull which faced outwards from her body, a memento mori. Her hands rested on top of it, with her fingers entwined.

I remembered what I'd read about Mary Magdalen. She was a woman in distress, who had demons cast out of her. And I remembered she was the first to see Jesus after his resurrection. Stepping into his tomb, she found two angels sitting where his body had lain, then mistook the risen Christ for a gardener.

Her face was turned away, mostly obscured, but it was obvious that she was still a young woman. The line of her gaze was directed into a space between the twin flames. It was as if she could see something beyond, at a different angle to the frontal view of the observer. Her lips were parted but not in a motion that indicated speech; instead they embodied stillness. It seemed to me that she had been sitting there, unflinching, for a long time.

'Why this one?' I said, eventually.

Esther didn't answer, but rather surprised me by laying her head on my shoulder.

'*Penitent* is such a strange title,' she said. 'She doesn't look regretful.' She spoke softly, not in a whisper but low enough that only I could hear what she was saying.

'You're right, she doesn't,' I said.

She moved off my shoulder and gazed again at the canvas.

'I found this painting by chance,' she said. 'Of course, I know it, I've seen it in books, but I came across it here one day and it helped me to understand something.'

She took a moment to gather her thoughts.

'At first I liked it because it's so intimate, such a private moment. I kept coming back because I found it calming. It's a woman reflecting on someone she loved and lost. And then after a few visits I thought again about the title. And I thought that maybe she wasn't reflecting on something she'd done but maybe it was something she hadn't done. She doesn't look regretful because she's made peace with it. She's paid her penance. That look on her face is one of acceptance.'

Then she turned to me and softly said, 'Simon, your pages are so full of guilt. You've invented a whole other life to try to understand why the bombing happened. But it doesn't change anything. What happened, happened. You're not responsible for those deaths, any more than you're responsible for the death of your mother.'

'I didn't invent him. I didn't just draw some character out of the ether. He came to me. And as regards my mother, it's not the same thing. I couldn't prevent her death, but maybe I could have prevented what happened that day in Enniskillen. I should have told someone.'

'You were scared. You were a young kid. The man you met on that island, you couldn't place him, put a name to him. You don't know what they were doing there. You don't know that they were linked to the bombing.'

'I know what I saw.'

'You know what you think you saw. And you had no one to talk to; you couldn't ask anyone for advice. You were trying to protect everyone around you – me, the Irvines, your father. You can't hold a fifteen-year-old boy accountable for all of that. It's too much to carry. You bore all that alone.'

'If I had told someone, they would have had to check it out. They would have had to investigate what was in those crates they carried. It might have prevented what happened.'

'All of it might well have happened anyway. Maybe not in Enniskillen, but somewhere else. A movement is a movement, it has its own line of direction. They would have found another way, another opportunity.'

'That's not true.'

'Simon, listen to what I'm saying. Peace comes only after the darkest days. Listen to what I'm telling you, I know about this. Things need to find their own course. You can't change the past, no matter how hard you might try.'

I felt a surge run through me. For a moment, I thought that another seizure was on its way, but instead I began to weep, freely, openly. I wept and shuddered, shuddered and wept. Esther held me and I settled into her arms and became a child again, years of sorrow pouring forth. Regret for my mother, for the fact that my father couldn't speak to me, for all of the strictures of my childhood, the loaded words, the dangerous inflections, the tensions that I had to hold within myself, finally came unloosed.

The grief that had stayed within me, unalloyed, unacknowledged, for decades.

I don't know how long we stayed there. New York is a city where you can weep openly without anyone raising an eyebrow. The security guard stood in his spot, not paying any heed. People walked around us, stared at the goats and the lute players, unwavering in their conversations.

Afterwards, I walked home, all the way down Fifth Avenue, to Washington Square Park, through the narrowing streets of SoHo, and then took a left on Spring Street, mannequins eyeing me from shop windows. And I thought again about *The Penitent Magdalen*, at the direction of her gaze. She stares at the space in between the two flames, to somewhere else, somewhere beyond the room she's in and its reflection, somewhere beyond binary states of being, where another kind of truth is possible.

Tonight the subway trains still trundle unhurriedly past my right shoulder, slipping away into the bowels of the bridge. People still look up at me, startled. Tomorrow I will be just a memory, no longer one of those film-flickering lives that provide the backdrop to an elevated ride. In the morning, I'll move my desk away from the window. Next week, or maybe the week after, I'll begin to look for somewhere more permanent, a place where I can hang pictures and put down some rugs. I might even become a true New Yorker and get myself a dog.

I once read a sentence somewhere that said: *The opposite of love is not to hate but to separate.* When I think of Camille, of those final months and that final near-fatal drive, I wonder what might have happened if I'd parked the car that night and walked back into our apartment in Clinton Hill and set about trying to repair all that had been broken. To walk away felt ruthless, cowardly, and it still does, even if it was the right decision. And I realize now, as I write this, that my window looks out towards Brooklyn, towards Clinton Hill, and that maybe all of these nights here, alone at this desk, are also my way of reaching out towards that memory of her, that woman, my wife, who walked from our car into our apartment and sat there, kettle on the boil, waiting for her husband to step through the door, to begin again.

The house in Lisnarick is up for sale again. On the auctioneers' website, I can see the changes that have been made to it. The people who bought it after my father died put a porch at the front door to keep out the rain. The front windows are flanked by trellises on either side, with clematis creeping up them, brightening its aspect. The kitchen has been knocked through to the breakfast room and large French windows have been put in. Light floods through. It looks so much more hopeful, free, and that awful fucking fluorescent striplight has been taken out, replaced by tasteful LED spotlights. The kitchen cupboards are modern, the worktops stainless steel.

The walled garden has been landscaped, and I'm pleased to say they retained the boundary walls and the grand chestnut tree I used to climb is still there. The bathroom has a full-length iron bath, painted lilac, and is covered floor to ceiling in large grey tiles. The wallpaper has been removed from my room; it's a cleaner space now, clearer, white walls and dark floorboards and a king-sized bed that I assume doesn't creak when you sit on it.

And I see myself in that vast, comfortable, king-sized bed, in that clean white room. The surroundings have changed but I'm the boy I once was. A gawky, lonely teenager. Fresh-faced. Greasy-haired. I throw back the duvet and step sleepily down the stairs and into the parlour and approach that gold carriage clock on our mantelpiece. I open the face of the clock and I turn its hands back to Saturday, 7th of November 1987, and, as I do so, the walls around me fade away and I am released into a vast white space, like those salt plains they have in Utah, open possibility stretching out in every direction. To my left, my father sits slumped in his chair. Behind me, in the mirror, Brendan McGovern approaches my right shoulder and whispers his question, asks me my name.

And my father says, *Simon.*

And my father asks me if I'd like to go to the Remembrance Day parade in the morning.

And I turn and face the mirror again, and, looking inside it, I see Belmore Street. It is night. The street is empty except for the two figures of Brendan and Joe McGovern, making their way towards the Reading Rooms. They're wearing dark clothes and soft-bottomed trainers. The soldier on his plinth gazes down on them, without reaction, a sentry asleep at his post. Joe carries the sportsbag and palms a gun in his pocket. Brendan has a torch in his left hand. The reach the door of the Reading Rooms. Brendan turns the knob slowly, puts his shoulder to the door. The main room, in darkness, is still laid out from the bingo.

Brendan clicks on his small torch. A weak light rises up from the basement, voices. They both pace heel to toe, the way they've practised, distributing their weight evenly across their stride. The boards creak beneath them.

Now would be the worst time to be caught; no way they could talk themselves out of it. Joe keeps the gun low, by his thigh. If they're disturbed, they've agreed that Brendan will do the talking. But Brendan is pretty sure it won't come to that. Joe would open fire if he had to, no remorse. Brendan hears voices downstairs, casual conversation. He can't make out the words, but it doesn't matter: as long as the tone of the conversation remains steady, they won't be disturbed.

They move a few more paces. The boards creak, the conversation stops, the two brothers freeze. Through the floorboards, Brendan can see the figures around the table. They're still. Silently, he pleads for them to stay that way. The conversation resumes.

They reach the stairwell. The boards here are shorter, less give in them, less likelihood of their creaking. Nearly there. In the room, Joe puts the bag on a bench, sets the timer, arranges the package, zips back up the bag and slides it into a small room under the staircase. He nods, gestures with the gun: time to leave. Brendan steps back, lets his elder brother lead the way.

He looks again at the bag. Looks at it resting there. Dormant. Ready to destroy everything around it.

Brendan, on impulse, lifts the bag. He lifts it gently. He knows its weight – not so heavy, considering its purpose, its potential. He lifts it and turns. Joe is halfway across the main hall. He has stopped, and is looking at his younger brother. Brendan can't see his face, only his silhouette. He knows that Joe can't put up any resistance. The bag is too delicate, the situation too poised. The younger brother is the one with all the power now, holding power in his hands. Joe puts up his hands to his head. Frustration? Fear? Astonishment? It doesn't matter. Now only the bag matters.

He passes his brother. Joe barks a whisper, but he ignores it.

As he nears the door, Brendan hears a chair being pushed back in the basement. He hears a voice calling out, from down below, from the bottom of the stairs. No urgency in it – he'll make it to the door all right. Joe won't want to open fire, not with everything so delicately poised.

Brendan reaches the door, pulls it open with his right hand. He steps outside. No one around. The stars are out. He steps out into the night, the bag steady in his left hand, a clock ticking inside it, a reassuring constancy to the noise, the whisper of a fragile heart.

Author's Note

While *Remembrance Sunday* is a work of fiction, it has at its centre a historical atrocity which – I have no doubt – is still very present for those who survived it and the loved ones of those who did not. Every act of violence destroys human possibilities. For the town of Enniskillen, November the 8th will always be linked with the IRA's brutality.

All of the characters who participate in the action of the novel are invented. A small number of real people are named, but I've been cautious not to imagine into these people's actions, thoughts or lives.

I'd like to acknowledge a number of books that were important to me in my research. *Killing Rage*, a memoir by the former IRA member Eamon Collins, was particularly crucial in my formation of the character of Brendan McGovern – in relation to historical context and the process of radicalization.

The section regarding the poker game in the basement of the Reading Rooms is informed by *Enniskillen: The Remembrance Sunday Bombing* by Denzil McDaniel. That detail and many others from McDaniel's book were invaluable in my re-creation of the bombing. *Lough Erne* by Alain Le Garsmeur and Keith Baker informed my imaginings regarding the life of the young Simon Hanlon. For general background on the IRA and life in Northern

Ireland during the Troubles, I benefited from reading *Making Sense of the Troubles* by David McKittrick and David McVea, *Bandit Country* by Toby Harnden, *Rebel Hearts* by Kevin Toolis, *The Troubles* by Tim Pat Coogan and *The Lost Soul of Eamonn Magee* by Paul Gibson.

Many of my thoughts regarding neuroscience were influenced by an extraordinary pair of books by the neuropsychologist Paul Broks, written fifteen years apart. The first, *Into the Silent Land*, greatly informed my descriptions of the Wada test and provided an excellent companion through the landscape of the brain. The second, *The Darker the Night, the Brighter the Stars*, changed my understanding of consciousness, as did the writings of Riccardo Manzotti, in particular his thoughts articulated in *Dialogues on Consciousness*, a collaboration with Tim Parks.

A Smell of Burning by Colin Grant and *Behavioural Neurology and the Legacy of Norman Geschwind* edited by Steven C. Schachter and Orrin Devinsky were very useful regarding the history of epilepsy and our current thinking about the subject, and I'd particularly like to thank Orrin Devinsky for his assistance. His and Kate Picco's recounting of their personal experiences around the condition were very valuable to me.

The story regarding Adeline Ravoux and Van Gogh comes from *Van Gogh in Auvers* by Wouter van der Veen and Peter Knapp.

The lines from *The Idiot* are drawn from the translation by Richard Pevear and Larissa Volokhonsky. The quotations of Marx and Engels are from *The Classics of*

Marxism: Volume One published by Wellred Books. The line 'the opposite of love is not to hate but to separate' is from *And Our Faces, My Heart, Brief as Photos* by John Berger.

For hospitality and guidance regarding Chinatown, I'm very grateful to the Knickerbocker Village Senior Center, in particular Mary Springer. I'm also thankful for the assistance from my former colleagues at the Visiting Nurse Service of New York, particularly Hing Sit and Erica Chan, and to Charles Leung for his generosity in introducing me to the residents of Chinatown.

Thanks to a number of very supportive readers: Isobel Harbison, John Ptacek, Sujata Shekar, Téa Obreht, Hari Kunzru, Nathan Englander, Leo Duncan, Caroline Ast, Tanya Ronder, and my editors Mary Mount and Brendan Barrington.

Nora Hickey M'Sichili, Nick Laird and Carlo Gébler were invaluable in providing me with guidance regarding details of life in and around Enniskillen.

Thanks to the Civitella Ranieri Foundation, the Centre Culturel Irlandais, the Dora Maar Institute and the Villa Marguerite Yourcenar for providing me with time and space to write when it was particularly needed. I'm grateful to the Arts Council of Ireland for their financial assistance.

Thanks to Caspian Dennis, and all of the team at Abner Stein. And a special thank you to Frances Coady, who has been a constant and unwavering support throughout the entire writing and publication process.